Dear Readers,

Many years ago, when I was a kid, my father said to me, "Bill, it doesn't really matter what you do in life. What's important is to be the best William Johnstone you can be."

I've never forgotten those words. And now, many years and almost two hundred books later, I like to think that I am still trying to be the best William Johnstone I can be. Whether it's Ben Raines in the Ashes series, or Frank Morgan, the last gunfighter, or Smoke Jensen, our intrepid mountain man, or John Barrone and his hardworking crew keeping America safe from terrorist lowlifes in the Code Name series, I want to make each new book better than the last and deliver powerful storytelling.

Equally important, I try to create the kinds of believable characters that we can all identify with, real people who face tough challenges. When one of my creations blasts an enemy into the middle of next week, you can be damn sure he had a good reason.

As a storyteller, my job is to entertain you, my readers, and to make sure that you get plenty of enjoyment from my books for your hard-earned money. This is not a job I take lightly. And I greatly appreciate your feedback—you are my gold, and your opinions do count. So please keep the letters and e-mails coming.

Respectfully yours,

William W. Johnstone

Trade this book back to
Phil's Book Exchange
N.M.B. Flea Market - Bldg. A
North Myrtle Beach, S.C.

WILLIAM W. JOHNSTONE
with FRED AUSTIN

THE FIRST MOUNTAIN MAN:
PREACHER'S FORTUNE

PINNACLE BOOKS
Kensington Publishing Corp.
http://www.kensingtonbooks.com

PINNACLE BOOKS are published by

Kensington Publishing Corp.
850 Third Avenue
New York, NY 10022

Copyright © 2006 by William W. Johnstone

All rights reserved. No part of this book may be reproduced
in any form or by any means without the prior written consent
of the Publisher, excepting brief quotes used in reviews.

If you purchased this book without a cover, you should be aware
that this book is stolen property. It was reported as "unsold and
destroyed" to the Publisher and neither the Author nor the Publisher has received any payment for this "stripped book."

This novel is a work of fiction. Names, characters, places, and
incidents are either the product of the author's imagination, or
are used fictitiously. Any resemblance to actual persons, living
or dead, or events is entirely coincidental.

All Kensington Titles, Imprints, and Distributed Lines are available at special quantity discounts for bulk purchases for sales pro-
motions, premiums, fund-raising, and educational or institutional
use. Special book excerpts or customized printings can also be
created to fit specific needs. For details, write or phone the
office of the Kensington special sales manager: Kensington
Publishing Corp., 850 Third Avenue, New York, NY 10022,
attn: Special Sales Department. Phone: 1-800-221-2647.

Pinnacle and the P logo Reg. U.S. Pat. & TM Off.

First Pinnacle Books Printing: January 2006

10 9 8 7 6 5 4 3

Printed in the United States of America

ONE

As with life itself, beauty and ugliness existed side by side in the country through which the lone man traveled. Stretches of barren desert alternated with bands of rich green vegetation that bordered the occasional stream. Ranges of pine-covered mountains shouldered up out of the arid landscape surrounding them. Some of the mountains were capped with snow that sparkled a brilliant white in the sun, a tantalizing reminder of coolness while down below the heat had set in, despite the fact that it was still early in the summer.

From time to time the traveler reined in his horse and sat there staring at the mountains. His only other companion, a massive, shaggy creature that appeared to be as much wolf as dog, sat down and waited patiently, tongue lolling from his mouth. The big cur was happy as long as he accompanied this particular human.

With their typical sanguinity, the Spanish explorers who had first come to this land more than a hundred years earlier had dubbed the mountains the Sangre de Cristos—the Blood of Christ. The man called Preacher could see how the mountains got the name. When the sun hit them just right, they did have a certain reddish hue to them that might remind somebody of blood. To Preacher, though, they were just mountains. One more obstacle to cross.

He had come up out of Texas after wintering there and was anxious to get back to his beloved Rocky Mountains, where he had spent so much of his life after running away from home as a boy. Texas had been all right. . . . A mite too humid for his tastes, maybe, especially over east in those thick, piney woods. But the American settlers who were moving in, such as that big strapping McCallister boy and his pretty, yellow-haired wife, seemed to be fine, feisty folks. If the Mexican authorities who ran the place didn't trod careful, they would have some real trouble on their hands in a few years. Americans wouldn't stand for being mistreated for too long. They were a peaceful people at heart, but they loved freedom and would fight for it if they had to, by God! Preacher expected those Texicans wouldn't be any different. He wouldn't have minded being around to watch the fun when they finally got tired of ol' Santa Anna's high-handed arrogance.

By that time, though, he would probably be back up in the mountains, trapping beaver. That was his true calling.

Well, that . . . and getting into trouble, seemed like.

"Come on, Horse," Preacher said as he heeled his mount into motion. "There's bound to be a pass up there somewheres, and I reckon we better start lookin' for it." He rode toward the mountains at an easy lope, with the big wolflike dog bounding along ahead of him and the horse.

This Nuevo Mexico was part of Mexico, too, but the government didn't have the same problems here that it did over in Texas. There weren't nearly as many Americans around, although more traders and trappers from the States were drifting in all the time. Many of them had come to stay, too, unlike Preacher, who was just passing through. Charles Bent and Ceran St. Vrain had established a regular trade route between Santa Fe and St. Louis, and over the past few years, hundreds of wagons had gone back and forth over what folks had started to call the Santa Fe Trail. Preacher thought it a certainty that there would be trouble sooner or later between the American settlers and the Mexican government in Texas. Over here in New Mexico, it was just a likelihood.

But again, the possibility didn't worry Preacher overmuch. He liked a good scrap as well as the next man—well, better than some, to tell the truth—but he didn't go out of his way to look for a fight. It would be fine and dandy with him if nothing happened to delay his return to the Rockies and those clear, cold, high-country streams where there were scads of beaver just waitin' for him to take their pelts.

First, though, he had to get through the Sangre de Cristos, and before that he figured to stop for the night at a trading post he had heard about in Taos. It was supposed to be located at the foot of the mountains and was the last stop for travelers on their way north, the last outpost of any sort of civilization in that direction.

As a rule, Preacher wasn't that all-fired fond of civilization, but as he rode toward the mountains, he had to admit to himself that a drink of whiskey, a hot meal, and a soft place to lay his head for the night might not be such bad things.

There might even be a pretty woman at that trading post. He purely did love the sight of a pretty woman.

"Bring out the whores, old man!" Cobey Larson bellowed as he slammed a knobby fist on the bar. The rough planks that had been laid down between two whiskey barrels to form the bar jumped a little under the impact.

"I have told you, Señor," said the stocky Mexican man behind the planks. A worried frown creased his sweating forehead. "There are no women like that here, only my wife and daughter."

One of the other Americans, the barrel-shaped Arnie Ross, laughed and said, "That sounds all right to me. I don't care who the hell they're related to, as long as they's soft and bouncy in bed."

The proprietor of the trading post, whose name was Vincente Ojeida, struggled to keep his composure in the face of these vulgar, insistent *americanos*. Their words were offensive to him and inflamed his blood with their insult to his honor, but he maintained a tight rein on his temper as he said, "If you wish supplies or whiskey, I can help you, but otherwise I cannot."

Larson leaned closer, a scowl on his whiskery face. "Are you tellin' me there ain't even any squaws around here we can lay with?"

Vincente shrugged eloquently. "I am sorry, Señor. Such is the way of things."

"Well, that may be all right for you. . . ." Larson reached to his waist and pulled a pistol that had been tucked behind his belt. It was already loaded and primed, and as he raised it he drew back the hammer. "But I ain't so philosophical. I been on the trail a damn long time, and I want a woman." He pointed the barrel of the pistol at Vincente's nose. "You get my drift, pepperbelly?"

Larson's companions laughed as they enjoyed the show their leader was putting on. There were four of them: the rotund Ross, Bert McDermott, Hank Sewell, and Wick Jimpson. McDermott and Sewell were cut from the same cloth as Larson, lean, buckskin-clad men with hawklike faces. Jimpson was bigger, towering over the others. His shoulders had filled the doorway of the trading post from side to side when he came through it. His brainpower didn't match his size, though. He was little better than a halfwit, devoted to Cobey Larson and willing to do anything Larson told him to.

Vincente had sensed that the five gringos were trouble as soon as he saw them saunter into the trading post. They arrived on horseback, with no wagons, so he knew they weren't traders. They could have been fur trappers or even prospectors—some people believed there was gold to be found in the mountains, and there would always be men who searched for precious metals—but they did not have the look of men accustomed to such hard labor.

That left only one real possibility as far as Vincente could see: The men had to be *bandidos,* robbers who preyed on the trade caravans.

There were no other customers in the trading post at the moment, which emboldened the Americans even more. They crowded up to the bar, and Larson repeated his demand. "Bring out your wife and daughter! I want to see 'em!"

Elgera and Lupita were in the storage room at the back of the trading post. It was mere luck that they had not been in the big front room when the Americans entered. But Vincente knew the door behind him was open a crack, and Elgera would have heard the loud voices of the visitors and realized that the best thing for her and her pretty fourteen-year-old daughter to do was to stay out of sight. She was smart as well as beautiful, and that was one more reason Vincente considered himself a very lucky man to have married her. He himself was not so intelligent, else he never would have mentioned the very existence of a wife and daughter to these beasts who walked like men. The words had slipped out before he could recall them. Now he had to try to repair the damage.

"They are not here, Señor," he said, trying to make his voice sound forceful. That wasn't easy when he was staring down the barrel of a pistol.

"You just said they were!"

"They live here with me, of course, but they are not here *now.*"

"Well, where the hell are they?"

Vincente wished he was better at thinking up lies. "They have gone to the mission," he said.

"Mission? What mission?"

"In the mountains," Vincente said, gesturing vaguely in the direction of the peaks that loomed over the trading post. "They have gone to pray in the church. A . . . a pilgrimage."

Larson brought the pistol closer to Vincente's face and prodded the tip of his nose with it. With an ugly grin on his face, Larson said, "I think you're lyin'. I think them women are here, and you just figure they're too good for the likes of us. Well, that's where you're wrong, pepperbelly. Trot 'em out here, or I'll blow your damn head off."

Vincente's heart slugged heavily in his chest. Elgera must have heard that threat, and he knew his wife well enough to know what she would do next. Unwilling to stand by and let her husband be murdered, she would rush out and take her chance with the *americanos*. He just hoped she would have the sense to hide Lupita somewhere in the storeroom first.

But it didn't come to that because, at that moment, another man said from the open front door of the trading post, "I wouldn't do that, friend. You shoot him and I'll have to pour my own drink, and I ain't in much of a mood to play bartender."

All five of the men swung around to look at Preacher. That meant the one who had the gun in his hand was sort of pointing it toward him, and Preacher didn't like that. Generally, whenever a fella pointed a gun at him, Preacher shot the son of a bitch before the son of a bitch could shoot him. It seemed only reasonable.

This time, however, he restrained the impulse to draw one of the pistols at his waist. He had been in the saddle all day, and he was tired. Killin' meant buryin', and digging graves was hard work.

"Who the hell are you?" the man with the drawn gun demanded.

To a bunch of hard cases like these, he probably didn't look like much. He was tall and lean—enough so that some folks might call him skinny—and dressed in buckskins that had seen better days. He hadn't trimmed his dark hair and beard in a while, so he supposed he looked a mite shaggy. A felt hat with a big, floppy brim was cocked back on his head. He looked almost sleepy as he leaned a shoulder against the door-jamb, but anybody who took the time to look close at the deep-set, piercing eyes under bushy brows would see that they told a different story.

"Who, me?" Preacher said mildly. "I'm just a pilgrim passin' through these parts, friend. Not lookin' for any trouble. Thought maybe I'd rest myself and my horse here for the night before we start over the pass in the mornin'."

"This ain't any of your business, so you'd be wise to keep your nose out of it."

"I expect you're right." Preacher brought his left hand up and laid a finger alongside his nose. "But this here proboscis of mine is too big to keep out of things sometimes. You like that word? Means long nose. I heard it once from a fella who had a lot of book learnin'."

"Ah, hell, Cobey," the short, round man said. "He's just a half-wit of some sort. Probably dumber than Wick." He jerked a thumb at the biggest member of the group, a huge young man with a dull expression on his face.

The one with the gun grunted and said, "Yeah." Addressing himself to Preacher, he went on. "Turn around and ride out of here, mister, if you're smart enough to know what's good for you."

Preacher chuckled. "You've sure got me figured out, friend. I'm nosy *and* I'm dumb."

"I ain't your friend, damn it! Quit callin' me that!" The man turned back to the stocky Mexican, who Preacher assumed was the proprietor of the trading post. "Now, are you gonna bring them women out here, or do I have to shoot you?"

"Women?" Preacher called. "What women? There's women here?"

Cobey looked back over his shoulder and said through gritted teeth, "Are you still here? This greaser's got a wife and daughter stashed somewhere, and we aim to have 'em!"

Preacher's left hand rubbed his bearded jaw. "I sure am glad you told me we ain't friends."

"What?" The gunman half-turned toward Preacher again, his annoyance showing plainly on his face.

"If we ain't friends," Preacher said, "then I don't have to feel bad about doin' this."

He drew his pistol and shot the man called Cobey.

Two

The bullet ripped through Cobey's arm, missing the bone but gouging out a considerable hunk of flesh and splattering blood. It was his gun arm, which meant that the pistol in his hand flew across the room. It hit the wall and went off, but the heavy ball buried itself harmlessly in a barrel of flour.

Preacher hadn't been expecting trouble, so his pistol wasn't double-shotted. If it had been, Cobey probably would have been dead by now, but the fella was lucky. He got to live, as long as he didn't do anything else stupid.

The same went for his companions, so to keep them from getting frisky, Preacher pulled his second pistol and leveled it at them. He did it fast, while they were still gaping in surprise.

"You boys stand still," Preacher told them. "Fat boy, see to your friend. The rest of you, don't move."

Cobey had slumped to his knees in front of the makeshift bar and clutched his wounded right arm with his left hand. His face had gone gray under its tan, but Preacher had to give him credit for toughness. He hadn't yelled in pain, hadn't made a sound, in fact, other than breathing hard.

His round friend hurried over to him and knelt beside him. He pulled a dirty bandanna from a pocket in his buckskins and tied it tightly around the wound, trying to stanch the flow of blood.

The air in the trading post smelled like burned powder. Preacher looked at the proprietor and said, "Sorry about the mess, amigo. I know blood can be mighty hard to get up out of floorboards."

"That . . . that is all right, Señor."

The door behind the man swung open far enough for a woman to peer out into the front room. Preacher saw dark eyes and a mass of thick raven hair. When the woman rushed out and threw her arms around the proprietor, she revealed just how pretty she was. She was followed by a younger, smaller version of herself. The wife and daughter he had heard mentioned, Preacher decided. Nobody else they could be.

It would have been better if the two of them had stayed in the back room, out of sight. Preacher could understand, though, why the woman had wanted to rush out and make sure her husband was all right. She would have heard that shot and not been sure exactly what had happened.

But as it was, her presence, and especially that of her daughter, immediately made things worse. Because the biggest of the hard cases, who was built sort of like a mountain, stared at the girl for a couple of seconds and then said, "I want her." He took a lumbering step toward the bar.

"Hold it!" Preacher snapped. "Unless you boys want me to shoot him, you better grab your pard."

One of the men took hold of the giant's arm, but the big man shook off the grip like it was nothing. He took another step toward the girl, who shrank back with a look of horror on her face.

"Come here," the giant said to her. "I want to kiss on you."

The proprietor pushed his wife aside and moved quickly between his daughter and the big man. He reached onto a shelf and plucked a knife from it. The blade shone red, as if already drenched in blood, in the late afternoon sunlight that slanted through a window.

"Get back, Señor!" the proprietor said. "Get back, I tell you!"

Without waiting, he slashed at one of the giant's outstretched hands. The knife ripped a gash across the back of it. Blood welled from the wound as the giant snatched his hand back and howled in pain. "You hurt me!" he roared. Furious, he lunged forward, crashing into the bar and swinging his malletlike fists at the proprietor.

Preacher didn't have any choice then. The Mexican was half the size of the giant. He would wind up being beaten to death if Preacher didn't stop it.

The pistol in Preacher's left hand blasted. The ball hit the giant in the back of the leg, knocking it out from under him. He reeled and went down, finishing the job of demolishing the bar. Planks scattered around him and one of the whiskey barrels overturned. The bung popped out and the Who-Hit-John began to leak, glugging onto the floor and forming a puddle. The sharp reek of the stuff mixed with the tang of the gunpowder.

The other three men, knowing that both of Preacher's guns were now empty, rushed him.

Preacher was expecting that. He flung the left-hand gun as hard as he could, and in these close quarters, when the gun hit one of the men in the face, it pulped his nose and sent him staggering backward, blood gushing down over his mouth and chin. Preacher ducked under a roundhouse punch thrown by one of the other men and grabbed the front of the hombre's homespun shirt. A heave and an outthrust leg to knock his feet out from under him, and the man found himself sailing through the air to crash heavily to the puncheon floor.

That left Preacher only the short, round man to deal with, but to his surprise he quickly discovered that it was a little like fighting a buzz saw. The fella was a lot faster than he looked, and a flurry of hard punches seemed to come from every direction when he closed in. A couple of them landed solidly, knocking Preacher back a step. He caught his balance, set his feet, and swung a blow of his own, driving a fist into the man's belly. That was another surprise. The man was built like a barrel, and punching him in the stomach was about like hitting a barrel, one made of thick, stout oak. He didn't even grunt.

The fella with the broken nose was back in the fight, too. His bloody face was contorted in a snarl as he circled and grabbed Preacher from behind, pinning his arms to his sides. "Get him, Arnie!" he yelled thickly at the fat man. "Beat the hell out of him!"

Preacher figured he ought to consider himself lucky that they were all mad enough to fight with their fists, rather than pulling their guns. Dealing with three-to-one odds in a gunfight, and him with a couple of empty pistols at that, would have been a mite tricky. He was confident that he would have figured out a way to do it, but hell, a brawl like this was more fun, anyway.

He stomped back on the instep of the man holding him and then jerked his head back, too, snapping it into the man's face. More cartilage crunched in the already injured nose. The man screamed and let go just as the fat man charged Preacher again. Preacher dropped to the floor and went forward into the fat man's legs in a rolling dive. The fat man's momentum carried him over Preacher and into his howling friend. Both of them went down in a tangle of arms and legs.

Preacher rolled on over and came up on hands and knees in time to see that the man he had shot had gotten back on his feet. He had grabbed up an ax from a table where several of them lay, and now he swung the double-bitted tool at Preacher's head. Preacher dived aside at the last second. The ax head bit deeply into the wooden floor and lodged there.

Preacher came up from the floor, uncoiling like a snake as he threw an uppercut that landed on the wounded man's jaw. The impact of the blow shivered all the way up Preacher's arm, and he hoped he hadn't busted a knuckle or two. The punch lifted the wounded man off his feet and sent him slamming down onto his back. Preacher didn't think he would be getting up any time soon.

But that still left three men—well, two, since the one with the broken nose was lying huddled on the floor, his hands pressed to his face, whimpering—but those two might want to tussle some more. Preacher clenched his fists and waited to see if they were going to attack again.

He heard a familiar, ominous, metallic clicking sound from behind him. "Step aside, Señor!" the proprietor cried. "Step aside, and I will deal with these animals as they deserve!"

Preacher threw a look over his shoulder and saw the owner of the trading post standing there with a double-barreled shotgun in his hands. The man's face was dark with outrage, and Preacher could tell that he wanted to pull the triggers and blast all five of the hard cases into bloody shreds.

That didn't sound like such a bad idea, but Preacher knew it wasn't the right thing to do. He said softly, "Hold on there, amigo. I don't reckon you want to kill these men."

"Oh, but I do, Señor, I do!"

Preacher shook his head. "Right now you do, but I can tell by lookin' at you that you ain't the type to kill a man in cold blood. If you do, it'll eat on you from now on, and you wouldn't never know a minute's peace."

"The law would not blame me! I am defending my home and my family and my honor!"

"I ain't talkin' about the law. I'm talkin' about what's in your own heart."

The man hesitated. Preacher knew he had read him right. The barrels of the shotgun lowered slightly.

"That's right," Preacher said. "What you need to do is give me the shotgun. *I'll* kill 'em, and I won't never lose a second's sleep over it."

The man seized the opportunity and pressed the shotgun into

Preacher's hands. He leveled it at the five men. From the terror-stricken looks on the faces of four of them—the giant with the wounded leg lay there sobbing in pain, not really knowing what was going on—they thought they were about to die.

"I will kill you," Preacher went on, "unless you pick yourselves up, get the hell out of here, and never come back. If you do, if you cause these good folks even one second of trouble or grief, I'll hear about it, and I'll hunt you down and kill you slow. I've lived with the Injuns, boys, and they taught me all their tricks. I can keep a fella alive for days, sufferin' more pain than you ever dreamed a man could suffer. It's up to you. Die now, die later . . . or be smart and live."

Cobey, the one Preacher had shot in the arm, looked at him and grated, "Who the hell are you?"

A grin stretched across the mountain man's lean face. "They call me Preacher."

The name meant something to a couple of the men, including the short, fat one. He said, "Damn it, Cobey, I've heard of Preacher. The Injuns call him Bear Killer. He fought a grizzly with just a knife."

The other one who recognized Preacher's name added, "We better do what he says. I ain't hankerin' to die today."

Cobey didn't look happy about it, but he couldn't ignore what his companions had told him. He struggled to his feet, clutching his wounded arm again, and said, "Get Wick, and let's get out of here."

It took all three of the other men, including the one who was still blubbering about his nose being busted, to lift the giant off the floor. All three of them supported him as he limped toward the door. As he went out, he twisted his head around to look one last time at the girl. "Pretty," he muttered. "Mighty pretty."

From the corner of his eye, Preacher saw a shiver go through the girl's slender form.

Cobey was the last one to back through the door onto the trading post's porch. "I ain't gonna forget you, Preacher," he said. "Our trails will cross again one of these days."

"You'd best hope not," Preacher said. "Next time, I might just shoot you on sight."

"Not if I shoot you first."

With that threat, Cobey turned away and stumbled after his friends, who were struggling to get the giant mounted on a rangy mule tied up outside along with the horses belonging to the rest of them.

Preacher stepped into the doorway and kept an eye on them as they mounted up. The shotgun was tucked under his arm now, but he could bring it into play in an instant if he needed to, and they knew it. He stood there, tall and vigilant, and watched as they rode away. He didn't go back inside until the five men were out of sight.

The proprietor and his wife and daughter had already started trying to clean up the mess that the brawl had made. Preacher set the shotgun on a counter at the side of the room and moved to help them.

"No, Señor," the proprietor said. "You have done enough already." He pulled a chair over. "Please, sit. Would you like something to eat or drink?"

"Maybe later," Preacher said as he nudged the chair aside. "Right now I'd like to help you straighten up. I'm partly to blame for that ruckus, I reckon."

"Not at all," the Mexican insisted. "Those gringo dogs deserve all the blame. No offense," he added quickly.

Preacher flashed a grin. "None taken. I can't speak for my dog, though. He might be insulted by the comparison."

That made him look around. Dog had trotted off into a nearby stand of pines as they rode up, probably sniffing out a rabbit or something, so he hadn't been around to take part in the fracas. Having the big cur at his side would have evened the odds considerably, but Preacher figured he had done all right on his own. He didn't see Dog, but he knew the animal would be back later.

Together, he and the Mexican righted the whiskey barrel before all of the fiery stuff could leak out. The fumes were still potent. Preacher waved a hand in front of his face and said, "A fella could get drunk just takin' a few deep breaths."

"Lupita, open all the windows," the proprietor said. "We must let more air in."

"Sí, Papá," the girl said as she hurried to carry out his command.

The Mexican turned back to Preacher and extended his hand. "I am Vincente Ojeida. That is my wife Elgera and my daughter Lupita."

Preacher shook hands with the man and said, "Glad to meet you, Vincente. I reckon you heard my name."

"Sí. The fame of the mountain man called Preacher has reached even here."

Preacher waved a hand. "Fame's just a matter of luck, usually bad. You run into enough trouble and live through it, folks start to talk about you."

"Like killing a grizzly bear with only a knife."

"What folks don't mention," Preacher said dryly, "is that that ol' griz came might dang close to killin' me, too."

"And yet you live."

"I got an advantage some folks don't," Preacher said. "I'm just too blasted stubborn to die."

THREE

Preacher and Vincente put the planks on the barrels to form a bar again while Elgera and Lupita mopped up the spilled whiskey as best they could and straightened the chairs and tables that had been knocked over. Both of the females fussed over Preacher, sitting him down at one of the tables and hurrying off to the kitchen in the rear of the building to prepare a meal for him. Vincente poured a couple of drinks, brought them over to the table, and sat down with Preacher. He sipped the whiskey, licked his lips, and said in satisfaction, "Ah."

"I thought you fellas drank tequila, mescal, things like that," Preacher commented.

"As a young man I ate many worms from the bottom of a bottle," Vincente said, "but as I grew older and began to trade with Señors Bent and St. Vrain, I have learned to appreciate a good Scotch whiskey."

Preacher laughed. "I don't reckon I can argue with that."

Vincente grew more serious. "I cannot thank you enough for what you did, Señor Preacher. I knew those men were trouble as soon as they came in, but I could not reach my shotgun in time. They were between me and it."

"I'm a little surprised you don't carry a pistol."

"I am not a good shot," Vincente said with a shrug. "The fact of the matter is, I am a man of peace, more suited to running a trading post than I am to fighting. I need a shotgun if I want to hit anything." He drank a little more of the whiskey. "But you are right, Señor. From now on, I will always have a pistol close at hand."

"That's a good idea, out in the middle of nowhere like this. You never know when Injuns might come raidin'."

"The Indians in the area are peaceful, for the most part. It is the white men I worry about. Again, I mean no offense."

Preacher leaned back in his chair and cocked an ankle on the other knee. "I imagine there are a whole heap more gringos around here than there were before the Santa Fe Trail opened up."

Vincente nodded. "*Sí*. The wagon trains pass through here every few weeks. Also, trappers who run their lines in the Sangre de Cristos come here for supplies. This is the closest place they can trade their pelts."

Preacher's interest perked up at the mention of trapping. "Many beaver to be found up in them mountains?"

"Some. Not the same as farther north. But there are fewer men trapping this far south, so it evens out, so to speak."

"I was on my way back up to the Tetons, but I might tarry for a spell in the Sangre de Cristos, sort of check out the streams."

Vincente beamed at him. "You will always be welcome here, Señor Preacher."

"Make it just Preacher. Señor means mister, and I ain't never been too comfortable with that."

"Very well, Preacher. My house is your house."

Elgera and Lupita came in then with platters of tortillas and bowls of beans and a pot of stew that smelled enticingly of chilies. Preacher and Vincente dug in, and although the stew was so hot it bid fair to blister his innards, it went down well and Preacher thoroughly enjoyed it. He had such a good time eating and visiting with the Ojeida family, in fact, that he almost forgot about the violence that had taken place earlier in the trading post. He was mighty glad he had decided to stop here for the night.

Later, he tended to Horse and left the big stallion in a shed behind the main building. Dog came dragging in, licking his chops, so Preacher knew he had filled up on rabbit and prairie dog, more than likely. Vincente had offered to let Preacher have the trading post's one bedroom, saying that he and his family could make pallets for themselves in the main room, but Preacher wouldn't hear of it. The weather was warm, although at this elevation the temperature would cool off considerably by morning, and he had a good bedroll that would suit him just fine. He told Vincente that he would spread his robes under the nearby trees.

"That'll let me keep an eye on the place, too," Preacher added in a low voice as he and Vincente stood on the porch after supper. Night had fallen, and the heavens were ablaze with a canopy of bright, twinkling stars. "Just in case that bunch decides to come back."

"You do not think they would, do you?" Vincente asked with a worried frown on his face.

"No, I don't," Preacher answered honestly. "Shot up and beat up like they are, I reckon they went off somewheres to lick their wounds for a while. I don't think they'll bother you again. But you can't never tell for sure what two-legged skunks will do. They're worser than the four-legged kind."

"*Gracias,* Preacher. Sleep well."

"I always do. That's the sign of a clear conscience, I reckon."

Vincente hesitated. "I have heard it said that you have killed many men. . . ."

"Only them that needed killin'," Preacher said.

The five men sat huddled around a small campfire, not far from the foot of the pass. They passed around a whiskey bottle. Most of the time, the only sounds were the crackling of flames and an occasional muttered curse.

Cobey's arm hurt like blazes. Once they had made camp, he had ordered Arnie to clean out the wound with some of their whiskey. Arnie had been reluctant to use good liquor for that purpose, but Cobey had insisted. He'd told Arnie to clean the wound in Wick's leg the same way. Wick had whimpered and mewled like a hurt kitten the whole time.

There wasn't much they could do for Hank's busted nose. Arnie had tried for a while to push everything back into place, but he had given up because Hank was howling so much and thrashing around. "Let it heal crooked, for all I care," Arnie had said in disgust.

Bert McDermott, who had been lucky enough to come through the brawl with only a few bruises, had laughed and said, "Yeah, Hank, it ain't like you're so handsome the gals are linin' up for you. The rest of you is so ugly, chances are they'll never notice a little thing like a crooked nose."

Hank had taken offense at that, of course, and there might have been a fight if Cobey hadn't growled at them to put a cork in it and settle down. They did what he said. None of the others really wanted to cross Cobey Larson, especially when he was mad to start with.

Now, as they sat around the fire, being careful not to stare into the flames and ruin their night vision, Cobey took a nip from the bottle and said, "That bastard's gonna be sorry he ever crossed our trail."

"I'm already sorry he crossed our trail," Arnie said. "I was lookin' forward to some beans an' tortillas."

"I wanted some tequila," Bert said. "I can't stand greasers, but they make some fine booze."

Wick said, "That little girl sure was pretty. I wanted to comb my fingers through that long black hair of hers."

"That ain't all you wanted to do to her," Bert gibed.

Wick looked down at the ground and flushed in embarrassment, although it was hard to tell that in the ruddy glow of the campfire. "I wouldn't'a hurt her," he said. "I'd'a been real careful with her, like she was a little doll or somethin'."

Cobey wanted to tell them all to shut up their yammering. He was in no mood for it. But he suppressed his anger. These men were his partners, after all, and it wasn't their fault that they had run up against the man called Preacher.

As if reading Cobey's mind, Arnie asked, "You reckon it was really him?"

"Preacher, you mean?" Bert asked.

"Yeah. I've heard about him, but I never saw him before."

"I did," Hank Sewell put in, his voice sounding odd because his nose had swelled up and was closed off completely. "Saw him at a Rendezvous a few years ago, not long after he picked up the name Preacher. It was him, all right."

"How come you didn't know him right off?" Cobey asked.

Hank shrugged. "Well, it's been a while. And it ain't like him and me was ever friends. I just saw him once at a Rendezvous, that's all."

"Is he a bad man?" Wick asked. "He must be, because he hurt me."

"He's a dangerous man," Arnie said. "That's for damned sure."

Cobey snapped, "He's just a man. He can be killed like anybody else. And I intend to do it."

Arnie leaned forward and said anxiously, "We got a job to do, Cobey. We can't meet that fella at the tradin' post like we was supposed to. How're we gonna handle it now?"

"We're going to wait here," Cobey answered without hesitation. "The main trail passes right by here. If everything's goin' accordin' to plan, he ought to pass by in a few days, and we'll meet him then. No reason we can't go right ahead with the thing and get it done."

"And when it's done?"

The bottle had made its way back around the circle to Cobey. He lifted it to his lips and took a healthy slug. When he lowered it, he said, "By then we'll all be healed up, so we'll find Mr. High-and-Mighty Preacher and make him rue the day."

"Rue the day," Wick repeated. "It sounds nice."

Preacher meant to leave the trading post early the next morning, but after a peaceful night's sleep, Vincente Ojeida asked him for some tips on handling a pistol, and Preacher was in such a good mood that he agreed to spend the morning there.

Followed by Dog, Preacher and Vincente walked out to a large open space behind the trading post, where Preacher placed several fist-sized chunks of rock on the trunk of a fallen tree Vincente had been meaning to split up for firewood. Then he moved back about twenty paces and drew both pistols. While Vincente watched, Preacher lifted both weapons and fired them without even seeming to aim. Two of the rocks on the log blew apart.

"Dios mio!"

Preacher lowered the pistols and smiled. "Don't go gettin' the idea that I can do that ever' time," he cautioned. "Along about ever' seven or eight shots, I'm liable to miss one, 'specially if somebody's shootin' back at me."

"You can teach me how to do this?" Vincente asked enthusiastically.

"I seriously doubt it. Some hombres, and I happen to be one of 'em, are what you might call freaks o' nature. The Good Lord blessed us with the speed to get a gun into action in a hurry, and the steady hand and eye so that most of the time all we have to do to hit somethin' is to look at it. It's a God-given talent . . . although sometimes when there's so much killin' goin' on, it seems to me almost like the Devil might've had a hand in it, too. There's times, though, when it comes in mighty handy."

Vincente looked disappointed. "But you cannot teach me?"

"Not to do what I just done. With practice, though, you can be as good a shot, or better, than most folks you'll ever run into. Let me see your pistol."

Vincente held out the gun he had brought from the trading post. Preacher looked it over, nodded in satisfaction, and handed it back to him.

"That's a fine weapon, and it's been taken care of. It'll shoot true. Now load 'er up and let 'er rip."

"You want me to shoot at the rocks?" Vincente asked as he loaded and primed the pistol. His movements were fairly slow, but he didn't fumble with what he was doing. That was a good sign.

"Just pick one of them and aim at it," Preacher told him. "Don't get in a hurry, but don't waste a lot of time, either. The longer you stand there holding your arm outstretched with a gun in your hand, the heavier it's gonna get."

Instinctively, Vincente took a deep breath without Preacher having to tell him to do so. He aimed for a couple of seconds and then pressed the trigger. The pistol boomed and bucked upward in his hand. He lowered it, squinted through the cloud of powder smoke that floated in front of him, and said, "I missed!"

"The rock's still there, all right. Look right underneath it, though." Preacher pointed at a scar in the wood.

"Is that where the shot hit?"

"Sure is. You didn't miss but by a few inches. Try again."

Vincente began reloading. The look of disappointment that had been on his face a moment earlier had vanished swiftly. When he was ready, he took aim and fired again. This time one of the rocks shattered, the pieces flying apart as the heavy lead ball struck it. Vincente let out an excited whoop.

"There you go," Preacher said. "You got a good eye. I can tell that about you. All you need is practice, and you'll be a lot better shot than you ever thought you could be."

"I cannot thank you enough, Señor Preacher—I mean, Preacher. Can I shoot again?"

Preacher waved a hand. "It's your powder and lead. Have at it."

For the next half hour, Vincente practiced, with Preacher setting up more rocks on the log for him to use as targets. He still missed about as many shots as he made, but Preacher thought that was pretty good and said as much. When Vincente was ready to call a halt to the practice, he said, "You will stay and eat with us, and then this afternoon, after siesta, we will shoot again, no?"

Preacher rubbed his jaw. He'd been planning to ride out, but Vincente was good company and his womenfolks were good cooks, there was no doubt about that. And Preacher figured there were still more tips he could give Vincente that would make him an even better shot. For one thing, Vincente needed to understand that shooting at rocks on a log and shooting at a man who was trying to kill you as hard as you were trying to kill him were two entirely different things. Preacher figured that a good grasp of that truth was at least as important as knowing how to stand and hold the gun and aim.

"Sure," he told the eager Vincente. "I reckon I can tarry a while longer. That's one good thing about livin' wild and free—nobody's waitin' for you."

But even as the words came out of his mouth, a memory flashed through his mind, a memory of a girl with long dark hair and a gentle touch and a sweet smile . . . a girl long gone, who probably never would have been his, even if she had lived. Yes, living wild and free had its blessings. . . .

But it had its little curses, too.

FOUR

What with one thing and another, three days went by and Preacher was still at the trading post. There were things around the place, like repairing the roof and the corral fence, that Vincente could use the help of another man for, and their shooting practice continued, too. Lupita had made friends with Dog, and the big brute was acting almost like a pup again. Preacher had ridden fairly hard from Texas, and Horse could use the rest. Preacher's only real worry was that if he stayed here too long, he might get fat from Elgera's cooking. He couldn't hardly empty his plate at mealtime before she had it filled up again.

Every day when he rolled out of his robes, he told himself that he'd be moving on. But good intentions, and all that . . .

He and Vincente were behind the trading post on the third afternoon. Vincente was practicing firing two pistols at the same time and not getting the hang of it. He had just lowered the empty weapons when Lupita came running around the building, calling, "*Papá, Papá!* Wagons coming!" Dog trailed behind her, barking excitedly.

Preacher and Vincente turned to face the girl. "One of the wagon trains of Señor Bent and Señor St. Vrain?" Vincente asked.

Lupita shook her head. "No, there are only two wagons. They come from the south."

"Travelers," Vincente said. "But where are they going?"

"Only one way to find out," Preacher said.

The four of them walked back around the trading post. Preacher saw the wagons trundling toward them along the trail, drawn by teams of mules. They were squarish vehicles with canvas covers over the backs. As they came closer, Preacher saw that a well-dressed man and woman sat on the driver's seat of the first wagon. They appeared to be in their twenties. The young man handled the reins and was doing a decent job of it. The second wagon was being driven by a stolid-faced Indian in white tunic and pants. A blue sash was around his waist, and a matching strip of cloth was tied around his head, holding back his thick, square-cut black hair. Next to him on the seat of the second wagon was a priest in a brown, hooded robe. Three Indians who resembled the one driving the wagon followed on horseback.

"Ricos," Vincente said quietly. "Rich ones, from Taos or Santa Fe, or perhaps even Mexico City. Why are they here?"

Preacher agreed with Vincente's assessment. The young couple's fancy clothes were indicators of their wealth, as were the sturdy wagons and the fine mule teams. The Indians were probably their servants. But Preacher didn't know why they had come to the edge of the Sangre de Cristos, or what the priest was doing with them.

Elgera came out on the porch, too, and watched with the others as the wagons pulled up to the trading post and stopped. The young man climbed down easily from the lead wagon's high seat and then turned to help the young woman descend to the ground. Together, they came to the bottom of the steps leading to the log building's porch.

They made a fine-looking pair. The boy was handsome and the gal was beautiful. Preacher couldn't decide if they were married, or brother and sister. He thought he detected a family resemblance that made him lean toward the latter choice.

That was confirmed a moment later when the young man said, *"Hola, señores y señora."* He took off his flat-crowned hat, revealing thick, glossy black hair, and swept low in a bow to Lupita. *"Y muy bonita señorita."*

Lupita blushed at the compliment, making her even prettier.

The young man straightened and replaced his hat on his head. "I am Esteban Felipe Alvarez, and this is my sister Juanita Olivera Alvarez."

"Welcome to my trading post, Señor and Señorita," Vincente said. "I am Vincente Ojeida. This is my wife and daughter, and our amigo, Señor Preacher."

"Preacher?" The sharply spoken word came from the priest, who had climbed down from the second wagon and now came forward. The four Indians stayed deferentially in the background. "You are a man of God?" The priest's expression as he looked up at Preacher made it clear that he found that idea hard to believe.

"Not like you, Padre," Preacher replied, "although I reckon I'm on good enough speakin' terms with the fella you call El Señor Dios."

"If you are not a preacher, is it not presumptuous of you to call yourself one?"

Most of the time, Preacher got along all right with men of God, but he felt an instinctive dislike for this little priest. The padre had thrown back the hood of his robe, revealing that he was bald except for a fringe of hair around his ears and the back of his head. He wasn't all that old, though, probably no more than thirty.

Keeping his temper in check, Preacher said, "The Injuns tagged that moniker on me. I got captured by a bunch of Blackfoot who figured on torturin' me to death. I couldn't get away from 'em, so I done the only thing I could. I started talkin'. I'd seen a street preacher one time, back in St. Louis, so I done like him and spouted the Gospel for ten or twelve hours straight. By that time, the Injuns decided that I was touched by the spirits—"

"The Holy Spirit?" the priest interrupted.

"Spirits that they found holy, anyway." Preacher shrugged. "They let me go, and that was all I cared about. The story got around, and I been knowed as Preacher ever since."

Vincente looked up from beside him and said, "You never told me that story, amigo."

"Well, I've only knowed you a few days, and you ain't asked about it yet."

"This is true."

The priest said, "I still think it is improper for a sinner to bear such a name."

"Last time I checked," Preacher drawled, "we was *all* sinners, old son."

The priest glared and might have continued the argument, but Esteban Alvarez said smoothly, "You must forgive Father Hortensio. He takes his calling very seriously."

The priest sniffed. "How else should I take it? What else in life could be more important than doing the work of our Holy Mother Church?"

As if he hadn't been interrupted, Esteban continued. "We have journeyed far, all the way from Mexico City, and would like to buy some supplies before we continue on our way. Can you accommodate us, Señor Ojeida?"

"Of course, Señor. Please, you and your sister come in."

So far, Juanita Alvarez had not spoken. But as she and her brother stepped onto the porch, Lupita came up to her and said, "Señorita, your dress is so . . . so beautiful! I have never seen anything like it!"

Juanita smiled at the girl and said, "*Gracias*. I have others in the wagon. Perhaps you would like to try one of them on before we leave?"

Lupita turned her excited gaze toward her mother. "Did you hear that? Can I try on one of the señorita's dresses, Mamá?"

"Perhaps," Elgera said. "We will see." She was frowning slightly, as if she didn't totally approve of the visitors. Preacher could understand that. Elgera probably didn't want her daughter's head getting filled with notions. Life out here on the Santa Fe Trail was hard, and there wasn't much time for extravagances.

Everyone went inside the trading post except Preacher and the Indians. Father Hortensio gave the mountain man an unfriendly look out of the corner of his eye as he went past, but Preacher ignored him. He didn't give a hoot whether or not some priest approved of him.

Preacher lingered on the porch instead and kept an eye on the Indians. He wondered what tribe they belonged to. Down in Texas, there were Comanches and Apaches, but these Indians didn't belong to either of those tribes. Navajo, maybe, he decided, although that didn't seem exactly right, either. He wasn't going to ask them. He didn't know if they even spoke English, and his Spanish, while good enough for him to get by, wasn't fluent by any means. They paid no attention to him. The three on horseback had dismounted, and now all four of them squatted on their haunches next to the second wagon and talked among themselves in guttural voices too low for Preacher to make out the words. He probably wouldn't have been able to understand their lingo, even if he knew what they were saying.

Vincente came back out onto the porch a few minutes later. "Señor Alvarez is picking out his supplies," he said. "I think he must be the richest man who ever stopped here."

"Did he say where they're bound?"

Vincente shook his head. "Up over the pass, that is all I know."

Preacher rubbed at his jaw as he frowned in thought. "Sort of out of place up here, ain't they?"

"It is true," Vincente said with a shrug. "The señorita, I can tell she is tired. The journey has been hard on her."

"They must have some mighty important reason to come

all the way from Mexico City and go on up into the mountains like they're plannin'."

"*Si*, but it is no business of mine."

"Mine, neither," Preacher said.

But he had a nagging feeling in the back of his mind that it might not stay that way.

Since it was already fairly late in the day, it came as no surprise when Esteban Alvarez decided that he and his sister and their companions would camp there at the trading post that night before moving on to the pass the next day. Vincente explained apologetically that he had no rooms to rent to the travelers, but Esteban told him not to worry.

"My sister sleeps in our wagon, and I have a tent for myself and Father Hortensio," he explained. "The Yaquis sleep under the wagons."

"Yaquis, eh?" Preacher said. "I wondered what tribe they belonged to."

"They come from the mountains of Mexico," Esteban said, "and are fierce fighters. But once they have declared their allegiance, there are no more loyal servants to be found anywhere."

Preacher hoped the young man was right about that. He had kept a close eye on the Yaquis, and they didn't look all that trustworthy to him. They had a sort of mean look in their eyes, like they would have enjoyed staking him out on an anthill and carving his eyelids off with their knives. The feeling was enough to make Preacher's hand itch to close around the butt of a pistol.

He kept his suspicions to himself, though, not wanting to alarm Vincente and Elgera without any reason. And he had to admit that the Yaquis had been on their best behavior so far. After dinner that night, everybody bedded down just like Esteban had said they would.

Preacher was restless and kept waking up during the night

to check on the group camped near the trading post. As far as he could tell, everything was quiet and peaceful. The travelers rose early the next morning. While the Yaquis prepared the teams for leaving, Esteban, Juanita, and Father Hortensio went into the trading post for breakfast. Juanita carried one of her dresses, which she gave to Lupita. "It will be a little large on you, *chiquita,* but your mamá can take it up," she said with a smile.

Lupita clutched the dress to her and asked excitedly, "Can I keep it, *Mamá?*"

A little reluctantly, Elgera said, "That will be fine. *Muchas gracias, señorita.*"

"De nada," Juanita said casually.

Father Hortensio watched the exchange with a frown of disapproval on his face. "Vanity is a sin," he proclaimed to no one in particular.

Preacher was leaning against a pickle barrel beside the priest. In a quiet voice, he said, "So's bein' a sour-faced jackass who acts like he's got a corncob stuck up his butt."

The priest turned sharply toward him and hissed, "You dare—"

"These are good folks," Preacher cut in. "I don't mean to be disrespectful, Padre, but I won't stand by while they're bad-mouthed, neither."

"You *do* mean to be disrespectful," Father Hortensio sneered at him. "You are a heathen, Señor!"

Preacher shrugged. "I disagree, but even if you're right, I been called worse in my time."

The priest just scowled, shook his bald head, and turned away. Preacher let him go. He sort of liked Esteban and Juanita, who didn't seem quite as spoiled as they might have been, given their wealth, but he was more than ready for the unpleasant little priest to move on.

After breakfast, that was what happened. The Indians had the wagons ready, so the Alvarez siblings climbed on board, as did Father Hortensio, and the little caravan moved out with waves and shouts of farewell from the Ojeida family. Preacher stood off to the side with Dog and watched the wagons roll toward the mountains. It took them a while, but eventually they were out of sight.

Vincente came over to Preacher. "You will stay again?" he asked.

"Sure. I wouldn't mind givin' those folks a good head start before I leave. I'm headin' the same direction, and I don't want to ride up on 'em and wind up havin' to travel with them. I've had enough of that priest."

Vincente crossed himself. "Father Hortensio is a man of God. He should be respected."

"Fella's got to earn my respect," Preacher said. "He don't get it just because he wears a padre's robes."

Vincente changed the subject, clearly not wanting to argue with this tall, lanky mountain man who had become his friend. They walked around behind the trading post and Vincente resumed his target practice, with Preacher making a suggestion from time to time that might improve his marksmanship.

More than an hour had passed fairly pleasantly in that manner when Preacher suddenly stood up from the tree stump where he had been sitting and cocked his head. Vincente noticed his reaction and asked, "What is it, Preacher?"

"I thought I heard somethin'. . . . There it is again!" Distant popping sounds came to his ears.

Vincente frowned. "I hear it, too. What is that?"

A grim look settled over Preacher's rugged face. "Those are gunshots, Vincente," he said, "and it sounds like they're comin' from the pass."

Vincente's eyes widened. "*Caramba!* Señor Esteban and Señorita Juanita . . ."

Preacher nodded and said, "Yeah. It sounds like those young folks are in trouble. Bad trouble."

FIVE

After the first flurry of gunshots, the sounds settled down to more regularly spaced intervals. Preacher heard them plainly enough as he was getting Horse ready to ride. It sounded to him like somebody had bushwhacked the Alvarez wagons and now had their occupants pinned down.

Of course, it was possible the shots had nothing to do with Esteban and Juanita and their companions. Preacher figured that was pretty unlikely, though.

Vincente came up to him as he finished tightening the saddle cinch. "I will go with you, Preacher," he declared. He had put on a sombrero and had two pistols tucked behind his belt.

Preacher shook his head. "No, I reckon that ain't a good idea. You've got a family and a business to look after, Vincente. Handlin' gun trouble is more in my line."

"But I can help you," Vincente protested. "I am a much better shot now. You have said so yourself."

"Maybe so, but there's things you don't know yet, and I ain't got time right now to teach you." Preacher saw hurt feelings flare in Vincente's eyes at that blunt statement. He reached out and squeezed the man's shoulder. "You're a damn fine fella, Vincente, but there's liable to be killin' work up there in the mountains, and you just don't know how to do that yet."

If you're lucky, Preacher added to himself, *you never will.*

He swung up into the saddle while Vincente stood there frowning. From atop Horse's back, Preacher said, "If I don't come back, you might ought to get word to Santa Fe about those young folks. The army might want to come up here and have a look around for 'em."

Vincente nodded. "*Sí.* I will do this."

Preacher returned the nod and heeled Horse into a fast trot. Dog bounded along beside them. Without looking back, he rode toward the Sangre de Cristos and the high pass that led through the mountains.

It wasn't hard to follow the wagon tracks leading to the pass. The Alvarez wagons were far from the first ones to use this trail. Over the past few years, hundreds of vehicles belonging to Bent and St. Vrain had traversed this path, carrying heavy loads of goods both ways between St. Louis and Santa Fe. The wheels of those wagons had etched ruts in the softer ground and had even left marks on the rockier stretches. Preacher still heard the faint popping of gunshots as he reached the base of the mountains and started up the trail to the pass.

At first the route swung back and forth and the slope was fairly gentle. The trail reached a point, however, where the climb was sharper. Horse managed it without much trouble, but Preacher sensed that even the valiant animal underneath him was laboring a bit more than usual. For mules or oxen pulling wagons, it would be a long, slow climb. It probably took most of a day for a wagon train to reach the top.

Preacher wondered how far Esteban and Juanita had made it before they were ambushed.

Again he cautioned himself not to jump to conclusions. Maybe it was one of the trade caravans that had been attacked. He figured they must be tempting targets for *bandidos* or renegade Indians, what with all the supplies they carried. Vincente hadn't said anything about expecting a caravan to come through today, but that didn't mean it was impossible.

He would find out soon enough, Preacher told himself grimly. The shots were louder now. He would be coming to the site of the trouble before too much longer.

About forty-five minutes had passed since he left the Ojeida trading post when he spotted a puff of smoke from a rocky bluff that shouldered out from the side of the mountain and overlooked the trail. The smoke was followed an instant later by the crack of a rifle, the sound traveling clearly through the thin air. Preacher reined Horse to a halt and studied the face of that bluff. Several more puffs of smoke spurted out from different points. There must be a ledge running across there, Preacher decided, and half-a-dozen or so gunmen were hidden up there, firing down at the trail. From where he was, a hump of ground shielded the trail itself from his sight. Preacher dismounted and, taking his rifle with him, strode up the rise so that he could see the trail.

His mouth tightened into a thin line at the sight of the two wagons stopped on a fairly level stretch about two hundred yards ahead of him. They were the Alvarez wagons, all right; he had no trouble recognizing them. One of the lead mules on each team had been shot and collapsed in its traces, bringing both vehicles to a halt. Preacher didn't see anyone on or around the wagons, but as he watched, a shot came from underneath one of them. The members of the party must have taken cover underneath the wagons when the shooting started.

Preacher wondered if any of them had been hit. There were no bodies lying around, at least not that he could see, and he told himself that was a good sign. Those pilgrims were in a bad fix, though. At the point where the wagons were stopped, the trail was about twenty feet wide. To the right, the bluff where the bushwhackers were hidden rose sharply. To the left of the wagons was a steep drop-off that fell several hundred feet to a canyon. There was no cover around the wagons themselves.

The people hiding underneath them were pinned down, good and proper.

They weren't putting up much of a fight, either. An occasional shot came from under the wagons, but each time it drew heavy fire in return. The thick planks of the wagon bodies would probably stop most bullets, but the lead balls might ricochet from the stony surface of the trail and bounce around under the wagons, wreaking havoc.

Somehow, Preacher had to figure out a way to stop those ambushers, or the people with the wagons were doomed.

His brain, trained by years of living in dangerous situations despite his relative youth, swiftly considered and discarded several options. Riding down to the wagons wouldn't do any good; if he did that, then he'd just be trapped, too. He might have been able to climb above the ledge where the riflemen were concealed and fire down into their midst, but that would take too long. He was looking at a climb of an hour or more that way. And taking potshots at them from down here might annoy them, but he doubted if he could do any serious damage that way. The angle was such that the ledge shielded them.

Preacher lifted his gaze higher on the bluff. He saw several outcroppings of rock that were littered with boulders. He frowned as he studied the angles and did some rough figuring in his head. He thought that if he could get some of those rocks to moving, they might just roll down onto that ledge and cause some real problems for the bushwhackers. Of course, that would put the people even lower down with the wagons at some risk, too, but Preacher thought the slope was such that any falling rocks would fly out beyond the ledge and plummet on into the canyon far below. And there weren't enough boulders up there to cause a full-fledged avalanche.

It was worth a try, he decided. He couldn't see any other way to help the pilgrims trapped under those wagons.

He moved to the side of the trail and rested the barrel of his rifle on a rock, steadying it as he drew a bead on a likely boulder. His shot had to hit right under it, where the rock rested on the ground. If his aim was too high, the ball from his rifle would just splatter against the face of the boulder itself. He pulled back the hammer, sighted in as best he could, and pressed the trigger. The flintlock snapped, the priming powder went off with a hiss, and then the main charge exploded with a loud roar. The stock kicked hard against Preacher's shoulder.

The distance was too great. He couldn't tell where his shot had hit, or if it had done any good. But he knew it might take several more tries to dislodge the boulder. With quick, practiced movements, he reloaded the rifle, rested it on the rock again, and fired a second time.

By now the men on the ledge must have heard his shots and figured out that somebody else was taking cards in this game. Preacher wasn't surprised when a ball struck the rock wall above his head, causing a little shower of dust and rock splinters. The shot had missed him by several yards, so he didn't worry overmuch about it. He just finished reloading, brought the rifle to his shoulder, and let off another round.

This time he saw the boulder lurch forward a few inches before it came to a stop.

Something whined past his ear like a big insect. The ball kicked up dust in the trail behind him. He finished reloading and lifted the rifle again, nestling his beard-stubbled cheek against the smooth wood of the stock as he drew a bead. He pressed the trigger, and once again the rifle roared and kicked.

The boulder was poised on the bluff in a delicate balance. The men who had hidden themselves on the ledge to ambush the wagons had seen that it was a good place for a trap, but they had neglected to notice that they were placing themselves in harm's way as well. Now, as the boulder lurched forward again and began to roll, Preacher thought he heard faint shouts of alarm from the bushwhackers.

The boulder toppled headlong, bounced off a couple of

other rocks, and started them rolling, too. With a rumble like distant thunder, the rockslide grew in breadth and power.

Preacher saw men leap to their feet and race for the far end of the ledge, where it curved back out of sight. Smaller rocks smashed down around them as they fled. Preacher finished reloading the rifle yet again and snapped it to his shoulder. Aiming quickly, he fired. He thought one of the bushwhackers staggered as if hit, but he couldn't be sure about that. Dust was beginning to rise, obscuring his view of the ledge.

He saw one of the men struck by a falling boulder, though. It swept the luckless victim right off the ledge and out into empty space. Screaming, the man plummeted toward the trail some fifty feet below. He fell past it, though, along with the rock that had knocked him from the ledge, and disappeared into the canyon. His scream faded away.

Preacher reloaded the rifle yet again and ran back to Horse, where he hung the weapon on its sling attached to the saddle. He swung up onto Horse's back, called, "Come on, Dog!" and rode hard for the wagons.

Clouds of dust hung in the air around the ledge. It wouldn't take long for them to blow away. But for the moment, even if the bushwhackers dared to venture back out onto the ledge, they wouldn't be able to see to shoot down at the trail. They would have to fire blind, if at all. Preacher wanted to take advantage of that momentary respite and get the wagons moving again.

The Yaquis must have heard the pounding of Horse's hooves on the trail, because they scrambled out from under the wagons, rifles in their hands. Before they could blaze away at Preacher, Esteban Alvarez followed them out and called, "No! Hold your fire!"

Preacher reached the wagons a moment later and didn't bother to dismount. He swept an arm toward a bend in the trail about a hundred yards ahead of them and shouted, "Let's go! Cut them dead mules loose and get the hell out of here! Once you're around that bend, maybe they won't be able to fire down on you!"

Esteban caught at his stirrup. "Señor Preacher!" he said. "We were attacked—"

"I know that, and them buzzards are liable to come back and make a second try at you if you just sit here waitin' for 'em!" He called out to the Yaquis in his rough Spanish, hoping they understood as he repeated his orders to cut the dead mules loose from the rest of the animals and move the wagons around the bend.

The Yaquis got to work while Esteban helped his sister and Father Hortensio crawl out from under the lead wagon. Preacher didn't think any of them had been wounded, which was mighty lucky. The bushwhackers had killed the mules first to stop the wagons, and that had given the travelers just enough time to scurry to safety underneath the heavy vehicles.

Preacher rode ahead, scouting around the bend. As he had hoped, there was enough of an overhang shielding the trail so that another ambush would be impossible right here. He wheeled Horse around and trotted back, glad to see that the Yaquis had gotten the dead mules cut loose from their harness. Two of the Indians had taken the reins and began pulling the wagons around the slaughtered animals. "Climb on!" Preacher urged Esteban, Juanita, and Father Hortensio. "We can't afford to slow down!"

Esteban had to help Juanita and Father Hortensio clamber up onto the wagons. The priest was clumsier and needed more assistance than the young woman. They managed, though, and the wagons rolled on toward the bend in the trail. The Yaquis who were driving had to saw on the reins and tug hard to make the mules cooperate. It wasn't easy with unbalanced teams. The other two Indians rode behind the wagons, leading the extra saddle horse. Preacher rode in front, his rifle now in his hands again in case he had to make a quick shot at the first sign of another attack.

There was no ambush, however, and slowly the crippled wagons made their way around the bend and into the shelter of the overhang. Preacher waved for the Yaquis to stop and called, *"Alto!"* The Indians hauled back on the reins.

Preacher rode over to the lead wagon. Esteban and Father Hortensio peered out the back of it, their faces pale and drawn. "Anybody hurt?" Preacher asked.

Esteban shook his head. "Only the two mules who were killed. When we heard the shots and saw the mules stumble, we knew we were under attack and got under the wagons. Luck was with us."

"God was with us," Father Hortensio corrected.

"You better hope he still is," Preacher said, "if you ever want to make it to the top of this pass alive."

Six

Juanita Alvarez climbed out of the wagon, following her brother and Father Hortensio. She was as pale and frightened as they were, but she kept her back straight and her head up. Preacher saw that and admired her grit.

"Señor Preacher," she said. "You saved our lives. How did you manage to make the mountain fall on our attackers?"

"Well, it weren't hardly a whole mountain, just a few rocks," Preacher explained. "That slide probably looked and sounded worse'n it really was. But it spooked those old boys enough to make 'em turn tail and run, and that's all that matters."

"It did more than that to one of them," Esteban said. "I saw him knocked over the edge. He fell past us, all the way down into that canyon." A shudder ran through the young man's frame, and Father Hortensio made the sign of the cross and muttered a prayer.

"You're wastin' your breath, Padre," Preacher told the priest.

"Does not any man deserve to have his soul commended to God upon his death?" Father Hortensio challenged.

"If that bushwhacker shows up at the Pearly Gates, I expect St. Peter'll tell him to skedaddle, that there ain't no place for him. More than likely he's toastin' himself on the fires o' hell right about now."

"You cannot presume such a thing."

Preacher bit back the retort that almost came to his lips. He had bigger problems on his plate than arguing theology with a stiff-necked priest. "You folks fort up here for a while," he told them. "I'm gonna do a little scoutin' on ahead."

"You wish to join our party?" Esteban asked with a frown.

"I didn't say that. I reckon for the time bein', though, we're in this mess together, at least until we all get to the top of the pass."

With a warning for them to keep their eyes open and stay ready for trouble, he rode on up the trail, which soon resumed its steep climb.

Preacher didn't see any sign of the bushwhackers, and wondered if they could have given up. That ledge must have led to another trail that they had followed out of these rugged peaks and valleys. It didn't take long for his experienced eyes to see that the spot where the wagon had been attacked was the best place for an ambush in the pass. Anywhere else, the bushwhackers would have been exposed to any return fire.

That increased the likelihood that the wagons might be able to make it to the top without running into another assault. Preacher turned, rode back down to where the party of travelers waited, and urged them to get moving.

"Esteban, can you shoot a rifle?" he asked the young man.

"*Sí, señor.*"

"Let that Yaqui handle the team. You take a rifle and mount up on that extra horse. You'll ride up front with me. The other two Injuns can bring up the rear. Tell 'em to be ready to fire."

Esteban nodded and passed along the orders.

Preacher turned to Father Hortensio. "How about you, Padre? Ever shot a rifle?"

The priest drew himself up and glared. "Of course not. As a man of God, I am also a man of peace."

Juanita spoke up. "I can use a rifle, Señor Preacher."

"Give your sister a gun," Preacher said to Esteban. "If those varmints come after us again, we'll hand 'em a warm welcome."

Esteban didn't look all that happy about giving Juanita a rifle, but he took one from the wagon, loaded it, and handed it to her, along with a powder horn and a shot pouch. He armed himself the same way, climbed onto the extra horse, and followed Preacher out to a point about fifty yards ahead of the lead wagon.

"How will we go on without the other mules?" he asked.

"Worry about that once we're on top of this here hill," Preacher advised him.

"Perhaps we should have turned around and gone back down."

Preacher shook his head. "Easier said than done. There wasn't room to turn those wagons and teams around. Sometimes the best thing to do is to bull straight on ahead."

"I suspect you know a great deal about bulling ahead, Señor Preacher."

"I been accused o' bein' bullheaded often enough," Preacher said with a chuckle. Despite the lighter moment, his eyes were always moving, roving over the rocky slopes around them, searching for any telltale signs of trouble. His rugged face grew more serious as he asked, "Who do you reckon those fellas were?"

"The men who attacked us? Thieves, of course. They had to be thieves, after whatever is inside our wagons."

The answer came quickly from Esteban. Maybe a little too quickly, Preacher thought as his eyes narrowed. His question had been mostly an idle one. From the start, he had assumed that the bushwhackers were highwaymen of some sort.

But Esteban's reaction made him wonder, and for the first

time his instincts warned him there might be more to all of this than he had suspected.

Hank Sewell wouldn't have to worry about his broken nose anymore. He had a lot more broken now. Probably every damn bone in his body, after that fall into the canyon. That grim thought was in Cobey Larson's brain as he led the men into the camp about a mile from the top of the pass.

Wick Jimpson was there, along with the man they had met the day before, down below the pass. Their employer had shown up on schedule, along with three other men he had hired as guides and bodyguards. Since Wick's wounded leg hampered him too much for him to take part in the ambush, he had assumed the role of bodyguard. He could still get around well enough for that. The extra three men—Hardy Powers, Chuck Stilson, and George Worthy—had been placed under Cobey's command. That gave him seven men, including himself, to stop the wagons carrying those Mexicans. It should have been plenty.

But nothing had worked out, and now Cobey was furious. He had lost Sewell, and Stilson was wounded. A rifle ball had clipped him on the hip. He had bled like a stuck pig, but Cobey thought he was going to be all right. Wouldn't be much good for a while, though, injured like that. Cobey's own wounded arm was still stiff and sore, but it was healing all right and he could handle a gun; that was all that mattered.

The man who had hired them hurried out from the camp to meet them. He was an Easterner, a tall, skinny fella who dressed fancy and liked giving orders too much, especially considering the fact that he didn't know all that much about the West. Still, he had already paid them some decent wages, just for meeting him, and promised more if they helped him get what he wanted.

"What happened?" he demanded as Cobey and the others

rode up. "Did you stop the wagons? Where's the Alvarez girl?"

Cobey swung down from the saddle and said wearily, "We stopped the wagons, but then they got away."

"Got away?" the Easterner echoed. "You didn't kill Esteban Alvarez?"

"We didn't kill anybody," Cobey snapped. "Fact is, we lost a man, and got another wounded. You'd know that if you'd just open your eyes."

The man looked angry that Cobey would talk to him that way, but he held his temper. His intense gaze played over the other men for a moment, and he said, "Yes, I see now that one of you is missing. What happened?"

"Somebody else took a hand. We had those greasers and their wagons pinned down, just like I planned. But then some other fella came along and started some rocks rollin' down on us. We had to hightail it outta there, or risk havin' what happened to Hank happen to the rest of us."

"What did happen?"

"One of those rocks knocked him off the ledge where we set up our ambush," Cobey answered grimly. "He fell past the trail and into a canyon a couple of hundred feet deep."

"Did you find his body?"

Cobey snorted in disgust. "We never looked for it. Nobody ever survived a fall like that. Hate to say it, but the wolves'll have to take care of ol' Hank."

The Easterner grimaced. "This is truly a savage wilderness, isn't it?"

"Your choice to come out here," Cobey said.

"So the Alvarezes got away?"

"That's right. They're likely on their way up to the top of the pass now. It'll be a hard climb for them, since we killed two of their mules, but I reckon they can make it."

The other man nodded. "So we'll have to stop them up here. I suppose that'll have to be all right. All that really matters is they don't reach their goal before I do."

"I thought you didn't know exactly how to find what it is you're lookin' for. That's why you needed us to grab the girl and kill her brother, so you could make her take you to it."

"Finding the location would certainly be easier with her help, but if it becomes necessary, I'll conduct a search of my own. I'm confident in my abilities."

Cobey was glad somebody was confident in the fella. As for himself, he didn't fully trust anybody from east of the Mississippi.

"Well, you'd best tend to your wounded man," the Easterner went on. "There's nothing more we can do today, I suppose." A thought occurred to him. "You said that someone interfered in your plans. Who was it?"

"I ain't sure," Cobey said. "I never got a good look at him. But he's a hell of a shot, I know that. And I know that if I ever find out who it was and cross trails with the son of a bitch . . . I'll take great pleasure in guttin' him, up one way and down the other."

The slow process of climbing to the top of the pass was made even slower by the loss of the two mules. More than once, the two Yaquis who weren't driving had to dismount and put their shoulders against the back of a wagon to help push it farther along the trail. After a while, Preacher called a halt and decided that one of the mules should be taken from the second wagon and hitched into the empty spot in the first team. Then two of the Yaquis' saddle horses were hitched side by side in the second team. Mixing horses and mules often didn't work out, but in this case they didn't have much choice.

That made things go a little faster, and by late afternoon the wagons were finally nearing the top. Preacher sat on Horse and looked back down the trail. To his right, the mountains tailed on farther south. To his left, they petered out and turned into a vast sweep of mostly flat land that stretched all the way over into Texas. That was Comancheria over there, hundreds of miles where few if any white men had ever set foot. Bands of fierce Comanches roamed that territory, hunting buffalo and making war on their enemies. Preacher had heard plenty about them, enough to know that they were best avoided. But he was intrigued anyway and told himself that one of these days he would ride through that country, just to see what it looked like.

Beside him, Esteban Alvarez sat on his horse and said, "At times I wondered if we would ever make it. The journey has been a long one."

Preacher grunted. "All the way from Mexico City? I'd say so."

Esteban turned to him and went on. "I cannot express my gratitude enough, Señor Preacher. If not for your help, we would have died today. Those bandits would have killed us all and looted our wagons."

There he went, talking about thieves again. Preacher still wasn't convinced that was all there was to it. But he didn't want to press the issue at the moment. It was more important that they finish the job of getting the wagons through the pass and then make camp for the night.

The wagons trundled up the last few hundred yards of the trail and came out on a high, windswept plateau. The Sangre de Cristos continued to rise to the west. To the east were some ranges of smaller mountains and hills, with more flat land visible beyond them. Ahead, to the north, were the ruts of the Santa Fe Trail. Though Preacher had never been over it, he knew the trail continued in that direction until it reached the Arkansas River, where Bent's Fort was located. The trail turned east there and followed the river for a good long distance before it veered off to the northeast toward the Missouri settlements where it originated. While he was in Taos, Preacher had talked to several men who were familiar with the trail, and he had filed away in his brain the details of everything they said. Out here on the frontier, information was a little like gold: A man could never have too much of it.

"It's late enough in the day we'd better think about findin' a good place to camp," Preacher told Esteban. "Stay with the wagons and keep them movin' north. I'll find us a likely spot and ride back to show you the way."

"Do you think those men will come back?" Esteban asked worriedly.

"You don't never know," Preacher answered bluntly and honestly. "But this is pretty open country right around here. If they show up, you ought to be able to see 'em comin'. Use the wagons for cover and put up the best fight you can. I'll hear the shots and come a-runnin'."

"I hope it does not come to that," Esteban said with a frown.

"You and me both." Preacher turned Horse and trotted off to the north with Dog following.

He rejoined the wagons in less than half an hour with news that he had found a good campsite. He led the party off the trail to a small hollow ringed with trees. "They'll give us some cover, in case we have to fight off an attack," Preacher explained to Esteban.

"Do you think that is likely?"

"Don't matter whether it's likely or not. I figure to be ready in case it does happen."

After the wagons rolled through a gap in the trees into the hollow, Esteban dismounted and helped his sister and Father Hortensio climb down from the lead vehicle. The Yaquis set about efficiently caring for the animals and getting ready to spend the night here. One of them arranged some rocks in a circle and soon had a fire going. Preacher wasn't sure that was a good idea. The group had been ambushed once already today, and with the exception of the man who had been knocked into the canyon, the varmints responsible for the attack were still out there somewhere. A fire would tell them exactly where the wagons were.

Preacher soon saw that the Yaquis didn't intend to leave

the flames burning, though. One of the Indians quickly prepared supper and heated a pot of coffee, and then put out the fire before full darkness settled down. That came closer to meeting with Preacher's approval.

As they all gathered around the remains of the fire, which still gave off a little warmth, and began to eat, Juanita said, "It seems that you are now a member of our little company, Señor Preacher."

"Impossible," Father Hortensio snapped before Preacher could respond.

Esteban said, "We cannot ask Señor Preacher to inconvenience himself by traveling with us. I'm certain he has other destinations in mind."

"Well, I can't rightly say," Preacher drawled, "seein' as how I don't really know where you folks are bound. But it might be a good idea if I was to stick with you for a while. The bunch that jumped you is liable to try again, and you'll likely need every gun you can get to help fight them off."

"I am sure they will find some other group of travelers to rob—"

Preacher interrupted Esteban by saying, "That's another thing. I don't reckon those fellas were regular thieves. I think they were after something mighty particular—and I think you know what it is." Ignoring the surprised looks on the faces of Esteban, Juanita, and Father Hortensio, he went on stubbornly. "I reckon it's time one of you told me the truth."

SEVEN

Father Hortensio glared at Preacher and sputtered, "I will not be called a liar by an uncouth heathen—"

"I wasn't really talkin' to you, Padre," Preacher broke in, silencing the priest with a look. He switched his gaze to Esteban and Juanita. Most of the light had faded from the sky, but enough remained for Preacher to make out the expressions of surprise and confusion on their faces. "I'm talkin' to these two."

"I . . . I take offense at your words," Esteban began. "To imply that we have somehow concealed the truth from you . . ."

"Those men were thieves, bandits," Juanita put in. "Why would you think otherwise?"

Preacher took a sip of his coffee and then said, "Mainly, it's the way you've been tryin' to convince me they were just *bandidos*. I've knowed fellas who could quote most of Mr. Bill Shakespeare's plays, and I recollect one of 'em sayin', *Methinks thou doth protest too much.* That's the way it sounds to me when you start talkin' about those bushwhackers bein' simple thieves. On top of that, you've got the fact that a couple of rich young folks would come all the way up here from Mexico City, draggin' along a priest and some Injun servants. Seems to me like you'd have to have a mighty good reason to make such a trip. And then there's the way the whole lot of you acted just now, when I brought it up. You folks are after something, and those bushwhackers were tryin' to stop you from gettin' to it." Preacher leaned back on the log where he was sitting. "If I had to make a guess, I'd say we're talkin' about gold."

Father Hortensio caught his breath with a sharply indrawn hiss. "He knows!"

"I reckon I do now," Preacher said dryly.

With a sigh, Esteban said, "No, you had figured it out already, Señor. But it is not just gold we seek. It is silver, too, and precious gems."

"It is more than that," Juanita added quietly. "It is our history, our legacy."

"Why don't you start from the beginnin'?" Preacher suggested.

The Alvarez siblings looked at each other, but before either of them could speak, Father Hortensio said, "No! Tell him nothing more! I forbid it!"

"With all due respect, Padre, it is not your place to forbid me to speak," Esteban said.

"I am an instrument of the Lord! Defy me and you defy Him!"

"I am sorry," Esteban said with a shake of his head, "but I think Señor Preacher has a right to know."

Father Hortensio glared for a moment, then folded his arms across his chest. "It is your decision, Esteban," he said coldly. "I wash my hands of the matter."

"I remember hearin' about another fella who was big on hand-washin'," Preacher said. "Name of Pilate."

Father Hortensio puffed up until Preacher thought he might bust a blood vessel. The priest didn't say anything else, though. He just stood up and walked stiffly over to one of the wagons, where he stood and glowered off into the growing darkness.

"The father means well," Esteban said in a low voice. "He takes his responsibilities to the Church very seriously."

"Nothin' wrong with that. I just think it's best that I know what we're dealin' with here, so I can lend you young folks a hand."

"You would join us in our quest, Señor?" Juanita asked.

"Suppose you tell me about it, and then we'll see."

"Very well." Esteban took a deep breath. "The story goes back a little more than a hundred and fifty years, to a time when one of our ancestors, Don Francisco Ignacio Alvarez, was a military commander here in the province of Nuevo Mexico. Word reached the governor in Santa Fe that the Pueblo Indians were planning an uprising that would force out all the Spaniards in the province and destroy the missions that had been set up by the priests."

Preacher nodded. "The Pueblo Uprisin'. I've heard tell of it. Led by an Injun name of Popé, or somethin' like that."

"Yes, that is right. You know the story, then. You know how the Indians did rise up as they planned and drove out the Spanish soldiers, forcing the settlers to flee all the way to El Paso del Norte."

"I've heard yarns about it. I ain't an expert on the subject or nothin' like that."

"We *are* experts," Esteban said. "The story has been in our family for many generations of how the Indians fought with the soldiers and slaughtered every priest they could lay their hands on, desecrating and destroying the missions as well. It was a time of blood and fire, Señor Preacher, of torture and death."

"What's it got to do with you now?" Preacher asked bluntly, knowing that with Esteban's Latin flair for the dramatic, the story would probably take a long time in the telling if he didn't speed things up.

"As I said, our ancestor Don Francisco was a soldier. Before the uprising, the governor sent him to this area, to the Sangre de Cristos, to see if there was anything to the rumors of trouble. When he got here, he met a priest named Father Alberto."

Over by the wagons, Father Hortensio had turned around and was listening to the story, Preacher noticed. At the mention of his fellow cleric, Father Hortensio crossed himself and muttered something in Latin that Preacher took to mean *rest in peace*. Old Father Alberto must have come to a bad end.

"Some of the priests believed that the Indians would never rise against them," Esteban continued. "But Father Alberto knew there was great danger. He had established a mission near here. He sent word to the other missions in the area that the priests should bring all their holy artifacts to his mission."

"And them artifacts was made of gold and silver, I reckon," Preacher murmured.

Esteban nodded. "Of course. Some of them were even encrusted with gems. And there were many gold bars as well. Father Alberto gathered them all at his mission, and when our ancestor arrived with a troop of soldiers, he placed the responsibility for the safekeeping of this fortune in his hands. It was up to Don Francisco to save those things for the Church and keep them out of the hands of the marauding Indians, Father Alberto said. Our ancestor had no choice but to comply."

"What did he do with the stuff?"

"The Indians had not yet risen, but violence was imminent. There was no time to take the artifacts and the gold back to Santa Fe or even to Taos. So with a small group of his men, Don Francisco rode west into the mountains and concealed them, thinking to come back later and retrieve the cache once the uprising had been put down."

"Only it wasn't put down, was it?" Preacher asked. "Not for a good many years, anyway."

"*Sí,* that is correct. By the time Don Francisco and his men returned to Father Alberto's mission, the place was already under attack. The Pueblos killed Father Alberto and his servants, and the soldiers were forced to flee, fighting a running battle as they tried to reach the pass. Many of them were killed. Don Francisco was badly wounded. The few survivors from his troop finally got him to safety, and none of them were from the group that accompanied him into the mountains."

"So this Don Francisco was the only one who knew where he had cached all the mission loot."

Father Hortensio sniffed a little at Preacher's use of the word "loot," but he didn't say anything.

"Yes, and he was too badly hurt to do anything about it. He almost died, and he was never the same after that. He returned to his family home in Mexico City after being discharged from the army due to his injuries. No one knew what he had done except him."

"But he must've told somebody sooner or later, else you wouldn't know about it now."

Juanita said, "Don Francisco was an educated, cultured man, despite being a soldier. His health was always poor after that, but not so poor that he could not write."

Preacher nodded. "So he wrote it all in a book, includin' where to find the gold, and that book has been passed down from generation to generation, until now you two have decided to go after it."

"An excellent supposition, but it is not *quite* that simple," Esteban said. "No one in our family knew about Don Francisco's manuscript until fairly recently."

"That makes sense. Otherwise somebody would've likely tried to find the loot before now."

"Indeed. The Alvarez family has always been wealthy, but not so rich that it would have turned its back on such a fortune. Don Francisco never told anyone about what he had done or what he had written. Why he kept it a secret, we do not know. Shame, perhaps. A feeling that he had let down Spain and the Church."

"Pride's a good thing sometimes, but it's easy for a fella to have too much of it."

"*Es verdad.* Don Francisco's manuscript only recently came to light, and the secret was discovered at last."

"So the family sent you up here to recover the treasure," Preacher guessed.

Esteban laughed, but the sound had a bitter edge to it. "My sister and I are all that remains of a once-proud family, Señor Preacher. And our wealth was almost gone. We spent almost all we had left to buy these wagons and outfit them for the journey. Now we must find the treasure, if we are to have anything."

Preacher shot a glance at Father Hortensio. "I ain't sure I understand. Seems to me that when you get right down to it, all that loot really belongs to the Church. It was just turned over to your ancestor for safekeepin', not given to him."

Father Hortensio left his spot by the wagons and walked over to join them again. "This is true," he said in response to Preacher's comment, "but the Church is more interested in recovering the holy relics than in the gold bars. An arrangement has been made to give Señor and Señorita Alvarez a portion of the gold in return for their assistance in recovering the other things."

"Because they've got the book that their great-great-whatever-granddaddy wrote tellin' where the cache is."

Father Hortensio nodded solemnly. "Exactly."

"Unfortunately," Esteban said, "Don Francisco drew no map, and the directions he gives in his manuscript are rather vague. It may not be easy to locate the place where he hid the treasure. We will have to search for it, using the manuscript to give us clues where to look." Esteban sighed. "He was a bitter old man when he wrote it, and I think perhaps he was not quite right in the head."

Preacher rested his hands on his knees and said, "Well, that's all mighty interestin', and I appreciate you tellin' me the truth. But that don't answer all the questions. Who else knows about this?"

Esteban shook his head. "As far as we are aware, no one."

"But you're afraid somebody might have found out," Preacher said. "Otherwise you wouldn't think that the hombres who jumped you in the pass might be after the loot themselves."

"Don Francisco's manuscript was found by scholars from the university," Esteban explained. "It was among several trunks of old papers that . . . that we had sold to the university."

"Do not think badly of us for selling parts of our family heritage, Señor Preacher," Juanita said softly. "As Esteban told you, our fortunes have greatly declined."

Preacher shook his head. "I ain't here to pass judgment on nobody. That's more in the padre's line." He paused and then went on. "If you gave the manuscript to the university, how'd you get it back?"

"One of the teachers there recognized it for what it seems to be at first glance, merely an accounting of Don Francisco's life, and returned it to us, thinking that it might be of great sentimental value. That is when I read it and discovered what it really contained."

"You think somebody else could have read it before you got it back," Preacher speculated.

"It is certainly possible, though the teacher who brought it to us thought that no one had examined it thoroughly."

"No way of knowin' that for sure, though."

"No," Esteban agreed. "There is not."

Preacher thought about everything they had told him. He tugged on his earlobe and ran a thumbnail along his bearded jawline. It all made sense, except . . .

"How come you went to the Church?" he asked. "You could've gone after the treasure yourselves without bringin' Father Hortensio along."

"As you said," Esteban replied quietly, "everything truly belongs to the Church. It was our thought only to retrieve it and return it to its rightful owners. Don Francisco considered his failure to be a stain on his honor, and therefore on the honor of the Alvarez family. Juanita and I wished only to cleanse that stain. The bishop was the one who suggested that some of the gold be given to us in return for our service."

Preacher listened closely, but he didn't hear anything in the young man's voice except sincerity. He had known all along that Esteban and Juanita seemed like pretty good youngsters. It looked like his hunch about them was right.

"What will you do now, Señor Preacher?" Juanita asked. "If it is true that someone else opposes us and seeks the treasure for themselves, there may be great danger in attempting to re- cover it."

"Yeah, I reckon you're right about that."

"No one will think unkindly of you if you decide to leave," Esteban said. "We would not ask you to help us."

"We most certainly would not request the assistance of a heathen," Father Hortensio added.

Preacher chuckled. "You know, I'm right glad you said that, Padre. You helped me make up my mind." He came to his feet and tucked his rifle under his arm. "Right now, I'm goin' to scout around a mite and make sure nobody's lurkin' close by. Set up some watches with them Yaquis. We need somebody standin' guard all night."

"You mean. . . ." Esteban began.

"I mean, come mornin', we're goin' after that treasure, and this here heathen's gonna do whatever he can to help you find it."

EIGHT

The night passed quietly enough. Preacher's foray around the camp didn't turn up signs of anyone sneaking around and watching them, but that didn't mean they were in the clear. Despite everything Esteban and Juanita had said about no one else being aware of the treasure's existence, Preacher's gut told him otherwise.

While the Yaquis were preparing breakfast, Preacher stood at the edge of camp and looked toward the mountains in the west. They rose steeply, and as his experienced eyes searched them, he didn't see any passes.

"You look troubled, amigo," Esteban said as he came up to stand beside Preacher.

"I am, a mite," Preacher admitted. "We don't know how far into the mountains we'll have to go to find that loot. It's gonna be hard goin' with wagons."

"What would you suggest?"

"If there was a safe place to do it, I'd say we ought to leave the wagons and your sister and the padre somewhere with a couple o' them Yaquis for protection, whilst you, me, and the other two Injuns ride into the mountains on horseback to search for the treasure."

Before Esteban could respond to this suggestion, a growl

from Dog warned Preacher that someone unfriendly was approaching. As usual, Dog's instincts were good. Father Hortensio, who had been close enough to overhear the conversation, came up behind Preacher and Esteban and snapped, "This is impossible! I must be there when the holy treasure is found in order to take proper charge of it."

Preacher turned to look at the priest. "That sounds like you don't trust this boy," he said, inclining his head toward Esteban. "You best remember, after he found the old don's manuscript, him and his sister didn't even have to come to the Church and say anything about the loot. They could've gone after it and kept it all for themselves."

Stiffly, Father Hortensio said, "The Church commends Señor and Señorita Alvarez for their devotion and willingness to do the right thing. That is why the bishop proposed allowing them to retain some of the gold."

"But if it was up to you, you wouldn't give 'em nothin', ain't that right?"

"Such decisions are not mine to make."

"It is all right, Señor Preacher," Esteban said. "Father Hortensio is right. He should be there when the treasure is found. As for my sister . . ." He shrugged. "I would not want to try to persuade her that she should remain behind after coming this far. She has a mind of her own, that one, and is very headstrong in her opinions. I fear that is what has made it difficult for her to find a suitable husband."

Preacher thought that any man who wouldn't be interested in a gal as beautiful as Juanita Alvarez just because she held an opinion or two was a damned fool. He kept that to himself, however, and said instead, "Sooner or later, it'll come to that, because there's only so far you can take the wagons into the mountains. And unless we come across some horses, we've got only so many mounts. Somebody'll have to stay behind."

"What is it you Americans say?" Esteban asked. "We will cross that river when we come to it?"

"Close enough," Preacher said.

They pulled out a short time later, after a quick breakfast, leaving the Santa Fe Trail and striking out across country toward the Sangre de Cristos. By midday they were in the foothills, with the gray, snowcapped peaks looming ever higher above them. The air was cool, not summerlike at all despite the season.

Esteban liked riding one of the horses instead of a wagon. He willingly turned over the chore of handling the team to one of the Yaquis and positioned himself and his mount up front, riding along about fifty yards ahead of the wagons with Preacher.

"Them Yaquis ever talk except amongst themselves?" Preacher asked.

"Not often," Esteban replied. "They are a strange people, known far and wide for their cruelty to their enemies. But as I mentioned, they are also very loyal. These four have abandoned their heathen beliefs and converted to Christianity. They greatly admire Father Hortensio."

Preacher glanced over his shoulder toward the wagons, where the priest now rode with Juanita. "Seems more like a horse's ass to me," he muttered.

"You are not a religious man, Señor Preacher, despite your name?"

"I never said that. It's true I ain't a Catholic like you folks, but when I was a boy my ma took me to a few brush arbor meetin's whenever the circuit-ridin' preacher came through those parts. And since I come to the mountains, I've knowed fellas who could spout Scripture just like some can quote Shakespeare. I swear, there's some old boys who have got pretty much the whole Bible memorized. I've heard plenty of it around campfires here and there."

"But that is the extent of your religion?" Esteban persisted.

Preacher tilted his head back a little and squinted toward the mountains ahead of them. "Look up yonder," he said, pointing.

"What am I looking at?"

"You see that peak . . . that one right there . . . with the snow on top and all the different colors on its slopes and the big blue sky above it?"

"Of course."

"Mighty pretty, ain't it?"

"Beautiful," Esteban agreed.

"Well, the way I look at it," Preacher drawled, "man could never build somethin' that big and that pretty. The biggest, fanciest buildin' in the world is nothin' next to a mountain like that. And no matter what anybody says, I can't believe that it just happened that way. Somebody built that there mountain, and all the other mountains and deserts and forests and oceans, and whoever's responsible for all that has to be a whole heap bigger an' more powerful than folks like you and me—and the padre—can even imagine. That right there . . ." Preacher pointed again to the mountains. "That's my church. That's where I see the face of God in those slopes and hear His voice in the lonesome wind."

Esteban was silent for a moment, then said respectfully, "I see your point, Señor Preacher. And I believe you *are* a religious man, no matter what Father Hortensio may think."

"Why don't you just call me Preacher? No need to tag the señor on there."

"All right. Men who have fought side by side need not stand on ceremony, eh?"

Preacher nodded, even though he and Esteban hadn't really fought side by side . . . yet.

He would be mighty surprised if it didn't come down to that before all this was over, though.

The group pushed on, and during the afternoon they came to a river that flowed on a slightly southwest-to-northeast axis in a beautiful green valley. Preacher reined in, studied the narrow, fast-flowing stream for a moment, and then said, "I reckon this must be the river folks call the Picketwire. That ain't the real name of it, from what I understand. French trappers called it the Purgatoire, which I reckon must mean Purgatory. But since Americans come to this part of the country, it's been the Picketwire. We'll ride alongside it for a ways, but from what I've heard, we won't be able to follow it all the way up into the mountains. This little valley it's in narrows down to a canyon the wagons would never get through."

Esteban looked at him in admiration. "How can you know so much about this land if you have never before been here, Preacher?"

"I've talked to fellas who have, and I listened. A fella who keeps his ears open and pays attention lives a lot longer out here than one who don't."

They waited for the wagons to catch up to them, and as the vehicles pulled alongside, Father Hortensio said excitedly, "Is this the Purgatoire River?"

"That's what we was just talkin' about, Padre," Preacher replied. "There ain't no signs, of course, but I think this is the Picketwire, sure enough."

"That means we are not far from the Mission Santo Domingo. It was built on the banks of the Purgatoire River, in the shadow of the mountains."

"That's the mission where ol' Father Alberto worked?" Preacher asked.

Esteban nodded. "There are quite a few references to the mission in Don Francisco's memoir. Of course, there will be nothing left of it now, except perhaps some ruins."

"Once the matter of the treasure is settled," Father Hortensio said, "I would like to reestablish the Mission Santo Domingo. That is another part of my charge from the bishop, to investigate such a possibility."

"If you did, I don't know where you'd get your parishioners," Preacher commented. "In case you ain't noticed, this is a big country, and it's mostly empty. We ain't seen hide nor hair of anybody since we left the Ojeida tradin' post, except those bushwhackers. And they didn't strike me as the church-goin' sort."

"I am told there are many Indians in these mountains," Father Hortensio said. "Perhaps they are staying out of sight because we are strangers."

"Last time a bunch of priests tried to convert the Injuns up here in these parts, it didn't work out so good. That's the reason we're here, remember?"

"Things are different now. In those days, the Indians were still too close to their savage roots to fully embrace the Word of the Lord."

Preacher didn't figure things had changed all that much, but the priest wouldn't want to hear that. He would just sneer at whatever Preacher had to say.

"Maybe you're right," he muttered. "Anyway, we'll be pushin' on."

They followed the river, stopping a short time later for the noon meal, then pushing on westward. In the middle of the afternoon, they came in sight of something that, to Preacher's keen eyes, looked unnatural and out of place in these surroundings. After a moment he realized what he was seeing was the remains of some tumbled-down stone walls. It was seeing something man-made in the midst of all these natural wonders that struck him as odd. He knew he had to be looking at the ruins of Mission Santo Domingo.

None of the others had noticed the old walls yet. He drew back on the reins and brought Horse to a halt. Esteban stopped, too, and asked, "Is something wrong?"

"Nope," Preacher replied. "If you look up yonder, you'll see what's left of that ol' mission the padre was talkin' about."

Esteban looked where Preacher pointed, and his face grew excited. He turned in the saddle and called, "Juanita! Father Hortensio! It is the mission!" He rose in his stirrups and leveled an arm toward the ruins.

Father Hortensio urged the Yaqui driving the lead wagon to hurry. The stolid-faced Indian flapped the reins against the backs of the mules and struck them with a long, slender stick he used as a whip. The wagons quickly caught up with Preacher and Esteban. When they stopped beside the two horsemen, Father Hortensio scrambled down from the seat of the lead wagon and peered at what was left of the fallen mission walls. He looked more excited than Preacher had seen him so far. He made the sign of the cross and then began offering up a prayer of some sort in Latin. Preacher couldn't even come close to following the words.

"Now that we are here, where Don Francisco started when he rode out to conceal the treasure, we can study his manuscript more closely and see where to go next," Esteban said.

"You've got the manuscript with you?" Preacher asked.

"Of course. Did you think we would not bring it with us?"

Preacher shrugged. "For all I knew, you just wrote down the parts about where to find the church loot and left the manuscript someplace safe."

"No, we brought the entire document."

"The only copy?"

"Yes, but—" Esteban stopped short. "I see what you mean. If anything happened to it, our chances of finding the treasure would be much worse."

"That's what I was thinkin'. I reckon we'll stay here tonight and get a good start on the search in the mornin'. Whilst we're here, it might be a good idea to copy down what those old pages say."

Esteban nodded. "Yes, I will do that. An excellent idea, Preacher. We should have thought of it before we left Mexico City."

"Of course, in a way you might've had the right idea," Preacher mused. "If you'd left the manuscript behind, there was always the chance that somebody else could get hold of it and figure out where you'd gone and what you were after."

"This is true. Still, I should make a copy—"

Father Hortensio abruptly broke off his prayer and said sharply, "Listen! Do you hear that? There are cries coming from the ruins!"

Preacher narrowed his eyes and canted his head toward the old mission. He hadn't noticed the sounds before, even with his keen ears, probably because the priest's sonorous Latin had drowned them out. But now he heard them clearly enough. Somebody was up there in those ruins. . . .

And from the way they were hollering, they were in some sort of trouble.

NINE

"Stay here!" Preacher told the others. "I'll see what's goin' on up there."

"I can come, too," Esteban said.

"Stay here," Preacher said again, "and keep a hand on your gun!"

With that, he heeled Horse into a gallop toward the tumbled-down walls. Dog bounded along with him.

The shouts became louder and more strident as Preacher approached the ruins. Whoever was yelling must have heard him coming, because the sounds took on an added urgency. Preacher could make out the words now, and to his surprise, they were in English.

"Help! For God's sake, somebody help me!"

Preacher couldn't see anybody yet. Parts of all four walls of the mission's main building were still standing, and one of the walls seemed to be mostly intact. Off to the side were what was left of several smaller buildings, but Preacher could see that nobody was around them. The man yelling for help had to be on the other side of that biggest mission wall.

Suddenly, Preacher pulled Horse back to a walk. It had occurred to him that he and his companions probably had enemies in these mountains. He could be riding into a trap.

Instead of charging blindly around the corner of the old building, he stopped, dismounted, and drew both pistols from his belt.

"Hello, the mission!" he called. "What's wrong?"

The frantic shouts stopped for a second as the man heard Preacher's call. Then he said, "Please, sir, help me! There . . . there's a snake . . . I . . . I'm afraid it's going to strike! For the love of God, sir!"

Preacher walked closer with the guns leveled in front of him. As he neared the corner of the building, he heard something that confirmed at least part of what the frightened man had said. The fierce, buzzing rattle was unmistakable. There was a rattlesnake somewhere close by, and it was mad as hell.

Preacher thought the fear in the man's voice was as real as that rattle, too. He took another step and swung to his right, around the corner of the old mission. He saw a man with his back pressed up to the stone wall and his hands splayed against it. The stranger was staring at a jumble of rocks about five feet away from his feet. The snake was coiled in those rocks, his thick, mottled brown body wrapped tightly around itself, his head up and his tongue flickering from his mouth as the rattle at his other end buzzed madly.

"You're doin' fine, pilgrim," Preacher told the man quietly. "Just keep standin' still whilst I draw a bead. That rattler's a big son of a bitch."

Indeed, although it was hard to tell with the snake coiled up like that, Preacher figured it was at least six feet long, which meant that if it struck, it could reach the terrified man who stood by the wall. Moving deliberately, without too much haste but without wasting any time, either, Preacher extended his right arm and aimed the pistol in his hand. It was cocked and primed and ready to fire, just as soon as he was sure of his aim. . . .

The rattling rose to a crescendo. The snake started to strike just as Preacher pulled the trigger.

The pistol roared and bucked in Preacher's hand. He was afraid that the snake's movement had thrown his aim off a little, and as he stepped forward through the smoke, he saw that he was right. The pistol ball had struck the snake just behind the head, severing it from the body. With some momentum already established, the head itself kept going for a couple of feet before dropping to the ground.

"Stay away from that head!" Preacher snapped at the stranger. "That bastard can still bite you! He don't know he's dead yet."

He could see the snake's jaws still working, trying to sink his fangs into something and inject his venom into it. A couple of feet away, the headless body coiled and writhed and thrashed.

Preacher brought the heel of his boot down on the head and felt the satisfying crunch of bones as he stomped it. He ground the head into the rocky dirt, then picked up a stick and used it to flip the grisly remains away. He did the same thing with the snake's blood-dripping body.

The stranger was still leaning against the wall, but it was in relief now, not terror. His face was bathed in sweat despite the coolness. He said, "Thank God you came along when you did, sir!" and started to step away from the wall.

Preacher swept up his left-hand gun and fired again, aiming this time at the stranger's feet. The man shrieked and leaped in the air. When he came down, he landed awkwardly and fell to one knee.

Preacher leaned over and lifted the body of another snake on his pistol barrel. This one was smaller, only half the size of the monster Preacher had first shot, but he had no doubt it was just as venomous. His hurried shot had been accurate, striking the serpent in the head just as it launched itself at the man's leg. The heavy lead ball had completely disintegrated the head.

As Preacher tossed the second snake away, he said to the stranger, "Sorry there weren't time to warn you, friend. That snake come through a hole in the wall right next to your feet. Probably the mate o' that big son of a bitch. Figured I'd best just go ahead and shoot it whilst I had the chance."

The man was shaking. "Are . . . are there any more of those awful creatures around here?"

Preacher glanced around at the ruins of the old mission and said, "I wouldn't be a bit surprised. Snakes like rocky places like this. Plenty o' places for 'em to den up. If you watch where you're steppin', though, and don't start turnin' over rocks, chances are you won't get bit. Most times, a snake'll slither off without botherin' nobody when a man comes around, if he's got half a chance to. They only coil up and get angrified if they feel cornered, or if there's a lot of loud noise. All that yellin' you were doin' probably irritated the hell out o' them snakes."

The man pulled a handkerchief from his pocket and mopped his sweat-drenched face. "I wasn't too happy about it myself."

Preacher started to reload his pistols. As he did so, he glanced at the stranger, taking his measure. The man was tall and slender and dressed like an Easterner, in tight trousers and shoes instead of boots and a tweed waistcoat. He wore a beaver hat on his head and had muttonchop side-whiskers. All in all, he looked about as out of place in the foothills of the Sangre de Cristo Mountains as a man could possibly be.

"No offense, friend," Preacher said as he tucked the loaded pistols behind his belt again, "but what the hell are you doin' here?"

"I . . . I came to study this old mission. I'm a historian and scholar of religion. My name is Rufus Chambers. Dr. Rufus Chambers."

Preacher frowned. "You're a sawbones, too, besides all that other stuff you said?"

"My doctorate is in philosophy, not medicine," Rufus Chambers said. "I'm on sabbatical from Harvard."

"All right," Preacher said, not quite sure what a sabbatical was. Some kind of wagon, maybe. He had heard of Harvard and knew it was a fancy school back East somewhere. He couldn't for the life of him figure out how a greenhorn like Chambers had gotten from there to here without getting himself killed somewhere along the way.

He heard hoofbeats coming from farther west along the river and looked in that direction when Dog growled. "Is . . . is that beast tame?" Chambers asked. "It looks like a wolf."

"Naw, he's a dog . . . mostly," Preacher replied. "And he's tame . . . mostly." He saw two riders approaching the old mission in a hurry. They wore buckskin and homespun. One sported a coonskin cap, the other a trapper's hat with a wide brim, much like Preacher's hat. Each man carried a rifle.

"Ah," Chambers said. "My guides have returned."

So that was how he had managed to survive. He had hired a couple of experienced frontiersmen to look after him. That was a pretty good idea, considering the man's inexperience. Those two should have stayed closer, though, because Chambers had almost gotten himself killed wandering around by himself in these ruins.

The men rode up and reined to a halt, casting wary glances toward Preacher as they did so. "You all right, Professor?" the one in the coonskin cap asked. "We heard a couple o' shots."

"Yes, I'm fine, Mr. Powers," Chambers said. "I had a perilous encounter with a pair of angry reptiles, but this gentleman came along in time to dispose of them for me."

"I shot a couple o' rattlesnakes, is what he's tryin' to say," Preacher put in.

The man called Powers frowned at him. "Who are you, mister?"

"They call me Preacher."

The two guides exchanged a glance, and Preacher knew they had heard of him.

"Well, I'm certainly glad to meet you, Mr. Preacher," Chambers said. "Allow me to introduce my guides, Mr. Powers and Mr. Worthy."

Both men gave Preacher curt nods, which he returned in kind.

"They were scouting along the river and left me here to explore the ruins," Chambers went on. "I didn't think there would be any danger."

"Your guides there should've knowed better."

"How was we supposed to know he'd stumble into a den of rattlers?" the one called Worthy asked in surly tones.

"You never saw any snakes in a place like this before?" Preacher shot back.

"Gentlemen, gentlemen, there's no need to argue," Chambers put in. "The important thing is that no one was hurt. Well, except for the snakes, of course. And I, for one, don't intend to lose any sleep over them."

Preacher turned to the Easterner again. "You plan on stayin' around here for a while?" he asked.

"Yes, indeed. I don't know for how long. I'm conducting a study of Spanish missions, preparatory to writing a volume of history concerning the spread of religion through uncivilized areas and the obstacles encountered in the inevitable collision with more primitive cultures, and I suppose I'll stay as long as my researches require." Chambers looked guilelessly at Preacher. "Why? My presence here doesn't represent a problem, does it?"

"That's one thing about the frontier," Preacher said, not answering the question directly. "A fella can go where he pleases, as long as he can stay alive doin' it."

"Oh. Of course. I thought perhaps you represented the Mexican government. I have permission from the government to be here, arranged through the university in Mexico City."

"I don't represent nobody but myself," Preacher said. "I sure as hell don't speak for any government, Mexican, American, or otherwise."

Powers spoke up. "Professor, when we were ridin' in, we

spotted a couple of wagons parked beside the river a few hundred yards east of here."

"Those folks are with me," Preacher said.

"I suppose you want to move on, then," Chambers said. He extended his hand. "Thank you for stopping and coming to my assistance, Mister . . . Preacher, was it?"

"Just Preacher." He ignored the professor's hand. "Fact of the matter is, we were bound for this old mission, too."

"Oh." Chambers's face lit up. "Are your companions scholars, too?"

"You could say that. One of 'em's a priest."

"Excellent! I can question him directly about the expansion of the Church into the province of Nuevo Mexico. It's quite a bloodstained tale, from what I understand."

Preacher rubbed his chin. He didn't like Powers and Worthy, and Rufus Chambers seemed like the sort of fella who would get mighty annoying to have around after a while. Not only that, but the presence of these three Americans at Mission Santo Domingo could complicate the search for the missing treasure that much more.

Still, Preacher thought that watching the professor and Father Hortensio going at it hammer and tongs might be pretty entertaining to watch. There was nothing he could do about it, either. If he tried to run off Chambers and the two guides, that would likely just make them suspicious.

He and Esteban and Juanita would have to come up with some reasonable story to explain why they were here. Then he and Esteban could carry on with the search while Juanita, Father Hortensio, and the Yaquis stayed here at the mission to keep an eye on Chambers and the other two men. The whole situation was trickier now, but not impossible.

"I'll ride on out and bring the wagons in," Preacher said. "You watch your step, Professor, hear?"

"Indeed I shall! I don't want to stir up any more poisonous snakes."

"Venomous," Preacher said as he gathered Horse's reins.

"I beg your pardon?"

"Them rattlers ain't poisonous. I've eaten rattlesnake meat more'n once in my life. Tastes a mite like chicken. They can't hurt you unless they bite you, so they're venomous."

"I see," Chambers said with a frown. "Perhaps you should be teaching the natural sciences back at Harvard, Preacher."

The mountain man swung up into the saddle. "Professor Preacher?" He shook his head. "I don't reckon that'd be a good idea."

He had his doctorate, whatever that was, in staying alive.

TEN

Esteban and Juanita were worried about the news that Preacher brought back to the wagons, but Father Hortensio was absolutely livid.

"Impossible!" the priest declared. "Those men have no right to be here!"

"They claim they got permission from the Mexican government."

"Impossible!" Father Hortensio said again. "The government and the Church work closely together. If there was some sort of American expedition bound for Mission Santo Domingo, I would have heard about it."

"Maybe the arrangements were made after we left Mexico City," Esteban suggested. "We have been on the trail quite some time, after all."

That explanation made sense to Preacher. He didn't know how long it took to get from Harvard to Nuevo Mexico. To tell the truth, he wasn't exactly sure where Harvard was. He was a mite foggy on his geography when it came to places east of the Mississippi.

"No matter what the arrangements were," he said, "Professor Chambers and them other two fellas are here, and I don't reckon we can run 'em off without causin' more trouble. We'll just have to keep an eye on 'em, that's all."

Father Hortensio muttered some more, but Preacher ignored him. It was Esteban who asked a more pertinent question.

"What do we tell them about why we are here?"

"I been thinkin' on that," Preacher said. "How about we say that you and your sister have an old land grant from the King of Spain that gives you the right to some land up here, and you're scoutin' it out for the family?"

Esteban nodded. "That sounds like it might be true. There were many such land grants, and they covered much of the territory in Nuevo Mexico."

"That's what I was thinkin'."

Juanita asked, "What if those men ask to see the papers pertaining to such a land grant?"

"Why would they?" Esteban replied. "They have no interest in that. Nor would they have any right to make such a demand. We could reasonably refuse it."

Preacher said, "It ain't likely to come to that. As long as we stay out of their way, I reckon they'll stay out of ours. That professor may talk your ears off, but that's the biggest danger."

"Very well, then," Esteban said. "Let us go."

They got the wagons moving again. By the time they reached the ruins, Preacher saw that Powers and Worthy had a campfire going, well away from the tumbled-down buildings themselves. They didn't want to run into any more rattlesnakes, and Preacher couldn't blame them for that.

"We'll set up our own camp over there," he said, pointing to another spot about a hundred yards away from the ruins of the old mission. There were some trees there to give them a little shade and form a windbreak of sorts.

While the Yaquis pulled the wagons up to the place Preacher had selected as their campsite, Preacher and Esteban rode over to Professor Chambers's camp. The professor had set up a tent for himself. He came out of it when he heard the horses and raised a hand in greeting to Preacher and Esteban.

Preacher performed the introductions. "Professor, this is Don Esteban Alvarez of Mexico City. Don Esteban, Professor Rufus Chambers of Harvard University."

Esteban dismounted and shook hands with Chambers. "It is an honor to meet you, Professor," he said. "I have heard of your great university Harvard. I myself attended the University of Mexico."

"Also known as the Royal and Pontifical University," Chambers said. "The oldest institution of higher learning in the New World."

"You know much about Mexico?" Esteban asked.

"I've studied your country quite extensively, Don Esteban, from the first Spanish colonies to the overthrowing of Spanish rule and the establishment of a sovereign Mexican government less than ten years ago. You come from a fascinating land."

"*Gracias*. I am afraid I know little by comparison about your United States of America."

Chambers waved a hand. "We're upstarts compared to the Spanish. Our country has been in existence a mere fifty years or so." He looked past Preacher and Esteban at the wagons and said, "My word! You have a lady with you. A very beautiful lady, at that."

"My sister," Esteban said, his voice hardening a little. "Doña Juanita."

"Please accept my apologies. I meant no offense. I was just startled to see such a lovely flower out here in the middle of this wilderness."

"I will introduce you to her later," Esteban said. "And to our other traveling companion, Father Hortensio."

"I would be most appreciative. I'm especially interested in discussing historical topics regarding the Church's development in Mexico with the good father."

Preacher pointed at the wagons with his thumb. "We best go see about gettin' camp set up."

"Of course." Chambers gave them a toothy grin. "So nice to meet you, Don Esteban."

Esteban just nodded and walked back to the wagons with Preacher. Both of them led their horses. Under his breath, Esteban said, "The professor is a strange man."

"He's a fish out o' water, that's for sure," Preacher agreed.

The Yaquis were doing their usual efficient job of setting up camp. Juanita and Father Hortensio were waiting for Preacher and Esteban. "Did they ask questions about why we are here?" Juanita wanted to know.

Esteban shook his head. "No, the professor did not even seem concerned about that. He is very interested in talking to Father Hortensio about the Church, however."

The priest folded his arms across his chest. "I have nothing to say to him."

"You might want to be friendly," Preacher suggested. "That'll keep 'em from wondering about us, maybe."

"There will be no time for such conversation. We will be spending our days searching for the lost treasure."

"Well, now," Preacher said, "I was thinkin' that maybe you and the señorita and them Yaquis might stay here whilst Esteban and I do the searchin'."

Father Hortensio shook his head. "No, I have already said that this is unacceptable. I must be there when the treasure is found."

"What do you reckon Esteban and me are gonna do, run off with it?" Preacher felt himself getting angry, even though he tried to rein in his temper.

Esteban moved between the mountain man and the priest. "Father," he said quietly, "I think Preacher is right. It will be safer if you and Juanita stay here. We cannot forget that we were attacked. The men responsible for that may still be after us. This place will be easier to defend than if we were caught out in the open."

"That's right," Preacher said. "You could fort up in that old mission. You'd just have to be careful and watch out for snakes."

Father Hortensio sniffed and said, "Sometimes the most treacherous serpents are those who go on two legs rather than on their bellies."

For once, Preacher couldn't argue with him.

They were sitting around the remains of their campfire that night when Professor Chambers and his two guides walked over from the other camp. "Hello, there!" Chambers called. "That's the accepted protocol, isn't it? One should always sing out when approaching another man's camp?"

"If you don't want to get shot, it's the smart thing to do," Preacher agreed. He was on his feet, having stood up when he heard the three men coming. His right hand rested lightly on the butt of a pistol.

Esteban stood up, too, and waved toward the log they were using for a bench. "Join us, Señores," he said graciously.

Chambers stopped in front of Juanita and swept off his hat. He bent low in a bow. "Señorita," he said respectfully. "It is my great honor to make your acquaintance."

"My sister," Esteban said. "Doña Juanita Olivera Alvarez. Juanita, this is Professor Rufus Chambers."

"Good evening, Professor," Juanita said as Chambers straightened from his bow. "We did not expect to encounter a man of culture and learning out here so far from civilization."

"Nor did I think to encounter such a charming, lovely young woman."

"You are bold, sir," she said sharply.

"My apologies, Doña Juanita. I mean no offense. We Americans are plain-spoken, though. We say what's on our minds."

Esteban stepped in, saying, "And this is Father Hortensio."

That distracted Chambers away from Juanita. He turned to the priest and said, "A great pleasure to meet you, Father. I have many questions about the Church."

Father Hortensio grunted and said with ill grace, "I will try to answer your questions, Señor."

Worthy and Powers had sat down at the other end of the log, not making a pretense of being sociable. They had taken out pipes and were filling them from their tobacco pouches. Preacher sauntered over to join them while Chambers kept chatting with Esteban, Juanita, and Father Hortensio.

Preacher sat down on the log, leaving a gap between him and Worthy. He took out his own pipe and pouch, and as he pushed tobacco into the pipe's bowl, he said quietly, "You boys are a long way from home."

"How do you know where we come from?" Powers asked.

"I don't, but I figure it ain't Nuevo Mexico. We're all gringos here, the three of us."

"I'm from Missouri," Worthy said. He seemed to be the slightly friendlier of the two. "Hardy here is from Louisiana."

"Louisiana, eh?" Preacher said. "I been there. I was part o' that dustup Andy Jackson had with the British down yonder at New Orleans, back in '14."

That got Powers's interest. "You was at the Battle of New Orleans?"

"Sure enough."

"You must not've been very old."

"Old enough to pull a trigger," Preacher said. "Never will forget it. We fired our guns and the British kept a-comin', but after a while there wasn't nigh as many of 'em as there was when they started out. After a while they turned tail and run off through the briars and the brambles." Preacher shook his head at the memory. "Hell, them redcoats was so spooked they ran through the bushes where a rabbit couldn't go! We chased 'em all the way down the Mississipp' to the Gulf, and they ain't come back since."

"Yeah, it was a good fight," Powers said. "I was there, too. We give them bloody British what for."

Worthy leaned closer and said, "We heard o' you, Preacher. You've got quite a rep."

Preacher just shrugged.

Powers asked, "How'd you come to be wanderin' around Nuevo Mexico with a couple o' fancy greasers and a padre?"

Preacher's voice was cool as he said, "It's a long story. And that boy and his sister are fine folks, even if they *are,* what you call 'em, aristocrats."

"No offense, Preacher," Worthy said quickly. "You got to admit, though, it's a mite odd, a fella like you throwin' in with the likes o' them."

"No more odd than a couple of ol' boys like you two takin' on the job of guidin' somebody like the professor."

Worthy chuckled. "Yeah, he is a funny duck, ain't he? Pays good, though. I reckon that explains it all right there."

"I reckon so," Preacher agreed.

"So, are them Mexes payin' you?"

Preacher hesitated. Worthy and Powers were being a mite more curious than frontier etiquette deemed acceptable. They were pumping him for some reason. Maybe they were just genuinely curious . . . or maybe they had some other motive for their questions.

"We just happened to be goin' the same direction and fell in together," he said. "They seem like good youngsters, and they could use a hand gettin' around."

"What are they after up here?"

Preacher shook his head. "You'd have to ask them. They ain't said, and I ain't asked."

"Well, it's none of our business," Worthy declared.

"We've got our hands full just lookin' after the professor," Powers added.

"Yeah, it would've been bad if he'd got hisself bit by them rattlers this afternoon." Worthy gave Preacher a friendly nod. "We're obliged to you for takin' a hand. It's a good thing you come along when you did."

Powers chuckled. "Otherwise we might never have got the rest o' the money he owes us."

"Glad I could help," Preacher said. He fetched a still-glowing stick from the fire and used it to light his pipe, then passed it along to Worthy and Powers. The three frontiersmen sat there and smoked in silence. They had already talked more than men of their ilk were accustomed to. The vast, empty distances of the frontier made a man get used to being quiet.

It was a companionable silence the three of them shared, but that was deceptive, Preacher thought. He wasn't sure how Powers and Worthy felt about him. . . .

But he knew that he didn't trust them worth a lick.

ELEVEN

When Chambers, Powers, and Worthy had gone back to their camp, Esteban called Preacher into the tent that he shared with Father Hortensio. The priest was still outside, talking to Juanita.

"They will say their prayers together before Juanita retires to the wagon for the night," Esteban explained as he lit a candle that sat on a folding table. "Meanwhile, I thought you might like to see this."

He took a wooden box from under his cot. It was old; Preacher could tell that with just one look. The dark wood had a sheen to it that no amount of polishing could achieve. The look came from decades of being handled. The corners were reinforced with brass caps, and a brass strap ran around the center of the box. A brass clasp held it closed. The box was fairly large, a little bigger than the dimensions of a family Bible, and Esteban handled it like it was heavy.

He set the box on the table and reached for an old brass key on a rawhide thong that hung around his neck. He lifted the thong over his head and then bent down to use the key to unlock the clasp. Then he replaced the thong and the key around his neck.

Preacher had a pretty good idea what he was about to see,

so he wasn't surprised when Esteban lifted the box's lid and revealed a stack of old paper. "Don Francisco never had the pages bound into a book," the young man said, "although he could have. Perhaps he thought that would be too vain a gesture. He left them as they were, a manuscript of his life."

The pages were thick vellum, heavily yellowed with age and densely covered with scrawled words in Spanish. Preacher leaned over to take a closer look. The ink had faded since Don Francisco had used it to tell his story more than a hundred years earlier. Preacher could make out some of the words, but some were too dim for him to read.

"There's so many pages, they can't all be about that loot he stashed up in the mountains."

Esteban shook his head. "Of course not. These are memoirs that cover Don Francisco's entire life up to the point when he wrote them. The pages about Father Alberto and the treasure of Santo Domingo are only a small section of the manuscript. In fact, it would be easy to overlook them. The only reason I found them is because I was trying to read the entire manuscript."

"Why'd you do that?" Preacher asked.

"I believe I was destined to do so," Esteban answered solemnly. "I wanted to learn about my ancestor. I learned more than I ever expected."

Carefully, he took the stack of pages out of the box and extracted several of them. Sitting down on a folding stool that went with the table, he went on. "I will copy those pages now, and then I want to give the copies to you, Preacher, for safekeeping."

"I ain't so sure that's a good idea," Preacher said with a frown. "Them pages are mighty important to you. Maybe you'd best hang onto the copies."

"No, in case of trouble, you would be more likely to be able to preserve them than I would be. No matter what happens, in the long run the treasure must be located and returned to the Church."

"Seems like that means a lot to you."

Esteban nodded. "It does. At one time I studied for the priesthood myself. The Church was going to be my life. Eventually, I realized that no matter what I hoped, I simply did not have the calling. But still I am devoted to the Holy Mother Church. Those relics must go back where they belong." He waved a hand in the direction of the ruins. "If their place is in a restored Mission Santo Domingo, I would gladly give my life to bring that about."

"Let's hope it don't come to that," Preacher said.

Esteban took sheets of paper, a pen, and an inkwell from an unlocked box that was also underneath his cot. He put them on the table and spent several minutes copying one of the pages from Don Francisco's manuscript. Preacher watched him, noting the intent, serious look on the young man's face and the care with which he inscribed the words on the fresh sheet of paper.

"I'm curious about one thing," Preacher said.

Esteban looked up from his task. "What is that, *mi amigo*?"

"How come you decided to trust me with all this? I mean, sure I came along yesterday and gave you a hand when those polecats bushwhacked you, but how'd you know I wouldn't double-cross you and go after the treasure myself once you let me in on the secret?"

Esteban smiled. "Why, that is the simplest question of all to answer, Preacher. I knew you would never betray us because I can see the goodness in you. It shines like a beacon in your eyes."

"I got goodness shinin' in my eyes?" Preacher grunted in surprise. "Ain't nobody ever accused me o' *that* before."

Just as on the previous night, the Yaquis took turns standing guard. Preacher spread his robes under a tree, and several times during the night he got up and prowled around, just to make sure no enemies were lurking. The night passed quietly, and when he awoke the next morning it was to the smell of breakfast cooking.

After he had checked on Horse, Juanita welcomed him to the fire with a smile. "*Buenos dias,* Señor Preacher," she said as she offered him a plate of tortillas and beans and a cup of coffee laced with strong chocolate. Preacher sat down on the log and dug in heartily.

He didn't see Esteban or Father Hortensio. "Where's your brother and the padre?" he asked Juanita.

"Esteban is still asleep. He worked long into the night copying the pages from Don Francisco's manuscript. Father Hortensio has gone over to the mission to pray."

Preacher frowned. "He knows to keep an eye out for snakes, don't he? Them rattlers are liable to be stirrin' around at this time o' day."

"He said that God would protect him from the serpents."

Preacher's frown deepened. Faith was a mighty fine thing, but it was no substitute for being careful. There was an old saying about how God helped those who helped themselves. Preacher would have added that God watched over those who weren't damn fools to start with.

Some folks were funny about snakes and religion, though. When he was a boy, he had heard about people who handled snakes as part of their worshippin'. Never had made much sense to him. As far as he could see, wrappin' a rattlesnake around your arm didn't prove your faith in God; it just proved you were askin' to get bit. He believed that folks had a right to worship however they saw fit . . . as long as they didn't expect him to cuddle up to no rattlers.

He looked over at the other camp, which was located about seventy-five yards away, and didn't see anybody stirring around it. "Any sign o' the professor and his pards this mornin'?"

"I have not seen them," Juanita said. "Perhaps they are still asleep, too."

Preacher nodded and went back to eating breakfast. Not

everybody was used to getting up as early in the morning as he did.

He tossed the last bite of his tortilla to Dog, who caught it out of the air and gulped it down. After draining the last of his coffee, he stood up, motioned for the big cur to follow him, and walked toward the old mission.

He heard Father Hortensio before he saw him. The priest was intoning a prayer, as Juanita had said. The Latin words flowed like a river in Father Hortensio's deep, powerful voice. The mountain man thought that the priest could probably do some mighty fine preachin', if he was of a mind to.

Father Hortensio knelt inside what had been the sanctuary, before the spot where the altar probably had stood. Preacher hoped he had checked for snakes before getting down on his knees. Standing beside the wall, Preacher looked around for rattlers but didn't see any. He studied the old stones that had been crudely mortared together to form the wall. He saw darkened streaks on some of them and figured that must have come from the flames after the Indians set the inside of the church on fire. The walls themselves wouldn't burn, but most of the interior would, and so would the roof. Once it had collapsed, time and the elements had done their job on the walls, although it was possible the rampaging Indians might have been responsible for some of the damage. Stones from the collapsed walls were scattered around the inside of the old church, and grass grew up rankly between them. The ashes that had been left after the conflagration were long gone, having been reclaimed by the earth.

Father Hortensio stopped praying abruptly. Preacher looked at him and saw that the priest had turned halfway around to glare at him. He didn't think he had made any noise when he came up; he was in the habit of walking quietlike. But Father Hortensio had sensed his presence somehow.

"You would spy on me while I am at my devotions?" the priest demanded.

"Wasn't spyin' on nobody," Preacher said. "I just come over

here to make sure you was all right. I can see now that you are, so I'll be goin'."

"Yes, a heathen such as yourself must feel uncomfortable in the house of the Lord."

Preacher had turned away, but at Father Hortensio's smug words he stopped and swung back toward the priest.

"How come you got such a burr up your butt about me?" he demanded. "You ain't had a bit o' use for me ever since you laid eyes on me. I never done nothin' to hurt you, and I ain't been disrespectful of your callin'. Well, not too much, anyway."

"You are a heathen, and you are a gringo," Father Hortensio answered bluntly. "All white men are thieves. Esteban was a fool to trust you."

"You think I'm gonna back-stab those young'uns and steal the Church's loot?" Preacher laughed, remembering what Esteban had said the night before about being able to see the goodness in him. "I give you my word, Padre, that ain't never gonna happen."

"Esteban says you should have a share of the gold for helping us."

Preacher's eyes widened in surprise. "I didn't know that, and I sure never asked for it."

"You wanted to know what Esteban and Juanita are getting out of this. The implication is clear. You want to be paid off, as well."

"I never turned down honest money," Preacher said with a shake of his head. "The workman is worthy of his hire. It says that in the Good Book, if I recollect right. But hell, the only reason I come along is because I thought you folks needed help."

"Don't blaspheme," Father Hortensio said coldly.

"It's true my language is a mite rough," Preacher admitted. "I'm tryin' to hold it in these days, on account of I don't want to hurt nobody's feelin's. So I'll apologize for the way I said that, Padre. But what I meant is still true. I may not know these particular mountains, but I've spent a heap o' years on the frontier, and I know how easy it is to get yourself killed if you ain't careful. That's the only reason I come along, so that maybe you and those two young folks—and them Yaquis, too, I reckon—will stand a better chance of comin' through this alive."

"You are most kind and generous," Father Hortensio said, but the look on his face made it clear that the sentiments he expressed weren't genuine.

Preacher shook his head. "I give up," he muttered. He and the priest weren't ever going to get along, and he figured he might as well quit trying. It was like trying to teach a pig to sing—a waste of his time and a danged annoyance to the pig.

He stalked back to camp, leaving Father Hortensio praying in the old mission.

Esteban was awake by the time Preacher got there, and the young man had an eager look on his face. "Today we will ride up into the mountains and begin our search," he said to Preacher.

"I reckon. What about your sister and the padre?"

"They have agreed to stay here." Esteban gave Juanita a hard look. "Is this not true, Juanita?"

"Sí," she said grudgingly. "But the only reason I said that I would stay behind is so that Father Hortensio would, too. I still think I should be with you, Esteban."

"Preacher and I will be fine, and if fortune smiles on us, we will locate Don Francisco's cache today and our quest will be over."

Preacher had a hunch it wouldn't be that easy, but he didn't say anything. It wouldn't hurt to let Esteban feel optimistic for a while.

A short time later, while Preacher was getting Horse ready to ride, the sound of loud, angry voices came to his ears. He glanced toward the mission and saw Father Hortensio and Professor Chambers standing outside the walls, arguing about something. Preacher couldn't catch all the words, but it was something about the Catholic Church's role in helping Spain colonize Mexico. Chambers said something about the Aztecs, and Father Hortensio disputed it.

Preacher shook his head as he tightened the saddle cinch. He looked down at the big wolflike creature sitting near him and said, "I don't know about you, Dog, but I'm mighty glad we're ridin' out and won't have to listen to them two squabble all day."

Dog just sat there, tongue lolling out, but Preacher would have almost sworn that he nodded in agreement.

TWELVE

It was still fairly early when Preacher and Esteban rode out. Preacher let Esteban take the lead, since the young man was the one who had studied Don Francisco's manuscript and had some idea where they were going. After they had followed the river for a short distance, though, Preacher said, "Maybe you better give me some idea what the old don had to say, Esteban. I might see some landmark he mentions that you wouldn't notice."

"The same thought had occurred to me," Esteban agreed. "I was just waiting until we got away from camp, so that we could discuss the situation in peace."

Preacher thought about the argument between Father Hortensio and Professor Chambers and grinned. "Probably a good idea," he said with a chuckle.

"Don Francisco knew he did not have much time," Esteban began as he reached inside his short, charro-style jacket and brought out a sheaf of folded papers: the pages he had copied the night before. He unfolded them as he went on. "It was feared that the Indians would attack at any moment, so he had to move quickly. The relics were wrapped in cloth and placed in heavy bags. The gold bars were loaded in wooden chests. Don Francisco picked ten of his most trusted men to go with him, and they loaded the treasure onto pack mules. Then they set off from the mission into the mountains, following this river at first."

Preacher could see it in his mind's eye: the soldiers in their armor and plumed helmets; the proud grandee who was their commander, also wearing armor but set apart by his silks and finery; the line of heavily laden pack mules plodding over the rocky ground, bearing their load of treasure toward the rugged peaks.

"Do them papers say how far they followed the river?" he asked.

Esteban shook his head. "Not exactly. According to the manuscript, the party branched off into a dry canyon that rose steadily, taking many turnings, until it reached a high plateau. There they located a suitable hiding place and concealed the treasure before returning to the mission and the violence that awaited them there."

Preacher frowned. "That's all it says? No offense to your old ancestor, Esteban, but shoot, that ain't much to go on!"

"I know," Esteban said with a sigh. "Don Francisco was writing this not as directions for finding the treasure, but only as part of the story of his life. Therefore he was not as . . . specific . . . as he might have been."

"Any mention of any other landmarks besides the twisty canyon and the high plateau?"

"Only one. Let me see . . ." Esteban turned through the pages he had copied so laboriously, frowning as he searched for the reference he was looking for. His expression cleared a moment later as he said, "Ah, here it is. He says that the treasure will be protected by the wolves of God."

"The wolves of God," Preacher repeated. "Wonder what in tarnation he meant by that."

Esteban shook his head. "I have no idea. There is no explanation in the manuscript."

"Well, whatever he was talkin' about, maybe we'll know it when we see it."

"This is my fervent hope," Esteban said.

He put the papers away inside his jacket, and the two of them got their horses moving again. Preacher kept his eyes open for any likely-looking canyons. Some landmarks might change over the course of a century and a half, but he doubted if an entire canyon would just close up and disappear.

Unfortunately, anywhere there were mountains, there were also lots of canyons. It might take days, even weeks, to search all of them in the area.

But if it took that long, so be it. The Alvarezes had brought along plenty of supplies from the trading post, and if they ran low on food, there was abundant game in these parts, not to mention edible plants. Preacher had lived off the land many times in the past and had no doubt that he could do so again.

About an hour after they rode away from the wagons, Esteban pointed and asked excitedly, "What about that canyon there? Do you think that might be the one?"

"Only one way to find out," Preacher said. He had already noticed the canyon mouth, but had been waiting to see if Esteban would see it, too. He would have spoken up if the young man hadn't, but he wanted to find out just how keen-eyed Esteban was. The canyon mouth was partially concealed by brush, but Esteban had seen it anyway.

They rode around the brush and into the canyon, which cut into the side of a mountain like a knife slash. It didn't look to Preacher like it had any twists and turns, but maybe those started farther up. They couldn't afford to ignore any possibility, so he pushed on and Esteban followed.

After a mile or so, however, the canyon came to an abrupt end against a stone wall. Preacher studied the barrier. In a hundred and fifty years, a rock slide could have blocked the canyon they were looking for. However, this wall appeared to be a solid sheet of stone, making it unlikely that it had been formed by such an avalanche. This canyon had probably come to an end right here in this spot for untold centuries.

It couldn't have been the one that Don Francisco and his men had followed with their mule train.

"All right," Preacher said. "Looks like a dead end, so we turn around and head back."

Esteban couldn't conceal his disappointment. "I was hoping this would be the one."

"So was I, but I didn't figure it would be that easy. Most things in life that you're lookin' for take a whole heap o' time and trouble to find, leastways if they're worth havin'."

"What about you, Preacher? What are you looking for in life?"

Preacher flashed a grin. "I ain't quite sure. But like we said before, I'm hopin' I'll know it when I see it."

"That may require a great deal of searching."

Preacher thought about all the places he had never been before and said, "That's all right by me."

From the top of a pine-covered hill overlooking the Purgatoire River, Cobey Larson peered down at the old, abandoned mission through the lens of a spyglass. He followed the movements of Professor Chambers, Hardy Powers, and George Worthy, as the professor poked around the ruins and pretended to be studying them. Hell, thought Cobey, for all he knew, Chambers really was studying what was left of the mission. He was from back East somewhere, and a professor to boot, and everybody knew folks like that were all crazy.

Chambers was set on getting his hands on that treasure, though, and not only was he willing to pay good wages to the men who were helping him, he also didn't care who got hurt in the process, which made things a little easier. He wouldn't get squeamish if they had to get rough with the girl while they were trying to get the location of the loot out of her. Chambers didn't mind if they killed the boy and the priest and those Mexican Injuns, neither.

Preacher, now . . . Preacher might be a problem.

Cobey had heard of the rugged mountain man. Preacher was supposed to be as dangerous as a sack full of wildcats. He had survived numerous Indian fights as well as his legendary hand-to-paw battle with a grizzly bear.

But Cobey was tough, too, and he thought he could take Preacher if it ever came down to that. Maybe it wouldn't, though. Maybe they would be lucky and would find a way to kill him easier than that.

Arnie Ross came up and knelt beside the place where Cobey was stretched out. "What're they doin' down there?" he asked.

"More of the same. The professor's putterin' around, and Powers and Worthy are tryin' to stay out of the way."

"Is Chambers still arguin' with that priest?"

"No, that seems to be over with, at least for now."

"So what the hell are we supposed to do?"

Cobey grunted. "Wait, I guess. We could jump those Yaquis and kill them and the priest, but then we'd have Preacher and the boy to deal with when they get back."

Arnie licked his lips. "You think they went off lookin' for the treasure?"

"No place else I reckon they'd go."

"Maybe they'll find it and bring it back to the mission. Then we wouldn't even have to look for it. We could just take it away from 'em."

"Yeah, that'd be mighty pretty, wouldn't it?" Cobey laughed humorlessly. "I'll believe it when I see it."

Arnie hesitated and then said, "Speakin' of takin' that treasure away . . . we ain't gonna let the professor pay us some piddlin' wages and then ride off with that whole dang fortune in gold and silver and gems, are we?"

Cobey lowered the spyglass and turned his head to look over at his partner. An ugly grin spread across his face as he asked, "What do you think?"

* * *

The priest was insufferable, Rufus Chambers thought. Stiff-necked, judgmental, smug, and arrogant . . . Father Hortensio seemed to think that he knew more about the history of the Church in Mexico and South America than he, a professor at the greatest institution of higher learning in the Western Hemisphere, did. Father Hortensio refused to admit that the Church had been responsible for more bloody-handed conquest than the Aztec, Mayan, and Incan empires combined. It was a simple matter of history as far as Chambers was concerned. It did no good to deny the facts.

But soon the priest would be dead, along with the Yaquis and Esteban Alvarez and the man called Preacher. Chambers consoled himself with that thought. Soon he would have not only the fortune that old Don Francisco had hidden in these mountains, but he would have Don Francisco's beautiful great-great-great-granddaughter, too. Was that enough generations? Chambers asked himself with a frown. Well, it didn't really matter. What was important was that he would be rich, and Juanita Alvarez would be his to do with as he wished.

She was a bonus. When Enrique Gallardo, his friend from the university in Mexico City, had written to him about the lost treasure of Mission Santo Domingo, he hadn't said anything about a beautiful young woman being involved. Enrique had read about the treasure in an old manuscript written by Don Francisco Alvarez, and he had immediately thought of his friend from Los Estados Unidos, Rufus Chambers. Enrique could not, or would not, abandon his position in Mexico City just to go on a treasure hunt that might turn out to be futile, but Rufus Chambers might. After all, Chambers was at loose ends after having been dismissed from his teaching position at Harvard following that unfortunate incident with the daughter of a fellow instructor. He had left Cambridge and crossed the Charles River to Boston, where Enrique's letter had found him. For a percentage of the profits, Enrique was willing to pass along the secret he had discovered.

Chambers had agreed, of course. Whether or not he would ever live up to that part of his bargain . . . who could say? Perhaps he would; Enrique, like all Latins, was possessed of a fiery temperament and an easily offended honor. If Chambers double-crossed him, Enrique might hunt him down to the ends of the earth. Easier to just pay him, take the lion's share of the treasure, and the girl as an added treat.

Chambers paused in his study of the tumbled-down walls and cast a glance toward the camp where Juanita and Father Hortensio were talking. She was beautiful, as lovely in her dark, volatile way as any of the more pallid young women with whom he had dallied in Cambridge and Boston. He couldn't wait until the first time they were together. Taming a spitfire like that would be very enjoyable indeed!

Lost in those thoughts, he didn't hear George Worthy until the man came up behind him and said, "Professor, me and Hardy been thinkin'."

Chambers jumped a little, then turned and said, "You startled me."

"Sorry. Anyway, we been thinkin'—"

"Not your strong suit," Chambers cut in. "You should leave that to me."

The frontiersman frowned. "You got no call to talk to me that way, Professor. We're part of this business, too, and we know a lot more about some things than you do."

"Yes, of course, you're right," Chambers said easily. "My apologies, George. Now, what's on your mind?"

"Well, we were just wonderin'. . . . Seems to us we could go ahead and kill them Yaquis now, and the priest, too. They ain't expectin' any trouble, so we could take 'em by surprise."

Chambers nodded. "Yes, yes, no doubt. And Mr. Larson and the other men are close by in case you needed any assistance. But what about Preacher and Señor Alvarez? They might hear the shots and come rushing back."

"We'd have the girl to use as a hostage," Worthy said

stubbornly. "They couldn't do a thing, as long as they wanted to keep her alive."

"Didn't we have a long talk about this? The only real threat facing us is Preacher. We don't want him wandering around loose, knowing what we're really after. Right now he believes the lies he's been told. We need to keep him from becoming suspicious of us, and that way we can bide our time and strike at the proper moment, so that we wipe out all of our opposition at once."

"Waitin's all well and good, but sometimes you got to strike while the iron's hot."

"Yes, I've heard that old saying. It's not always applicable.' Worthy looked confused.

"Sometimes it's better to wait," Chambers went on, clarifying his position. "Trust me, George. Before we're through, the lost treasure of Mission Santo Domingo will be ours, and all of our enemies will be dead."

"Includin' Preacher?"

"Especially including Preacher," Chambers said.

THIRTEEN

Preacher and Esteban went up and down several canyons that morning without finding what they were looking for. None of the canyons led to the top of a plateau, and Preacher didn't see anything that looked like it would inspire the name "wolves of God." When they stopped to make a cold lunch on jerky and tortillas, Esteban was discouraged.

Preacher tried to cheer him up by saying, "You didn't really figure you'd find the treasure the very first mornin' you went to look for it, did you?"

"We could have," Esteban said.

Preacher nodded. "Yeah, I reckon we could have. Stranger things have happened, as folks sometimes say. But I ain't disappointed. We'll just keep lookin'."

"Do you really believe we will find the place?"

"Sure I do. Things change in a hundred and fifty years, but the big things are still the same. We'll find the right canyon and it'll lead us to that plateau, and when we get there we'll find the cave."

"I hope so," Esteban said. "I would feel like my life would be justified if I could do this thing."

"I reckon I never felt like I had to justify my life," Preacher said. "I just live it."

They moved on, checking canyons on both sides of the river. Some, they were able to eliminate fairly quickly; other, deeper canyons required them to spend more time riding to the end and back once it became obvious none of these were the one they were looking for.

"Does that manuscript say how long it took Don Francisco and his men to cache that loot and get back to the mission?" Preacher asked.

Esteban shook his head. "Unfortunately, no. Don Francisco speaks of the need for haste, but he does not say whether he means by that a matter of hours or days. He could have been gone from the mission for several days and still considered that acting quickly."

"Could be," Preacher agreed, looking around at the mountains that surrounded them. "Seems to me he would have been in more of a hurry than that."

"Then the canyon should be close," Esteban argued.

"You'd think so. We just don't know."

By late afternoon, it became obvious they weren't going to find what they were looking for on this day. Preacher said that they ought to head back to the camp at the old mission.

"Perhaps we should go a little farther," Esteban urged. "We have time to check one more canyon, surely. And it might be the one we seek."

Preacher thought it over and nodded. "All right. One more."

They rode along until they came to another opening leading away from the river. The canyon was narrow, and sure enough, it took a sharp bend to the right about fifty yards in. After another short distance, it bent back to the left. Preacher frowned, wondering what would cause a zigzag formation like this. In the straighter canyons, it was relatively easy to see that they had been worn out by the action of water flowing through them over the centuries and by the upheaval of the earth's crust in earthquakes and volcanic eruptions and suchlike. He supposed water had carved out the twists and turns of this canyon, too, but he had seldom seen one that twisted around quite this much. Esteban was getting excited, and Preacher's spirits started to lift, as well. Now he was glad they had decided to press on and check one more canyon before turning back.

"We are climbing, are we not?" Esteban asked. "It seems so."

"I reckon we are," Preacher agreed. "If we could look behind us, we could probably tell how far we've climbed. Way this canyon snakes around, though, you can't see very far in any direction."

He reined in suddenly as a sound came to his ears. He held up a hand and said to Esteban, "Listen."

"What is it?" the young man asked eagerly.

"Just listen," Preacher said again.

After a moment, Esteban's eyes widened as he realized what he was hearing. "Wolves!" he exclaimed. "It is the howling of many wolves!"

"The wolves of God," Preacher said softly.

"It must be! But—" Esteban's face fell. "How can it be, Preacher? That sounds like a whole pack of wolves. Even if my ancestor saw them where he concealed the treasure, how could they still be there, over a hundred and fifty years later."

Preacher shook his head. "That ain't real wolves you're hearin', even though it sure sounds like it. Somewhere up yonder above us on the mountain, the wind is blowin' through some sort of rock formation that's causin' those howls. I've heard such things before, though I don't reckon I've ever run across anything that sounds quite so much like real wolves as that does."

"We must go on!" Esteban started to urge his horse forward.

Preacher reached over to lay a hand on his arm and stop him. "Hold on a minute. Look up at the sky. We're losin' the light, amigo. Even if we turn around now and head straight back to camp, it'll be dark before we get there."

"What is wrong with that? Can you not find your way back to the mission after dark?"

"I reckon I can, sure enough. This canyon will take us right back to the river, and all we have to do is follow it to the mission."

"Then we should go on!"

"It may take an hour or more to get to the head of this canyon," Preacher said. "Once we get there, we won't have time to search for the treasure before nightfall. It makes a lot more sense to head back to camp and come here again first thing in the mornin'. We'll have good light and most of the day, and I reckon there's a real good chance we'll find ol' Don Francisco's hidin' place."

"But . . . but . . . to be this close and turn back!" Anguish was easy to hear in Esteban's voice. "I do not know if I can stand it, Preacher."

"It's still possible this ain't the right canyon. That sound could be carryin' for a long way."

"But everything fits with the description in the manuscript!"

"Yeah, it does, and I think there's a real good chance this is the one we been lookin' for. It'd still be better to wait until tomorrow to find out for sure." Preacher glanced at the sky again. "We're burnin' daylight just talkin' about it."

"All right," Esteban said, but he didn't sound happy about it. "I cannot believe I am saying this, but we will go back. Tomorrow, though, we will return here as soon as possible."

"Dang right we will," Preacher agreed.

They turned their horses and started back down the canyon, as somewhere above them, the wolves of God continued to howl.

Juanita didn't care very much for the way she caught Professor Chambers watching her a couple of times during the day. She knew what it was like to have men look at her with lust in their eyes. She had been familiar with that feeling for quite a few years, ever since she had begun to turn from a girl into a woman. She wasn't particularly worried about Chambers, though. He seemed rather mild-mannered, not dangerous at all.

The men called Powers and Worthy, though, they were different. They were frontiersmen, rough and accustomed to taking whatever they wanted. They looked at her with avid gazes, too, and it was because of them that Juanita made a point of staying near Father Hortensio and the Yaqui servants. They would protect her if the gringos tried anything, she thought.

Oddly enough, the most dangerous gringo she had ever encountered, the man known as Preacher, did not frighten her at all. She knew he was aware of her beauty, but she never felt that she might be in any danger from him. Despite his rough exterior, he was a true gentleman, every bit as noble in his soul as any of the grandees she had met in Mexico City. More so, in fact.

So she was glad that evening when Preacher and Esteban returned to the camp near the old mission. When it had grown dark, around an hour earlier, Juanita had begun to worry that something had happened to her brother and Preacher. It seemed unlikely that the mountain man would be caught unawares by anything—he was perhaps the most *alert* man Juanita had ever seen—but an accident of some sort could not be ruled out. However, it was only because of their search that they were late getting back.

Juanita knew as soon as she saw the excitement on Esteban's face that they might have found what they were looking for. Esteban dismounted quickly, came over to her, and took her hands in his.

"We have found it!" he said.

Juanita's eyes widened in joy. "The treasure of Mission Santo Domingo? You have it with you?"

"No, not yet, but tomorrow—"

"We found a likely place to look," Preacher put in as he strolled over, much more deliberate in his movements than Esteban was. He could move very swiftly when he needed to, of course, but the sort of high-strung nervous energy that Esteban was exhibiting at the moment seemed alien to Preacher's very nature. He went on. "We won't know for sure until we've had a closer look."

"But I am sure it is the right place," Esteban insisted. "My heart tells me it is so."

Juanita cast a glance toward the other campfire. "We should be careful how we talk of these things. Professor Chambers and the others do not know why we are really here."

"And that is the way it shall remain," Esteban declared. "This is our business, and none of theirs."

"Tell me about it," Juanita urged. "Sit down and tell me what you found."

They sat on the log, still holding hands, and Esteban explained about their day-long search for the right canyon. While he was doing that, Preacher tended to the horses.

"We were about to give up for the day because it was getting late," Esteban said, "when I asked Preacher if we could check one more canyon. That proved to be the one we were looking for. It matched the description in Don Francisco's manuscript perfectly! We even discovered what the wolves of God are."

"Not real wolves, surely," she said.

He shook his head and explained about the rock formations that caused the howling sounds when the wind blew through them.

"You saw them for yourselves?" Juanita asked.

"No, but Preacher knew what caused the sounds. He said that he has heard such things before."

"I am surprised you turned back and did not continue the search until you found the treasure."

"It was too late," Esteban said, but he sounded disappointed. "Preacher said it would be better if we returned in the morning, when there will be plenty of time and light." He shrugged. "I suppose it makes sense. But I wanted so much to keep going until we found the treasure."

"That settles it," Juanita said. "Tomorrow I go with you."

Preacher came up in time to hear that statement. "I ain't sure that's such a good idea," he said.

"Why not?" she asked as she looked up at him.

"For one thing, those wagons won't be able to make it up that canyon. It's too narrow."

"Could they reach the mouth of the canyon, by the river?"

"Well . . ." Preacher hesitated. "I reckon they might."

"Then we can take the wagons that far, and then I will join you and Esteban on horseback for the final part of the search."

"And I as well," Father Hortensio put in. Juanita hadn't heard him come up, but obviously he had overheard enough of the conversation to know what was going on. As he stepped into the firelight, his normally solemn visage was more animated than Juanita had ever seen it.

Preacher frowned. "I don't know that we need a crowd up there. If you folks stayed down at the mouth of the canyon with the wagons, Esteban and I could bring the loot down a little at a time, and the rest of you could stand guard over it."

"You would deny me the right to be there when those holy relics are uncovered for the first time in over a century? A prayer should be said over them immediately, to bless their rediscovery and to wipe out the stain of the violence that led to their being hidden."

"Well, I don't reckon it'd hurt anything if you went along to the mouth of the canyon," Preacher grudgingly agreed. "After that, we'll see."

Juanita squeezed Esteban's hands. "I can hardly believe that we are so close to our goal at last."

"Believe it," he said. "I do."

She might have asked him for more details, but at that moment Professor Chambers sang out from somewhere nearby, "Hello, the camp!"

"Say nothing more about the treasure," Esteban warned in a low voice.

Juanita nodded. She decided that she wouldn't say anything to Esteban about her uneasiness over Chambers and the two guides. He had enough on his mind already.

Besides, soon they would have the treasure, and they would be on their way back to Mexico City with it. Their quest was almost over.

FOURTEEN

Preacher had heard Chambers approaching before the professor called to them, and so had Dog, growling as he gazed off into the darkness. Preacher had been about to shush the two youngsters when they had quieted down about the treasure on their own. No point in tempting a couple of rough hombres like Powers and Worthy with talk about hidden gold and such.

Chambers came up and said, "Good evening, everyone. I hope you had a productive day. I know I did. I even enjoyed my discussions with the good padre here, spirited though they might have been."

Father Hortensio just sniffed. Evidently it was a toss-up who he liked the least, Preacher or the professor from back East.

Esteban was gracious. "Please join us, Professor. We were about to eat supper."

"I've already eaten, thank you. I certainly wouldn't mind sharing a cup of coffee with you, though, and the camaraderie that comes with it."

"You are welcome," Esteban said.

Chambers didn't seem to notice that his presence had put a damper on the conversation. He sat down on the log between

Esteban and Father Hortensio and filled a cup from the coffeepot that sat at the edge of the fire. Preacher was a little worried about that fire. He hadn't forgotten the ambush and the fact that somebody didn't wish the Alvarez party well. But there was a fire over at the professor's camp, too, so it wouldn't really serve any purpose to extinguish this one. Might as well let folks enjoy it, he decided.

He got a plate of tortillas and beans and sat off by himself while Chambers regaled Esteban and Juanita with stories about life back in Boston and asked them questions about Mexico City.

"Since my area of expertise is the Spanish conquest of the New World, I find everything about your country fascinating," he told them.

"Have you ever visited Mexico?" Esteban asked.

"No, I haven't had that good fortune as of yet, but I hope to someday."

Father Hortensio asked, "How can you claim to know anything about a land where you have never been?"

"Well, there are a great many books about the conquest—"

"Bah! The only book from which one can truly learn is the Holy Word of God."

"Perhaps you're correct as far as spiritual matters go, but when it comes to history, one has to rely on other books."

Preacher couldn't resist putting in a comment of his own. "There ain't been a history book yet that wasn't written by a fella who wanted you to believe *his* version of the way things were."

"History is written by the victors, is what you're saying," Chambers responded.

"Yep. Except when other folks come along years later and try to twist things around so that the way they tell the stories ain't exactly the way they really happened. Wouldn't surprise me a bit if someday you professors tried to say that these days was completely different than the way they really are."

"Oh, surely not. Scholars are supposed to be devoted to

the truth, not to some distorted version of the facts concocted simply to support some dogma of their own."

Preacher shrugged. "Wait and see, that's all I can say. It could happen . . . and it'll be a mighty sorry day for this country when it does."

He went back to eating, having put in his thoughts. When he was done, he got up and strolled around the camp, rifle tucked under his arm. Dog went along with him, sniffing the night air. If there were any predators out there, four-legged or otherwise, Dog would smell them out.

The night seemed quiet, though, and when Preacher went back to the camp, he saw that Chambers was gone. The professor had said his good nights and returned to his own camp. Esteban and Juanita sat with their heads close together, talking quietly but excitedly, and Preacher knew they were talking about the treasure again.

He hoped for their sake that he and Esteban had found the right place and the lost loot would soon be recovered. Then he could see them on their way safely and get back to his own business. He was starting to long for more northern climes. If he didn't know better, he would say that he was starting to get homesick for his old stomping grounds. It would be good to get back and start running his trap lines again, maybe see some old friends, or even some old enemies.

The mountains were calling him, no doubt about that, and Preacher hoped he would soon be able to answer.

It was far into the night when a hand touched Rufus Chambers' shoulder and shook him awake. Instinct took over and made Chambers react instantly. His hand snaked under his coat and came out with a little pocket pistol he kept loaded and primed. His thumb looped over the hammer as he withdrew the weapon from his coat, and it was ready to fire as it flashed into the open.

A big hand clamped over his, trapping the pistol's hammer.

"Take it easy, you damn fool!" an angry voice hissed. "You almost blew my head off!"

"Larson?"

"That's right. Now give me that gun." Cobey wrenched the pistol out of Chambers's hand.

Chambers sat up. The fire had died down to just embers, and the night was cold. The good thing about the chill was that the snakes would be dormant until the sun rose and warmed them in the morning. Cobey hunkered next to the professor's bedroll. The big frontiersman carefully lowered the hammer on the pistol and gave it back to Chambers.

"Be careful with that," he warned.

"I know how to handle a gun," Chambers said coldly. "Don't underestimate me, my friend."

"I don't intend to. Listen, Powers and Worthy tell me those pilgrims found what they were looking for."

"We don't know that for certain yet. Worthy was able to sneak up and eavesdrop on them while I approached more openly, as a distraction, so to speak. He heard them saying something about a canyon and the wolves of God—"

"What in blazes is that?"

"According to my friend in Mexico City, the phrase 'wolves of God' is connected somehow to the hiding place of the treasure, according to Don Francisco's manuscript. I believe, based on what Worthy overheard them saying, that Preacher and the Alvarez boy have solved the mystery of that phrase and have either actually located the treasure or have a good lead to it."

"Then we could go ahead and make our move, right? I got the rest of the boys close by, and we can wipe out all that bunch except the girl. She can tell us what we need to know, I reckon. Her brother will have filled her in on everything they've discovered."

Chambers shook his head emphatically. "There's no need for haste. Why not let them go ahead and recover the treasure? That way our work will be done for us. All we'll have to do is kill the others and take the treasure."

"And the girl," Cobey said.

"And the girl, of course. We shan't forget her."

Cobey thumbed his hat back on his head and thought about it. "I reckon that might be best. I got to tell you, though, the boys are gettin' a mite impatient, and so am I. We're ready to see that gold and get our share that you promised us."

"Soon, my friend, soon," Chambers assured him. "We'll all be rich men before too many more days go by."

"We'd better be," Cobey said, and there was no mistaking the threat in his voice.

As usual, Preacher and Dog made several patrols around the camp during the night. Several times, Dog looked off toward the other camp and growled. Preacher ruffled the thick fur at the big cur's neck and said, "I agree with you, fella. Somethin' about them hombres don't smell right to me, neither."

Chambers and the other two hadn't done anything openly suspicious, though, so there was nothing Preacher could do except to keep an eye on them.

Early the next morning, the Alvarez party began making preparations to break camp. Professor Chambers must have noticed the Yaquis hitching up the mules and the horses, because he walked over and said, "What's this? You're leaving?"

"Yes, there is more of the old land grant we must explore," Esteban said, falling back on the story they had told Chambers to explain their presence here in the Sangre de Cristos.

"Well, I'll certainly miss your company. Especially the lovely Señorita Alvarez, and the stimulating discussions with Father Hortensio. Will you be coming back this way?"

"Probably," Esteban said.

Chambers smiled. "Perhaps my companions and I will still be here then. I hope so."

He shook hands with Preacher and Esteban, tipped his beaver hat to Juanita, and said to Father Hortensio, *"Vaya con Dios, padre."*

"I will go with God," Father Hortensio said. "Can you make the same statement?"

Chambers didn't answer, but just smiled instead. He waved as Preacher and Esteban mounted their horses and the others climbed onto the wagons. The group moved off to the southwest, following the river. Preacher glanced back from time to time and saw Chambers, Worthy, and Powers moving casually around the old mission. The three men didn't seem to be making any effort to follow them.

They might later, though, after Preacher and the others were out of sight. Preacher didn't have to warn himself to remain alert. That was just a way of life with him.

Traveling with the wagons meant that they had to go slower than he and Esteban had the day before. They weren't wasting any time now on fruitless trips up dead-end canyons, though, so it tended to even out. It was still past midday before they reached the canyon that appeared to lead to the hiding place of the treasure. They wouldn't know for sure until they explored all the way to the end of it.

"This is it," Preacher said as he called a halt. "Esteban and I will ride up and see what we can find. Might take as long as an hour to reach the head of the canyon, so it'll be fairly late by the time we get back."

"I must go with you," Father Hortensio declared as he started to climb down from the lead wagon.

"There ain't an extra horse," Preacher pointed out.

"There are the two hitched to the other wagon," the priest said. "One of them can be unhitched and saddled so that I can ride."

"It'd be better to leave 'em both where they are," Preacher argued, "in case we had to move these wagons in a hurry."

"Please, Padre," Esteban said. "Preacher and I can handle this part of the task."

Stubbornly, Father Hortensio shook his head. "I must go. If you refuse, I will wait until you are gone and then order the Yaquis to prepare a horse for me to ride. They are good Christians and will do as I command."

Esteban sighed and looked over at Preacher. "He is right, amigo. The Yaquis are more his servants than mine. It appears we must allow him to accompany us."

"Maybe so," Preacher said with a frown, "but that don't mean I've got to like it."

With a self-satisfied smirk, Father Hortensio told the Yaquis to get one of the extra horses unhitched from the second wagon and put a saddle on it. The chore was performed quickly, and the sun was still high in the sky when Preacher, Esteban, and Father Hortensio were ready to start up the canyon.

Esteban rode over to the lead wagon and reached across to take his sister's hand for a moment. "You will be all right here with the Yaquis?" he asked.

Juanita nodded. "I wish I was coming with you, but I do not want to slow you down. Just be careful, Esteban, and I pray you find what we have so long sought."

"I will," he said. "I am certain of it."

He turned his mount and joined Preacher and Father Hortensio, who looked a bit ridiculous with his robe hiked up so that he could sit astride the horse. With Preacher leading the way, the three men started up the canyon. Dog trotted in front of them. The first turn took them out of sight of the wagons.

Preacher's nerves were taut. He rode with his rifle across the saddle. The twisting and turning of the canyon grew more and more pronounced, until it seemed almost like they were going around in circles.

"It is enough to make one dizzy," Esteban commented. "This must be the right canyon. No wonder its serpentine path impressed itself so strongly on Don Francisco, and he remembered it years later."

Father Hortensio said, "I hear no howling of wolves."

"The wind ain't blowin' hard enough, I reckon," Preacher explained. "You won't be able to hear the howlin' all the time, just when conditions are right."

"To refer to such a phenomenon as the wolves of God is a bit irreverent," the priest said disapprovingly. "Perhaps even blasphemous. To the best of my recollection, nowhere in the Holy Scripture is the Lord linked with savage creatures such as wolves."

"Don Francisco heard howlin', and it came from somewheres high up," Preacher said. "I reckon that's why he came up with the name he did."

"Still, a truly pious man would not think of such a thing."

"My ancestor was a soldier, not a priest," Esteban said rather sharply. "I'm sure he never considered things from your perspective, Padre."

Father Hortensio sniffed, and as usual, that marked the end of the conversation. If anyone ever dared to argue with him, he ignored them to the best of his ability.

A short time later, Preacher chuckled as the wind picked up and the distant howling could be heard. It sounded just like a pack of wolves baying at the moon. "There you go," he said.

"I wonder if we are getting close." Esteban sounded excited as he spoke.

"Ought to be. We've climbed quite a distance."

Preacher wasn't surprised when, a few minutes later, they rounded another bend in the canyon and saw that it emerged onto a broad stretch of flat land. Don Francisco had described it as a plateau, but it wasn't, not really. It was more of a shoulder that stuck out from the side of the mountain, maybe a mile long and half a mile deep. A rocky slope jutted up on the far side, and steep drop-offs bordered the other three sides. The only reasonably easy way to get up here was by following the zigzag canyon up the side of the mountain.

"This is it!" Esteban said. "It must be!"

"Looks like it, from the description you read," Preacher agreed.

"But where is the treasure?" Father Hortensio asked anxiously.

Esteban's hands shook a little as he dug out the pages he had copied from the old don's manuscript. He studied them for a moment, flipping through the pages, before he said, "There is nothing else. Only the canyon, the plateau, and the wolves of God."

"Look up yonder," Preacher said.

He pointed to the cliff on the far side of the open ground. It rose almost sheer for a couple of hundred feet, and on top of it were a dozen or more rocky spires pointing toward the sky. Preacher's keen eyes had spotted holes worn in the spires by time and the elements, and he knew that was what produced the sounds that so resembled the howling of wolves.

"I don't see what you mean," Esteban said.

"Them rocks up there don't just sound like wolves, they look a little like 'em, too," Preacher explained. "Them spires are like the snouts of a bunch of wolves, thrown back and pointed toward the moon."

"Toward heaven," Father Hortensio corrected. "That is why Don Francisco named them as he did. They sing their homage to God."

Preacher shrugged. "That explanation makes as much sense as any other," he said. "And seein' them so-called wolves up there is good enough for me. I'm convinced this is the right place."

"Then the treasure *is* here," Esteban said.

Preacher nodded. "Yep. Now all we got to do is find it."

FIFTEEN

That proved to be easier said than done. Even though the area was relatively small, there could be any number of hiding places here. Preacher suggested that they split up, so that they could cover the ground more quickly.

"See," Father Hortensio said. "It was a good thing that I came with you. Three men can search more places than two."

"You're right, Padre," Preacher said. He pulled one of the pistols from behind his belt and held it toward the priest.

Father Hortensio recoiled as if Preacher had just tried to hand him one of the rattlesnakes that made its home in the old mission downriver. "I have no need of a gun," he said. "The Lord will protect me from any danger."

"I ain't givin' it to you for protection. If you find the cache, fire off a shot into the air, and we'll come a-runnin'."

Father Hortensio hesitated. "I am not sure I know how to fire such a weapon."

Preacher reined in the frustration he felt. He had almost said *For God's sake!* but he knew that wouldn't have gone over well. Instead, he said patiently, "It's already loaded and primed. All you have to do is pull back the hammer until it locks, then point the barrel into the air and pull the trigger.

Don't point it straight up above you, though. If you do that, the ball's liable come back down and hit you. Aim off to the side a little."

Reluctantly, Father Hortensio reached out and took the pistol. "Very well. But I feel a bit unclean having such a weapon in my possession."

The old padres hadn't felt that way about having conquistadors armed with swords, pikes, and blunderbusses along with them when they first came over here from Spain to take over the place, Preacher thought, but again, he kept it to himself.

He looked at Esteban instead and said, "Same goes for you. If you find anything, fire a shot in the air and we'll come to you. I'll do likewise if I'm the one who runs across the hidin' place first."

"Of course," Esteban said. "Good luck, amigo."

Preacher said, "Padre, you take the near end of this shelf. Esteban, you've got the middle. I'll go down yonder to the far end."

The other two men nodded in agreement. Preacher wheeled Horse and put him into a trot that carried him toward the far end of the flat stretch of ground. Dog followed.

This shelf might look flat, but that was only in comparison to the mountains that rose around it. As Preacher rode over the ground, he discovered that it was more rugged than it appeared and was cut in places by gullies and ravines. They were dry now, but when it rained higher up, he imagined all those ditches ran full of water.

There were also patches of hardy grass and stands of pine trees. The elevation kept the trees from growing quite as well as those lower down, so they were a bit smaller.

Preacher didn't see any likely hiding places for the treasure out in the open. When he reached the far end of the shelf, he turned Horse and rode toward the cliff. The shelf had narrowed down here to no more than a quarter of a mile wide, so it didn't take him long to reach the wall of stone that reared up at the back of the shelf. He started along it, watching for clumps of boulders or cave mouths. The face of the cliff was almost sheer and appeared to be featureless, however. Preacher remembered Esteban saying that the relics from the missions had been placed in bags, and the gold bars in wooden chests. He didn't know how many of either there were, but it seemed to him that a good number would be required. That would take some room if they were going to be properly hidden.

He couldn't see Father Hortensio from where he was, but he could pick out the figure of Esteban in the distance, still mounted and poking around a grove of trees. Preacher stuck close to the cliff, figuring that would be the most likely spot for the cache. A couple of hundred feet above him, the wind blew harder and the "wolves" howled louder. The sound had a faintly mocking quality to it. Preacher felt his frustration growing as the minutes dragged by and his search continued to turn up nothing.

He kept one eye on the sun as that glowing orb dipped closer and closer to the peaks of the mountains on the western horizon. It had taken an hour to reach the top of the zigzag canyon, and it would take about that long to get down. Preacher wanted to get back to the wagons by nightfall so that Juanita and the Yaquis wouldn't be by themselves once it was dark. The Yaquis had a reputation as fierce fighters, but Preacher didn't know firsthand just how much they could be depended upon.

He crisscrossed his search area several times before he decided that it was getting too late. Knowing that Esteban was going to be disappointed, Preacher looked around until he spotted the young man about three hundred yards away. He rode toward Esteban.

With an eager expression on his face, Esteban came to meet Preacher. "Did you find anything?" he called when twenty yards still separated them.

Preacher shook his head. Both men reined in as their horses trotted up to each other. "I didn't see hide nor hair o' that loot, nor any place that looked like a good spot for a cache," Preacher said. "Don't seem to be nothin' up here except some grass and trees and a few rocks. Didn't even see any animal sign."

"But it *must* be here!" Esteban waved his arms. "The canyon that twists back upon itself, the rocks that look and sound like wolves . . . everything fits! This must be the place Don Francisco described."

"Sure seems like it," Preacher agreed. "Let's go see if the padre found anything."

"He would have fired a shot if he had, would he not?"

"I hope so, but you can't never tell with a fella like him."

Together they rode along the shelf, which led them in a generally easterly direction. Preacher kept his eyes open. Just because Esteban had already searched this area didn't mean that the young man couldn't have missed something.

By the time they found Father Hortensio, however, Preacher still hadn't seen anything promising. Esteban hailed the priest.

"Please tell us you have found something, Father," he said.

"No, if I had, I would have shot the gun that Señor Preacher gave me," Father Hortensio answered. "Am I to assume that neither of you found the lost treasure of Mission Santo Domingo, either?"

"You can assume that, all right, Padre," Preacher drawled.

Esteban dismounted, took off his sombrero, and walked around for a moment with a frustrated, pained expression on his face. He burst out, "I do not understand it! Everything is perfect! The treasure should be here!"

"It ain't like we found the hidin' place and the loot was gone," Preacher pointed out. "Then it really would be lost. Either this ain't the right spot . . . or we just ain't found the stuff yet and it's still here."

Father Hortensio said, "I searched everywhere in this area

and found nothing. Are you saying that I overlooked something?"

"Nope, I'm sayin' one of us maybe overlooked somethin', but until we find it, there ain't no way of tellin' which one of us missed it the first time around." Preacher swung down from Horse's back and went over to Esteban. He laid a hand on the young man's shoulder. "I know you're disappointed, but maybe the ol' don just hid the loot really good. Like I've said all along, sometimes it takes a while to find what you're lookin' for. We'll head back down to camp for the night and come up here again in the mornin'. We'll spend the whole day searchin' on foot, takin' a closer look at everything. Might take a few days, but if that cache is here, we'll find it."

Esteban looked at him. "You sound certain."

"I *am* certain. And if it turns out this *ain't* the right spot, we'll push on and see if we can't find somewheres else to look."

Esteban smiled faintly. "You seem almost as devoted to our cause as the father and I, Preacher, and yet you have no stake in this."

"Oh, I got a stake, all right," Preacher said. "Once I get started on somethin', I'm about as stubborn as one o' them mules down yonder. That's my stake!"

Juanita was disappointed, of course, when they didn't return with the treasure. She smiled bravely, though, and told Esteban, "I am sure you will find it tomorrow."

"I pray you are right," he said.

While Preacher and the others were gone, the Yaquis had set up camp just outside the mouth of the canyon. There was grass for the mules and horses, and the river was close enough so that fetching water wasn't a problem. They could stay here for a week if they had to.

But it wouldn't take a week to thoroughly search that

shoulder of ground at the top of the canyon, Preacher knew. If they hadn't found the treasure in another couple of days, they would have to consider giving up on this location and moving on. That meant he and Esteban would have to start searching the canyons again for another one that matched Don Francisco's description.

He warned himself not to borrow trouble. Tomorrow they might be lucky.

As usual, through Esteban he instructed the Yaquis to take turns standing guard during the night. Preacher rose several times to check on everything, and the rest of the time he slept lightly, with Dog beside him and Horse nearby. He knew that if there was trouble, his four-legged friends would probably be aware of it before anyone else and would warn him. The night passed quietly, however, and Preacher was fairly well rested when he rolled out of his robes the next morning.

Esteban didn't look so chipper, and Preacher figured he'd had a hard time sleeping. The young man confirmed it over breakfast. "I spent a long time studying Don Francisco's manuscript again," Esteban said. "I hoped that I had overlooked something that would give us more of a clue where to search. I was wrong, though. There is nothing more in the manuscript than I have already told you, Preacher."

"Then we just keep lookin'," Preacher said.

"And today I will come with you," Juanita declared.

Esteban was about to argue with her, but Preacher stopped him with a raised hand. "That probably ain't a bad idea," he said. "That'll give us another pair of eyes. Fact of the matter is, I was wonderin' if we ought to leave a couple o' them Yaquis here to watch the camp and take the other two with us to help search. They could double up on that extra hoss."

"I think that is an excellent idea," Juanita said, clearly glad that Preacher wasn't going to object to her accompanying them to the top of the canyon.

Esteban shrugged, still in the grip of his discouragement. "If you think that is for the best, Preacher, then we shall do it."

"The more eyes we got lookin', the better," Preacher said.

After they had eaten, the group got ready to ride. Esteban picked two of the Yaquis to go with them. Preacher thought their names were Pablo and Joaquin. Those were the names they had taken, anyway, when they converted to Christianity. Preacher doubted if they had been born with them. To tell the truth, though, he had trouble keeping the Yaquis straight. They were all grim, stocky, unfriendly-looking cusses, as far as he was concerned.

The group that rode up the canyon was twice as big as the one the day before. Preacher hoped that would make them twice as lucky, but he wasn't going to hold his breath waiting.

When they reached the top of the canyon, he split them up, telling Juanita to stay close to her brother. One of the Yaquis he sent with Father Hortensio, and he took the other Indian with him. Again they divided the shelf into rough thirds, but today there would be two people searching in each area, and on foot rather than from horseback.

"Which one are you?" Preacher asked his companion as they started their search along the face of the cliff.

"Pablo, Señor," the Yaqui replied.

"Well, keep your eyes open, Pablo. We're probably lookin' for a cave, or somethin' like that. It's a cinch all that loot ain't stashed right out in the open."

Preacher didn't know how much Pablo understood of what he was saying, but the Yaqui nodded and seemed to know what Preacher meant. They spread out. Preacher poked under rocks and prodded at the ground and pulled aside the scrubby bushes that grew out of the cliff in places. Dog bounded around enthusiastically at first, but then sat down and looked puzzled when he realized there weren't any rabbits up here for him to chase.

Why *weren't* there any rabbits up here? Preacher suddenly

asked himself. He hadn't seen any birds in the trees or any varmints of any kind, not even a lizard. There were no tracks to indicate that deer or bears ever came up here to forage. Why not? There had to be a reason for animals to avoid the place, didn't there?

He sniffed the air. He hadn't really noticed it the day before, but there was a lingering trace of brimstone in the air. It was very faint, so much so that if he hadn't been looking for something odd, he might not have smelled it even now.

More than once, he had been to the area up north of the Tetons known as Colter's Hell, because John Colter had been the first white man to lay eyes on the place. It suited its name. Boiling water shot up out of the ground, and there were molten pools of mud and ash that gave off such a noxious scent that they sure seemed like doorways to Hades. The scent that Preacher smelled now was a little like that, only nowhere near as strong.

He knew that the geysers and the stink in Colter's Hell came from volcanic action far below the earth. Maybe something was going on, on a much smaller level, in these mountains. Though he hadn't seen it for himself, he had heard about an area somewhere here in Nuevo Mexico where an ancient volcano had erupted far in the past and left a layer of black, razor-sharp lava all over the ground for miles around. Maybe there was another volcano around here, long dormant but still bubbling deep in its bowels, and from time to time some of the pressure that built up was vented off through fissures in this cliff. That might be enough to make animal life avoid the place.

That was interesting as all get-out, Preacher told himself, but it didn't put him any closer to finding the treasure. He looked along the cliff toward Pablo, who was poking around at the base of the cliff about a hundred yards away. As Preacher watched, the Yaqui suddenly straightened—

And then he was gone, vanished as if he had never been there.

SIXTEEN

Preacher stared for a second, unable to believe his eyes. Folks didn't just disappear like that. But Pablo sure had, and there was only one explanation Preacher could think of. A moment later, as he heard faint, muffled shouts for help, that guess was confirmed.

The mountain man's long legs carried him quickly toward the spot where Pablo had vanished. Preacher was running by the time he got there. When he reached the place, he dropped to his knees beside a hole in the ground, an irregular circle a little less than three feet in diameter. It was located right against the base of the cliff, and enough sunlight penetrated the hole so that Preacher could see that it sloped backward, underneath the huge stone wall.

He couldn't see Pablo. He could hear the Yaqui's frantic cries, however. He leaned over the hole and called, "Pablo! I'm here! Hang on, dang it!"

Preacher turned his head and saw that Horse and Dog had followed him over here, as he expected. There was a rope coiled on the big horse's saddle. Preacher sprang up and ran to get it.

He was uncoiling the rope as he reached the hole again. He

said, "I'm gonna throw a rope down to you, Pablo. Grab onto it, and I'll haul you out of there."

"H-hurry, Señor!" The Yaqui's usual stolid demeanor had deserted him. "I cannot hold on much longer! My hands . . . they slip!"

Preacher tossed the rope down the hole, paying out as much of it as he could and still keep a good grip on it. "There it is! Grab hold!"

"I . . . I cannot! Señor—!"

Pablo screamed as he slipped and fell. Preacher grimaced, knowing that this hole in the ground might be hundreds of feet deep. He expected to hear Pablo screaming for a long time as he fell. . . .

But a mere heartbeat later, there was a heavy thud and a pained grunt that echoed in the narrow shaft. After a moment, Pablo said, "Señor?"

"You all right, Pablo?"

"*Sí*. The fall, she was a short one."

"Can you see anything?"

"No, Señor. All is dark."

Preacher began pulling up the rope. "Well, if you're set good, don't move. No tellin' if there are any other holes down there. You go to rustlin' around and you might fall again."

"I will not move, Señor."

Confident that Pablo would be all right if he just stayed calm and still, Preacher hurried over to the nearest trees and found a branch that had broken off sometime in the past. He brought it back to the hole and pulled up some dry grass that he wrapped around one end of the branch and tied in place. He tied the rope to the other end of the branch. Then he gathered some more grass, took flint and steel from his pouch, and quickly struck some sparks to get a fire going. When he had a tiny flame and a little curl of smoke, he leaned over and puffed on it until it grew into a large enough fire so that he could light the makeshift torch.

He turned to the hole in the ground and called into it, "I'm gonna lower a torch to you, Pablo, so you can see where you are."

"Sí, señor."

Preacher lowered the torch into the hole. The glare from it lit up the slanting shaft. The rough walls told Preacher that it was a natural opening in the earth, not man-made.

But a man could have taken advantage of it. Don Francisco Alvarez, to be precise.

Preacher was trying not to think about that. The important thing right now was to get Pablo out of there. The torch dropped out of sight, but a second later he felt the tension in the rope change. "I have the torch, Señor," Pablo called, his voice echoing. *"Madre de Dios!"*

"What is it?"

"Señor," Pablo said, his voice shaking a little now, "we have found the treasure."

Preacher's heart pounded harder. "You're sure?" he called down.

"There are wooden chests and big bags, just as the padre told us there would be. What else could it be? Do you want me to open some of them?"

"No, just hang on a minute," Preacher said. "What's the cave like?"

"Not too big. Large enough for the treasure, but not much more."

"Any other holes that lead deeper?"

"No, only some small cracks in the rock." Pablo paused. "It smells bad in here."

Preacher could smell it, too, wafting up from down below. Gas from somewhere deeper in the earth had to be seeping through those cracks in the cave wall. If a fella was shut up in there, it might be potent enough to choke him to death. As long as the shaft to the surface was open, though, Preacher figured they could stand to breathe the stuff.

"Untie the rope from the torch," he told Pablo. While the

Yaqui was doing that, Preacher tied the other end to Horse's saddle.

"It is loose, Señor."

"All right. I'm comin' down. I'm gonna fire a shot first, though, so the others will come on over here. Just in case somethin' goes wrong and we need some help."

He pulled out one of his pistols, cocked it, and fired into the deep blue sky. Then he reloaded the pistol and tucked it behind his belt again.

With that done, he positioned Horse near the hole in the ground and ordered, "Stay right there, old hoss. Don't move."

He gripped the rope tightly and started lowering himself into the hole. Dog whined worriedly as his master disappeared into the earth.

The rocks scraped a little hide off Preacher as he slid over them. When he looked over his shoulder he could see a red glow in the darkness that came from the torch Pablo held. About fifteen feet below the surface, the slanting shaft turned and dropped straight down. Preacher's legs dangled over the edge, and the feeling of empty air underneath him made his hands tighten instinctively on the rope.

"It is not far, Señor," Pablo said. "Only a few feet."

Preacher hung over the edge, looked around, and saw that Pablo was right. The floor of the cave was only a couple of feet below his boots. He let go of the rope and dropped the rest of the way, landing lithely.

As he straightened, he looked around. The cave was a rough square, about fifteen feet on a side. Pablo stood holding the torch in front of a stack of about a dozen wooden chests. Next to the chests was a pile of sailcloth bags. Preacher stepped over to them and rested a hand for a moment on one of the bags. He could feel some sort of solid object through the cloth.

He had known about the lost treasure of Mission Santo Domingo for only a few days. Finding it had not been a long-held goal for him, the way it was for Esteban and Juanita and Father Hortensio. Yet Preacher still felt a fierce sense of exultation for a moment. As he had tried to explain to the priest, he was not an overly religious man in the traditional sense, but it would give him some satisfaction to see these artifacts returned to their proper place, instead of being hidden away underneath the ground.

"It is the treasure we seek, Señor?" Pablo asked.

"Yep, it sure is," Preacher replied. He moved over to one of the wooden chests. At this elevation the air was fairly dry, even in the cave, so the wood hadn't deteriorated much in a hundred and fifty years. A simple brass latch held the lid closed. There was no lock. Preacher turned the latch and lifted the lid. The guttering light from the torch shone dully on the gold ingots stacked inside the chest.

"Madre de Dios," Pablo said again, this time in a breathless half whisper.

"Yeah," Preacher agreed.

He lifted his head as he heard the swift rataplan of hoof-beats on the surface. A moment later, Esteban called, "Preacher! Are you down there?"

"We're here," Preacher said, raising his voice so that it echoed in the close confines of the cave. "And so is the treasure!"

"Praise be to God!" That exclamation came from Father Hortensio.

Juanita asked, "Are you all right?"

"And where is Pablo?" Esteban added.

"Pablo's here with me, and we're both fine," Preacher replied. "Hang on a minute, and we'll climb out."

"We leave the treasure here, Señor?" Pablo asked, sounding surprised.

"Just for now," Preacher assured him. "That torch ain't gonna last much longer. We'll have to get some better light down here, and then we'll figure out how to get the treasure up to the surface." He smiled. "Don't worry. . . . It ain't goin' anywhere until we move it."

At Preacher's urging, Pablo climbed out of the cave first. He set the torch aside and grasped the rope, and Preacher gave him a boost that enabled him to reach the slanted part of the shaft. From there he was able to scramble to the surface on his own, although Esteban and Joaquin stood ready to help him if need be. Preacher went up next. When he emerged from the hole, Juanita threw her arms around his neck and hugged him.

"Please, Señorita," Father Hortensio said stiffly in disapproval, "there is no need for such a display."

"Without Preacher we might never have found the treasure, Father," Esteban said. He extended a hand to the mountain man. "He deserves our thanks."

Preacher shook hands with the young man. "It was Pablo who found the cave," he pointed out.

The Yaqui grunted and said, "By falling into it, Señor. I thought I was a dead man."

"I was a mite concerned about you when you slipped off that edge," Preacher admitted. "Without any light down there, there was no way of knowin' just how deep the cave was or how far the drop was gonna be."

"Just far enough to twist my ankle a bit when I landed . . . a price I will gladly pay to do the Lord's work."

Juanita hugged him, too, making the grim-faced Yaqui look a little uncomfortable, and Esteban slapped him on the back. Father Hortensio was too busy praying to issue any congratulations.

Preacher knelt and studied the hole. Now that they knew where the treasure was, there was no hurry about retrieving it, so he decided to indulge his curiosity. "I rode along here yesterday," he said to no one in particular. "I should've noticed a hole this big."

"But it was not that big, Señor," Pablo said. "It was small, like the burrow of an animal, and I had to move a rock aside to get a good look at it. When I did, the ground gave way beneath my feet and I fell."

"Yeah, the way you dropped out of sight, I figured somethin' like that must've happened. Maybe ol' Don Francisco and his men filled in most of the upper part o' the openin' and rolled that rock over it as a landmark. They could've figured that they would dig back down to the cave when they came back for the loot."

Esteban took up the speculation. "But they never returned, and over the years rain washed out some of the earth they used to block the tunnel, until it was open again except on top."

Preacher nodded and said, "That's the way it looks to me. Pablo came along and moved the rock, which changed the stress on the ground, and then stepped where he shouldn't and it all went out from under him."

Father Hortensio stopped mumbling prayers and sniffed. It wasn't a sound of disdain this time, however. "What is that smell?" he asked.

"Volcanic gas would be my guess," Preacher said. "It's comin' up from underground somewheres. There are cracks in the cave wall down there, and the stink is comin' through them."

"It smells like the very fires of Hades itself," Father Hortensio said darkly. "To think that relics dedicated to the Lord have been sealed away in that hellhole for all these years. It is shameful!"

"Yeah, well, them Pueblo Indians would've melted 'em down if they'd got their hands on 'em," Preacher pointed out. "Then they would have been gone for good."

"Es verdad," the priest admitted grudgingly.

"What do we do now?" Juanita asked. "How do we get the treasure out of there?"

"First thing we need to do," Preacher said, "is to gather some dead branches and some brush and toss it down the hole. That way we can make a little fire down there so we can see what we're doin'. The torch we had down there is burned out by now. Once we've done that, somebody can climb down, get the fire started, and tie the rope to one of those bags. The rest of us can pull it up. It'll take a while, and we might have to use Horse to lift them chests full o' gold bars, but we'll get it all done."

"It is hard to believe we finally found it," Esteban said. "This has been a dream of mine ever since I first read that old manuscript, penned so long ago by my ancestor."

Preacher clapped a hand on Esteban's shoulder and grinned. "You can believe it, amigo. Now, let's get to work."

SEVENTEEN

Esteban and Father Hortensio both insisted on going down into the cave so that they could see the treasure where it had been hidden for the past century and a half. Preacher figured it wouldn't hurt anything, so he didn't argue the matter. Once they had thrown enough branches and dried brush into the hole, he shinnied down the rope again and got the fire started. He kept it small, not wanting the air in the cave to get stifling hot. Then he called up and told Esteban and the priest it was all right to descend the rope.

Father Hortensio came first, and Preacher looked away, not particularly enchanted by the view of the priest's hairy legs under the robe. When Father Hortensio reached the bottom, he dropped to his knees in front of the treasure, crossed himself, and began to pray as if he were kneeling in front of an altar. That made Preacher frown. It didn't seem right somehow for a holy man to be so impressed by a pile of riches.

Esteban climbed down and dropped easily to the floor of the cave. He crossed himself, too, and said a prayer of his own as he looked at the heaped-up treasure, but at least he stayed on his feet. He went over to one of the bags and untied the rawhide thong that held it closed. The thong had been in place for so long that Esteban had to struggle with it for a moment, but finally he got it loose. He opened the bag and reached inside to withdraw an object wrapped in oilcloth.

Father Hortensio got to his feet and said, "Esteban, what are you doing? It is not our place to disturb these relics. They should not be unwrapped until we have returned them to the mission where they belong."

Esteban shook his head. "I understand, Father, but after all this time, I must see for myself that we have succeeded. I will do nothing to dishonor whatever artifact this may be." He ignored Father Hortensio's scowl and continued unwrapping the object in his hands.

Underneath the oilcloth was another layer of coverings, this one of fine linen. Esteban unwound it carefully, and the firelight suddenly gleamed on the heavy candlestick that was revealed. It appeared to be cast of solid gold. Esteban's hands shook a little as he peered down at what he held.

"That candlestick should be on an altar, not in this cave that stinks of the very devil himself," Father Hortensio said. "Please, Esteban . . ."

Slowly, Esteban nodded. "You are right, Father." He began to carefully wrap up the candlestick again. Father Hortensio helped him.

Meanwhile, Preacher tried to heft one of the chests. He was able to lift it slightly, but he knew he could never climb up the shaft with it. He was confident that Horse could raise it, though. They would probably need a second rope, so that two of them could be fastened around the chest.

"We'll get the bags out first," he said as he brought the end of the rope over to where Esteban and Father Hortensio stood. Esteban had replaced the candlestick in the big sailcloth bag. Now he tied the rawhide thong around the bag again, closing it, and Preacher tied the rope to the bag.

He stepped over to the opening of the shaft, carrying the bag. He set it on the ground, cupped a hand at his mouth, and called up, "Haul away!" The rope grew taut as Pablo and Joaquin began pulling it up hand over hand. The bag of holy relics rose from the floor of the cave. Preacher took hold of it and reached above his head to guide it into the shaft. The bag disappeared from sight.

"You fellas might as well climb out when the rope comes back down," Preacher told his two companions. "I can handle this part of the chore, at least for now. Might need a hand when it comes time to boost those chests up."

Esteban shook his head. "I think you should go back to the surface, Preacher. It is still possible that the men who attacked us several days ago could have been trying to stop us from reaching the treasure, rather than simply intending to rob and murder us. If that is true, they could still be around, waiting to, how do you say, jump us again. I would feel better if you were up there to protect us while we work."

"Well, you might be right about that," Preacher allowed. "I'll climb up and keep an eye on things."

A few minutes later, the end of the rope came slithering down the shaft again and dropped into the cave. Preacher nodded to Esteban and Father Hortensio, then grasped the rope.

"I'm comin' up," he called, and he started to climb.

Professor Rufus Chambers could barely contain his excitement as he lowered the spyglass. "They've found the treasure!" he said. "I'm certain of it!"

Cobey Larson reached for the glass. "Lemme see."

"There's some sort of tunnel," Chambers went on. "Preacher and one of the Indians climbed out of it. There must be a cave down there, below the cliff. What better place for Don Francisco to have concealed the treasure?"

Chambers and his group of hired gunmen had followed the Alvarez party along the river that morning, and when everyone except the two Yaquis who had remained with the wagons had started up the canyon across the way, Chambers had suspected that was the one Don Francisco had talked about in his manuscript. Arnie Ross, who seemed to be more intelligent than he appeared, had suggested that some of them climb to this ledge on the opposite side of the river where they might be able to see what was going on at the head of the canyon where Preacher and the others had gone. The climb had been long and hard, but it had been rewarded. From this vantage point, with the help of the spyglass, they could see what was going on over there, a good half mile straight across the valley of the Purgatoire. A distant shot had drawn their attention and helped them to focus on the right place. Chambers, accompanied by Larson and Ross, had watched as the Alvarez siblings, the priest, and one of the Yaquis had converged on the spot. The professor had wondered where Preacher and the other Indian were, when lo and behold, the two of them had climbed into sight, apparently from out of the ground.

From there, it took no great reasoning skills to deduce that there was a cave over there, and from the excited attitude of the individuals gathered around it, Chambers knew they must have located the lost treasure of Mission Santo Domingo. That was the only thing that would produce such a reaction.

"Yeah, you're right," Cobey said. "They're throwin' branches and such down the hole, so they must be plannin' to build a fire in that cave."

"There's no point in waitin' any longer," Ross put in. "We need to climb back down, join up with the rest o' the fellas, and get over there to jump those folks before they know we're anywhere around."

Cobey nodded in agreement. "Sounds good to me."

"Wait just a moment," Chambers said. "Perhaps it would be better to wait and let them bring all the treasure out of the cave before we make our move."

"Hell, no," Cobey said emphatically. "I didn't have a problem with lettin' them *find* the cache, but there are plenty of us to haul it up outta that cave. We need to jump 'em now, while all their attention is on what they're doin'. If we wait until they've brought the treasure out and loaded it on the wagons, Preacher will be on his guard even more than he was before." He clenched a fist. "I want that son of a bitch dead before he knows what's hit him."

Chambers thought it over for a moment and then nodded. "I think you're right, my friend. Let's go. It will take us a while to climb down, and then we have to get up that canyon and take them by surprise."

"That'll mean killin' the two Yaquis they left with the wagons," Arnie pointed out.

Chambers just smiled and said, "Yes. So it will."

Preacher climbed out of the hole and saw that the first bag of treasure had been tied to the saddle of the horse that had carried the two Yaquis up here. Juanita said, "I thought we could go ahead and send Joaquin down to the wagons with it, but I wanted to be sure you approved of that first, Preacher."

After a moment's thought, Preacher shook his head. "We need to get all the loot out first, so we can carry as much down as we can at one time. We'll want to ride guard on it, too, in case anybody tries to take it away from us."

Juanita frowned. "You think that is possible?"

"Anythin's possible," Preacher said. "Especially when you're dealin' with a fortune in gold."

"Very well. I trust your judgment, Preacher."

He hoped she was right in doing so.

For the next hour, they worked steadily. Preacher checked the other horses, but none of them had a rope tied to the saddle, which put a minor crimp in his plans. They could pull the chests out with only one rope, but it would be a trickier chore and they would have to be careful not to break the rope or to let any of the chests slip out of the loop and fall while they were being hauled up. He was sure they could manage, though.

In the meantime, raising the bags of relics to the surface

one at a time was fairly easy, though time-consuming. They had to take a break from the work, too, while Father Hortensio climbed out of the cave. He was rather pale and claimed that the smell bothered him.

"I do not know what is sickened more, my stomach from the fumes or my soul from the reminder they carry of the infernal realm ruled by El Diablo."

"You figure Hell is really down there under the ground, Padre?" Preacher asked.

"Where else would it be?" Father Hortensio snapped.

Preacher scratched his bearded jaw. "I dunno. Don't reckon I've ever really thought about it that much."

"You should spend more time in religious contemplation."

"I'll keep that in mind," Preacher said dryly. Father Hortensio's skeptical expression made it plain that he didn't believe the mountain man for a second.

They got back to work, and the pile of bags on the ground near the entrance to the cave continued to grow. Finally, Esteban called up, "This is the last bag, Preacher."

"All right," Preacher replied. "We'll haul it up, and then I'll climb down and we'll see about bringin' those chests outta there."

A few minutes later, the bag was on the surface and added to the pile that had grown over the past hour. Preacher took hold of the rope and let himself down into the cave.

He found Esteban waiting for him with one of the chests open. The young man reached into it and took out one of the heavy bars of gold.

"I have been thinking, Preacher," he said. "You should take this." He held out the ingot.

Preacher frowned. "Why would I want to do that?"

"You deserve it for all the help you have given us. The Church is willing to let Juanita and me keep some of the gold, so that we can revive our family's fortunes. You are equally deserving."

Preacher shook his head. "A bar o' gold would just weigh me down. Anyway, it ain't like I'm headin' back to St. Louis or some other place where I could do anything with it. Once I get back to my old stompin' grounds in the Rockies north o' here, I wouldn't have no use for any gold."

"You are certain?"

"Certain sure," Preacher said. He added, "I might let the Church buy me some supplies once we get back down to the tradin' post, if Father Hortensio will go along with it."

"I will see that he does," Esteban promised.

Preacher knew the youngster meant well by that, but he wasn't sure Esteban was in any position to deliver on that promise. When Father Hortensio didn't want to do something, he seemed to be harder to budge than a Missouri mule.

Esteban replaced the ingot in the chest and closed it. He and Preacher got at each end of the chest and lifted it, carrying it over to where the rope waited. They set it down, and Preacher looped the rope around the chest so that it criss-crossed itself before he tied it securely. The chest couldn't slip out of that arrangement. The only question was whether a single rope was strong enough to lift the great weight of the chest.

"All right, somebody lead Horse away from the shaft!" he called to those on the surface. "The rest of you haul on the rope, too!"

As the rope grew taut, Preacher and Esteban lifted the chest as well, boosting it toward the opening of the shaft. They had to raise themselves on their toes to guide the heavy box into the opening. Then Preacher stepped back and motioned for Esteban to do the same.

"If that rope was to snap, we don't want that chest fallin' back down on us," he explained. "It's heavy enough to bust a fella's head wide open."

They heard the chest scraping against the sides of the shaft as it rose steadily. After a few moments, the noises stopped and Juanita called excitedly, "The chest is here. We have it!"

"Good!" Preacher replied. "Untie the rope and toss it back down, and we'll get the next one ready to haul up."

He stood underneath the opening now, waiting for the end of the rope to tumble back down to the cave. When it didn't appear after a moment, he began to frown.

"Juanita? Somethin' wrong up there?"

Suddenly, there was a muffled half scream, cut off abruptly, and somewhere above them a gun roared, the blast echoing down the shaft to the two startled men below the surface.

EIGHTEEN

For a moment, while they were on that ledge high above the river, Cobey Larson had considered pushing the professor over the edge. It would have been pleasurable to watch the arrogant bastard flail his arms and legs and listen to his terrified screams as he plummeted through empty air to his death. Cobey had kept Chambers alive until they found the treasure, but they didn't really need him anymore.

Still, you never could tell what might happen. A situation could arise in which it would be handy to have Chambers around, although for the life of him, Cobey didn't know what it would be. He supposed they could let the professor live a while longer.

They climbed down and rejoined Bert McDermott, Hardy Powers, George Worthy, Wick Jimpson, and Chuck Stilson. Wick and Chuck were still the walking wounded, and Stilson didn't mind bitching about how bad his hip hurt where one of Preacher's bullets had grazed it during the fight a few days earlier. Wick limped around in silence. He had complained about his wound at first, but after Cobey had lost his patience and snapped at the dim-witted giant to shut his pie hole, Wick had stayed quiet for the most part. In his doglike loyalty, he didn't want to upset Cobey.

"What did you find out?" Bert asked eagerly. "Have they found the treasure?"

"Yeah," Arnie Ross replied. "We saw 'em bringin' it up out of a hole in the ground, on a shelf up at the head of that canyon."

"Are we goin' to get it?" Powers asked.

Cobey nodded. "Yeah, mount up. They left a couple of the Yaquis with the wagons at the mouth of the canyon. We'll take care of them first and then sneak up on the others."

The men swung up into their saddles. Chambers was a surprisingly graceful rider for an Easterner. They started along the river toward the spot where the Alvarezes had left the wagons.

Cobey called a halt before they got there, and the men dismounted. "Arnie an' me will take care of those Yaquis, quietlike so the ones up at the other end of the canyon won't hear anything. Hardy, you and Bert come along, too, in case we need a hand."

"Yaquis are supposed to be pretty tough sons o' bitches," Arnie pointed out.

"That's why we're takin' Hardy and Bert along."

Arnie nodded, but still looked worried.

They set off on foot, slipping quietly through the trees. The Yaquis were from farther south in Mexico, Cobey reflected. They weren't at home up here in the Sangre de Cristos any more than the gringos were. He hoped that unfamiliarity with the territory would even the odds a little. It was important that they dispose of the Indians without warning the others.

Using every bit of cover they could find and moving with all the stealth they could muster, the four hard cases snuck up on the wagons. Cobey lifted a hand to signal a stop when they were about fifty yards away, crouched behind some brush. He peered through a gap in the dense foliage to study the layout.

The Yaquis had left the teams hitched and had hobbled the mules. One of the Indians sat on the lowered tailgate of the second wagon, a rifle across his knees. The other redskin prowled near the mouth of the canyon. He carried a rifle, too.

"How we gonna get 'em?" Arnie whispered in Cobey's ear. "We can't get close enough to jump 'em without them seein' us."

Cobey had already realized the same thing. He frowned as he tried to figure out what to do next. He and Arnie and Bert were good shots, he knew, and he supposed Hardy Powers was, too. If they all fired, they could cut down the two Yaquis before the Indians knew what was happening.

But the sound of those shots probably would reach the top of the canyon with little trouble in this thin air. That would alert Preacher and the others that something was wrong down here. Surprise was vital if they were going to deal with the deadly mountain man.

"We gotta lure 'em over here some way," Cobey breathed. "And when we jump 'em, we gotta kill 'em quick, so they don't even have time to yell."

Arnie and the other two nodded in understanding.

Cobey began making a faint rustling sound in the brush, the sort of sound that a small animal might make. He had to be careful not to make too much noise. If too many branches began to crackle, the Yaquis might decide there was a bear or a wolf or some other big varmint in here and just blaze away at it. He had to get them curious enough to investigate, but not worried enough to shoot first and check to see what they were shooting at later.

The Yaqui sitting on the tailgate heard the noise first. He looked toward the brush and frowned. Arnie, Bert, and Hardy lay utterly still while Cobey continued to shake the brush a little. Cobey stopped for several seconds while the Yaqui was watching, then started again, like an animal that had paused briefly in whatever it was doing.

After a minute the Yaqui said something to his companion. Cobey didn't understand the language. It just sounded like a bunch of grunts to him, mixed with a few barely recognizable

Spanish words. The Yaqui at the wagon stood up. The one over by the canyon mouth walked toward him. Together they started toward the brush where the gringos were concealed.

Cobey slid his knife out of its sheath and motioned for the others to do likewise. He gripped the weapon tightly, ready to throw it. Beside him, Arnie was tense with anticipation. Cobey knew that Arnie Ross was deadly with a knife; that was just one of many ways in which folks usually underestimated the round little man who was so much more dangerous than he appeared.

Cobey stopped making the rustling noise when the Yaquis were about ten feet away from the line of brush. The two Indians stopped as well and waited to see if the rustling would resume. When it didn't, one of the Indians shrugged, said something to his companion, and started to turn away. They thought that whatever was in the brush had gone on.

With a nod to Arnie, Cobey suddenly burst out of the brush and flung his knife. Beside him, Arnie did the same.

Cobey's knife buried its blade deep in the chest of one of the Yaquis. Arnie's throw was even better, the blade lodging in the other Indian's throat so that he couldn't cry out. The two white men followed their knives with a rush that bulled into the Yaquis and knocked them off their feet. McDermott and Powers charged out right behind them in case they needed help subduing the Yaquis.

Cobey ripped the rifle out of his man's hands and threw it aside. He slammed his knee into the Yaqui's groin and locked his hands around the man's neck.

A few feet away, Arnie Ross grabbed the knife he had thrown and ripped it across the other Yaqui's throat. Blood fountained high in the air, and the Indian's heels beat a grotesque tattoo against the rocky ground as he died.

Cobey kept choking his man until the Yaqui went limp underneath him. A fierce sense of satisfaction went through Cobey. Both of the Yaquis were dead, and neither of them had let out a shout or gotten a shot off. The small sounds of the deadly struggle could not have been heard up above on the shelf where the rest of the Alvarez party worked at recovering the lost treasure.

Cobey pushed himself to his feet and motioned the others forward. Arnie went back to fetch Wick and Chuck and the horses, as well as Professor Chambers.

When they were all together again, Cobey said quietly, "We'll leave the horses down here and go up the canyon on foot. We don't want the others to hear horses comin' and get spooked."

Chuck Stilson whined, "I don't know if I can make it that far on foot, Larson."

"You'd damned well better if you want a share of the loot," Cobey growled. "We're all goin' up there, so the odds will be as much on our side as possible. You, too, Professor."

Chambers nodded. "Of course. You can count on me. I'll do my part."

Cobey wasn't sure about that. He figured the professor might "accidentally" catch a stray bullet before all the shooting was over. He'd just have to wait and see about that.

Bert said to the giant, "Reckon you can make it, Wick?"

"I can go anywhere Cobey says to go," Wick replied without hesitation.

Cobey slapped him on the arm. "That's the spirit. Everybody check your pistols, and then let's go kill us some pilgrims and get us some gold."

"But not the girl," Powers spoke up. "We won't kill her."

"No." Cobey shook his head, thinking of Juanita Alvarez's thick dark hair and ripe figure. "We won't kill the girl."

The Yaqui's name was Benedicto. He had been born with a name that translated to Blue Eagle, but Benedicto he had become when he converted to Christianity and accepted the Spaniards' God. Now he called on Jesus, Mary, and Joseph to give him strength and help him ignore the pain that filled his body. Far in the back of his mind, he called on older, more savage gods as well. He would take whatever help he could get, as long as it allowed him to have his revenge on those who had done this to him.

He had no idea how much time had passed since blackness claimed him. When the gringo's choking hands had sent him into oblivion, Benedicto had believed that he was dying. He might die yet, of course, but somehow he had clung to life and now had made the long, slow climb back to consciousness. He drew rattling breaths through his bruised and painful throat, and each of those breaths seemed to add fuel to the fire that burned in his chest. The knife that had penetrated his body was gone, pulled back out by the man who had thrown it. Blood had followed, welling out of the wound so that the front of Benedicto's shirt was soaked with the stuff. Even though his chest was on fire, the rest of him was cold, as cold as a winter morning high in the mountains. He could barely feel his hands and feet.

But he managed to pull himself upright anyway, and as he stumbled to his feet he lifted his pain-blurred eyes and looked around.

The gringos were gone.

He did not know how many of them there had been. He remembered seeing two, perhaps more. They had killed Ismael and wounded him, then left.

Even through the fog of pain that shrouded his brain, Benedicto was able to think clearly enough to realize what must have happened. The gringos had sneaked up, attacked him and Ismael, and then gone up the canyon to kill the others and steal the holy treasure.

"Padre," he murmured, thinking of Father Hortensio. It was Father Hortensio who had shown him the light and led him to the Lord. Benedicto owed everything to Father Hortensio. He would gladly give up his own life to save the priest. Señor Esteban and Señorita Juanita were in danger, too, and Benedicto wanted to help them. He cared nothing for the man called Preacher. Preacher was a gringo and a heathen, and therefore less than nothing. But the others, including Pablo and Joaquin . . . Benedicto had to help them.

He looked around for his rifle, but even after he found it, he knew he lacked the strength to lift it and carry it up the canyon. His hand went to his waist. His knife was still there in its sheath. He could handle the knife. He drew it and stumbled toward the mouth of the canyon.

It never occurred to him to pick up the rifle and fire a warning shot. He merely shuffled along, clutching his knife, grimly determined to catch up to the evil gringos and avenge himself.

With each step, more of his life's blood dripped onto the canyon floor.

In the twisting canyon, men could move just about as fast on foot as on horseback. Cobey led the way, setting a quick pace. He had known the canyon twisted and turned, but he was surprised that it snaked around as much as it did. It was almost enough to make a man dizzy.

It took them over an hour to reach the top. That was longer than it had taken him and Arnie and the professor to get to the ledge on the other side of the river, but that had been a straight, relatively easy climb. As they trudged up the canyon, he heard Chuck Stilson muttering curses under his breath. Stilson was another one, like the professor, that they could probably do without, Cobey decided. Wick still didn't complain, even though he was really hurt worse than Chuck was.

When they neared the top, Cobey called a halt while they were still out of sight of the people on the shelf. For ten or fifteen minutes they waited there, catching their breath from the long climb. That gave Cobey a chance to go over the plan with the other men.

"Arnie, you and me'll take Preacher. He's got to go down

fast and hard, since he's the most dangerous of the bunch. We'll fire at the same time. Bert, you'll line your sights on Preacher, too, and if Arnie and me don't drop him right away, it'll be up to you."

McDermott nodded in understanding.

Cobey turned to Powers and Worthy. "It'll be up to you two to get them Yaquis, since they're probably the biggest threat after Preacher."

The two men gave grim nods of assent.

"That leaves you and Wick to take care of the Alvarez boy," Cobey said to Stilson. "I don't know how good a shot he is, so aim good and we won't have to find out."

"Yeah, I got it," Stilson said in surly tones.

"Wick, you understand?" Cobey asked the big man. "You're gonna take your gun and shoot at Esteban Alvarez. He's the young fella who'll probably be wearin' a sombrero."

"I understand, Cobey," Wick said with a frown, "but I don't know why we're doin' this. Why would I want to shoot at somebody who ain't shootin' at me?"

"Because we want what he's got. You remember me tellin' you about the gold?"

"Oh, yeah," Wick said, his expression clearing up a little. "The gold. I remember now."

"You just do what I tell you, and you'll get some of the gold."

"All right," Wick said. "I'll be good, I promise, Cobey."

"What about me?" Chambers asked. He took his pistol out of his coat pocket. "I can shoot, too, you know."

"You're like Bert, Professor," Cobey said. "If any of the rest of us miss with our first shots, it'll be up to you to step in and finish the job." But that wasn't likely to happen, of course, and anyway, Cobey didn't want to think about how badly things would have to be fouled up before their fate would rest in the hands of a professor from back East.

"Excellent," Chambers said. "Are we ready?"

"I reckon we are. It's half a mile or more to that cliff where the cave is. There are plenty of trees between here and there for us to use as cover, though. I figure we can get within fifty yards of them without 'em knowin' we're there. That'll be close enough to cut 'em down without any trouble." Cobey looked around at the other men, saw the greed and ruthlessness on their faces—well, with the exception of Wick, of course—and he was pleased. "Let's go," he said.

The gringos were fools, Benedicto thought an eternity later as he reached the top of the canyon and staggered after his quarry. They believed him to be dead, and they never looked behind them. All their attention was focused ahead.

They had no idea that death was dogging their trail, he thought as he smiled grimly and tightened his grip on the knife in his hand.

NINETEEN

Everything had gone as planned so far. Cobey, Arnie, and the others crouched in the trees, watching the people gathered around the mouth of the cave. No one had noticed their presence.

But now things began to go wrong. Cobey realized with a scowl that he didn't see Preacher anywhere, or the Alvarez kid, either.

That meant the two of them had to be down inside the cave.

There was a big pile of sailcloth bags near the horses. Professor Chambers slipped up next to Cobey and clutched his arm. He pointed with his other hand at the bags and whispered, "The artifacts from the missions. The gold ingots are supposed to be in wooden chests."

Cobey nodded. "They're still bringin' the stuff up. Haven't gotten to the gold yet."

That wasn't a problem. Once everybody except the girl had been disposed of, some of Cobey's men could climb down in that hole and see to bringing the gold out. The problem was that Preacher wasn't out in the open where they could shoot the son of a bitch first thing. Cobey didn't figure that Esteban Alvarez represented much of a threat, but Preacher, now . . . Preacher was different.

Cobey leaned over to Arnie and whispered, "Preacher's down in that hole. We'll have to wait for him to come up."

Arnie nodded. "Yeah. We got to kill him first."

Cobey motioned for the other men to just wait and be quiet. They had waited this long; they could be patient for a little while longer.

Meanwhile, the two Yaquis hauled on a rope that went down into the hole and brought up several more bags of loot, one at a time. The watchers were close enough so that Cobey could hear the girl calling down the hole to Preacher and Esteban. He couldn't hear what they said back to her, though. But he made out enough of the conversation to know that all the bags were now on the surface. That left the chests full of gold bars. Cobey licked his lips at the thought of all that gold. . . .

Juanita Alvarez lowered the rope into the hole in front of the cliff again and then waited. The other end of the rope was tied to the saddle of the big rangy horse that Preacher normally rode. One of the Yaquis went over to the horse and grasped its reins, being careful because the animal bared its teeth at him. That was a one-man horse, Cobey thought, but it looked like the animal was willing to let the Yaqui lead it, even though it wouldn't have tolerated taking the Indian on its back.

Didn't Preacher have a dog? That thought suddenly occurred to Cobey. He had forgotten about the damned dog! Where was the shaggy beast? Off chasing varmints somewhere, Cobey hoped.

"Look how taut that rope is," Arnie said as the Yaqui began to lead the horse away from the hole. "There's somethin' heavy on the other end!"

"Damn right," Cobey said. "A fortune in gold." Instinctively, he lifted his rifle.

That was when a blood-covered apparition reeled out of the brush behind Cobey, lunged toward him, and drove a knife at his back.

Instinct and keen hearing warned Cobey in time for him to turn halfway around toward the unexpected threat. Horror shot through him at the sight of the pain-crazed Yaqui who was supposed to be dead down at the mouth of the canyon. Pain jolted Cobey the next instant as the Yaqui's knife lanced into his upper left arm. The thrust would have gone into his back if he hadn't turned sharply when he did. The rifle slipped out of his hand and clattered to the rocky ground, and he let out a choked groan, unable to hold it back.

Over by the cliff, a heavy wooden chest had just emerged from the hole on the end of the rope. The priest and the other Yaqui grabbed it and wrestled it to the side. Evidently, they hadn't heard the disturbance in the trees.

But Juanita Alvarez had, and as she turned swiftly, she saw Cobey stumble into the open, knocked forward by the collision with the Yaqui who had just stabbed him. She opened her mouth to scream.

Cobey wasn't sure until later exactly what happened next. Arnie Ross streaked forward, moving faster than a short-legged fat man had any business moving. He covered the ground between the trees and the cliff in a flash and tackled Juanita, clapping a hand over her mouth as he bore her to the ground. Fast as he was, though, he was too late. She had already gotten out part of a scream.

Snarling, Cobey jerked his pistol from behind his belt and raised it, cocking the hammer as he did so. The blood-covered Yaqui ripped his knife from Cobey's arm and brought it back to strike again.

Cobey jammed the pistol in the Indian's face and pulled the trigger.

The fire that geysered from the pistol's muzzle burned the Yaqui's right eye out. The heavy lead ball shattered his cheekbone and bored on through his head to burst out the back of his skull in a grisly shower of gray matter and glistening white bone fragments. The Yaqui flopped to the ground, dead at last. Cobey breathed hard as he looked down at the corpse. The reaction was partially from the pain in his arm and partially from the atavistic fear that the Indian would rise again, shattered skull and all, and come after him again. He would have sworn the Yaqui was dead when they left him down below.

He was dead now, sure enough, and didn't move except for a few final twitches. Cobey twisted around as more shots blasted out. The whole plan had gone to hell.

And any second, Preacher might crawl up out of that hole and go to killin'.

Juanita Alvarez struggled madly in the stranger's grip, but he was much stronger than her and his hands were like iron as he grasped her. She managed to get one hand loose and clawed at his face, trying to gouge out his eyes. He jerked his head to the side so that she merely scratched his cheek. He grunted in pain but didn't loosen his grip. She felt her feet leave the ground as he lifted her and carried her toward the trees.

Several other men stepped out of those trees and fired rifles at Father Hortensio and the two Yaquis. Those shots were hurried, however, and all but one of them missed. The only one that hit its target just grazed Joaquin's upper left arm. The impact was still enough to slew him around sideways. He recovered and snatched his rifle from the ground. Pablo had already grabbed his rifle and was drawing a bead on their attackers.

Father Hortensio was behind the horses, using the animals as cover from any more shots.

Pablo's rifle blasted and one of the strangers cried out and went over backward. Joaquin knelt behind the pile of bags, knowing their contents might stop a rifle or pistol ball. Father Hortensio saw what he was doing and shouted, "No! The holy relics must be protected!"

Joaquin thought the world of Father Hortensio, but the priest did not always see the practical side of things. How could he, Joaquin, protect the holy relics if he allowed the gringos to shoot him? It made no sense.

So he dropped to a knee behind the sacks, raised his rifle to his shoulder, and fired. At the same time, one of the men loosed a round at him from a pistol. Sure enough, the ball smacked into the pile of sacks but didn't penetrate all the way through it. Father Hortensio let out a cry as if the ball had struck him instead of the relics.

Joaquin's shot passed close enough to the head of one of the men to make him duck frantically into the trees. All of the gringos were retreating now, including the one who had hold of Juanita. She continued to struggle until the fat gringo holding her drove a fist against the side of her head. Pain flashed through her skull, and she went limp in his arms, knocked unconscious by the blow.

There were two loaded pistols holstered on the saddle of Señor Preacher's horse. Joaquin grabbed the butts of the guns and jerked them from their holsters, but as he spun toward the trees and lifted them, Pablo caught one of his arms and stopped him from firing.

"They have the señorita!" Pablo said. "If you shoot, you risk hitting her!"

Joaquin hadn't thought of that. He nodded and lowered the pistols. Now that the shooting had stopped, Father Hortensio came out from behind the horses and began to harangue them.

"The gringos have stolen Señorita Juanita!" the priest said. "What will we do?" He crossed himself. "At least the holy relics and the gold are safe!"

But for how long? That was the question none of them could answer.

And from behind the three men came Preacher's outraged bellow. "What the hell!"

The moment when Juanita screamed and the shooting started was one of the worst in Preacher's life. He was used to trouble, having lived with it for many years, but in the past he had always been able to strike back at whoever was trying to hurt him and his friends. He had never been trapped down in a hole in the ground, able to hear what was going on but unable to do anything about it or even to be sure exactly what was happening.

The situation was intolerable, that was all there was to it. "Gimme a boost," he said to an equally worried Esteban.

"What?"

"Help me get up to where the shaft starts."

"But there is no rope—"

"That ain't gonna stop me," Preacher vowed grimly.

As more shots rang out on the surface, Esteban made a stirrup of his hands. Preacher put his foot in it, and Esteban grunted from the effort as he heaved Preacher upward. The mountain man was heavier than his lanky frame would indicate, since it was so packed with muscles. He reached for the lip of the shaft, stretching as high as his long arms could reach. His fingers closed over the edge and took some of the weight off Esteban. The young man lifted Preacher higher. Preacher's foot came off Esteban's hands as he pulled himself into the shaft.

It angled toward the surface, seemingly too steep to climb without a rope or anything else to hang on to. The shaft was a little less than a yard wide, however, and Preacher's arm span was wider than that. He pressed his hands against the sides and pushed with his feet. That allowed him to inch upward. It took an incredible amount of strength to brace himself against the walls of the shaft like that and keep himself from falling, but it was strength that Preacher had. His progress was slow but steady. He kept his head back and his eyes fastened on the ragged circle of light that marked the upper end of the shaft.

The shooting came to an end just before he reached the top. Not knowing if that was good or bad, he was prepared for anything as he levered himself out of the shaft and sprawled on the ground. As he scrambled to his feet, he jerked his pistols from behind his belt. The muscles of his arms and legs tried to tremble from the exertion they had just gone through, but he willed them to an iron steadiness as he shouted, "What the hell!"

Father Hortensio and the two Yaquis were standing beside the pile of sacks containing the artifacts that had been hidden below. One of the Yaquis—Joaquin, Preacher thought—had a couple of pistols in his hands. Preacher recognized the weapons as the ones from his saddle.

The only person missing was Juanita Alvarez. "Where's the señorita?" Preacher snapped.

"They . . . they took her," Father Hortensio said.

"Who took her?"

"The gringos!" The priest leveled an arm toward some nearby trees.

Preacher swung in that direction, his pistols held ready to fire. He didn't see anything moving in the trees, however. "Where are they?"

"They fled," Father Hortensio said. He seemed to be getting some of his wits back about him now. "After they took Señorita Alvarez and tried to kill the rest of us, they ran off."

"We tried to stop them, Señor," Joaquin said. He lifted his left arm. Blood stained the sleeve of his shirt. "I was wounded."

"You hit bad?" Preacher asked.

The Yaqui shook his head. "The ball barely touched me."

Preacher grunted. "You were lucky. Get the rope back down the hole and help Señor Esteban outta there. And gimme back my guns."

He replaced the pistols behind his belt and took the ones that Joaquin had been holding. All four guns were double-shotted and loaded with a heavy charge of powder. They gave him considerable firepower as he stalked toward the trees.

He saw quickly that he wasn't going to need it. Juanita's kidnappers were gone. The tracks they had left headed off straight toward the top of the canyon, and Preacher had no doubt they were on their way back down now, taking Juanita with them as a prisoner.

They had left behind a couple of dead men. One of them was a Yaqui. He had been shot in the face at close range, destroying most of his features. Preacher was still able to recognize him as one of the Indians who had been left with the wagons.

The other man's identity was a mite more interesting. He was Hardy Powers, one of the so-called guides who worked for Professor Rufus Chambers.

TWENTY

By the time Preacher stalked back to where the others waited, Esteban was on the surface, having climbed up the rope that the Yaquis had dropped down the shaft to him. He hurried anxiously to meet Preacher and asked, "Where is Juanita? Did you see her?"

Preacher shook his head, and he hated to see the devastated look that settled on Esteban's face in response. The young man had to know what the situation was, though. Preacher said, "They've got her, all right."

"But who are they?" Father Hortensio asked.

"I don't know about all of 'em, but I've got a pretty good idea one was that Professor Chambers."

"I knew it!" the priest burst out. "I thought I saw him for an instant in the trees. He had a pistol and fired at us, as did the others."

Preacher jerked a thumb toward the trees. "Hardy Powers is dead over yonder. I reckon that fella Worthy was probably with 'em, too." He looked at Pablo and Joaquin. "I hate to tell you fellas this, but one of your pards is over there, too, shot dead."

They looked a little puzzled, so in rapid Spanish Esteban clarified what Preacher had just said. Both of the Indians gave guttural exclamations and then hurried toward the trees.

Preacher turned back to Father Hortensio. "Tell me exactly what happened," he ordered the priest.

Before Father Hortensio could answer, Esteban said, "Should we not go after Juanita? Can you follow the trail they left?"

"I reckon I can," Preacher said. "First, though, we need to know what we're up against. Tell me what happened, Padre."

"I . . . I am not sure," Father Hortensio said.

That was probably the first thing the priest hadn't been absolutely certain of since Preacher had known him, the mountain man reflected.

"We had just brought up the first chest of gold," Father Hortensio went on. "Then Señorita Alvarez screamed, and when I looked around I saw a gringo running toward her. A fat little gringo, but he moved very fast."

That rang a faint bell in Preacher's memory, but he passed over it for now. "Go on."

"At the edge of the trees, there was another gringo struggling with one of the Yaquis. I think it was Benedicto."

"The Yaqui, you mean?"

"Sí. The gringo, I had never seen before."

"What did he look like?"

Father Hortensio frowned in thought. "He was tall. A big man, strong-looking. He wore buckskin clothing, much like yours, but with more beads and decoration on them. He had long, fair hair and a beard."

Preacher nodded. That jibed with the memory that had cropped up at Father Hortensio's mention of the fat man. "The bunch from the trading post," Preacher said.

"Que?"

Preacher shook his head. "Never mind. Go on."

Father Hortensio rubbed his hands over his clean-shaven face and took a deep breath. "The tall gringo shot Benedicto. Then other gringos stepped out of the trees and began shooting at us. I could not say how many there were. A half dozen, perhaps. I thought one of them was Professor Chambers, but

I was not sure. We tried to fight back . . . or rather, Pablo and Joaquin did. I, of course, could not."

"You let them steal Juanita while you stood by and did nothing?" Esteban asked.

Father Hortensio drew himself up straighter. "I am a man of God," he said. "A man of peace. I cannot allow my hands to be stained with blood."

Esteban's face darkened angrily, and Preacher felt more than a mite irritated himself. But they didn't have time to waste, so he put a hand on the young man's shoulder and said to the priest, "Go on, Padre."

Father Hortensio shrugged. "There is not much left to tell. The fat man carried Juanita into the trees, and then all of the gringos fled."

"Why would they take her?" Esteban asked, his voice shaking. "Why?"

There was one pretty obvious reason, but Preacher figured there was a lot more going on here. He might be lacking much of a formal education, but he had a keen native intelligence and the ability to put things together quickly.

"Don't worry, Esteban, we're gonna get her back."

The young man turned an anguished look on him. "How can you know this?"

Preacher nodded toward the sacks of artifacts and the single chest of gold that had been brought up so far and said, "Because we've still got something that they want."

Never in his wildest dreams would Cobey have thought that so much could go so wrong so fast. They had lost another man—Hardy Powers, drilled dead center by a lucky shot from one of those damned Indians—and they didn't have any of the treasure they had set out to steal. Worst of all, Preacher was still alive. At least, Cobey supposed he was. From what they had seen before all hell broke loose, it had looked like

Preacher and the young Mex were down in the hole under the cliff where the loot was hidden.

The only good thing to come out of this debacle was that they now had the girl.

That had been quick thinking on Arnie's part to rush out there and grab her like that. Once Cobey had seen that, he'd realized that their best course of action was to cut their losses and get out of there, taking Juanita Alvarez with them.

Unfortunately, Hardy Powers had been hit and killed by that shot before they could pull back. Cobey hadn't known Powers for long, but he had seemed like a good enough fella. Too bad it couldn't have been the professor who caught that ball through the guts. Cobey wouldn't have minded that at all.

They were about halfway down the canyon when Cobey called a halt. Chambers objected, saying, "Shouldn't we keep moving? What if Preacher comes after us?"

"He knows by now we've got the girl," Cobey replied. "He's not gonna crowd us too much. From everything I've heard about him, he's a smart bastard. He'll have figured out by now that we're gonna have to work a swap."

"A swap?" Chambers echoed.

Cobey nodded. "That's right—the treasure for Señorita Alvarez."

The light of understanding dawned on Chambers's thin face. For a professor, he was dumb as a rock sometimes. The idea of trading Juanita for the treasure had sprung fully formed into Cobey's brain as soon as he saw Arnie grab her.

It wasn't as good as killing everybody else and just taking the girl and the loot . . . but once things had fallen apart, it was the best option they had left.

Juanita was starting to come around now. While Arnie hung onto her, Cobey took some rawhide thongs from his possibles bag and used them to tie her wrists. That would make her easier to handle. As consciousness returned to her and she realized what was going on, she began to spout a torrent of furious Spanish at them. Cobey put his face a couple of inches from hers, glared at her, and warned, "You better shut up, gal, or I'll gag you, too!"

That made her fall silent, although she still looked daggers at Cobey and all the other men. When her gaze reached Chambers, her eyes widened and she gasped, "Professor! You must help me!"

Chambers smiled and said, "I'm sorry, my dear, but I'm afraid I can't do that. You see, these men are my business associates."

"Then . . . you are a thief and a murderer, too!"

"Sadly, true."

"Why have I been abducted? I have never done anything to harm any of you men."

"You know better than that," Cobey snapped. "You know damned good and well why we grabbed you."

"You're our key to obtaining the lost treasure of Mission Santo Domingo, Señorita," Chambers said. "Surely, in order to insure your safety, your brother will turn over the treasure to us."

"You want to . . . trade me for the treasure?"

"That is essentially correct."

Juanita began to laugh. Cobey and Chambers frowned. "What's so damned funny?" Cobey demanded.

"You do not know Father Hortensio. He will not allow anything to divert him from his holy quest, not even my life."

"You're saying he won't turn over the treasure?" Chambers asked.

"Of course not. My life means nothing to him, in comparison to his devotion to the Church."

"He's just one man, and a priest, to boot," Cobey growled. "He won't be able to stop your brother from dealin' with us, and he sure as hell won't be able to stop Preacher."

"And do you think Señor Preacher will meekly go along with your plan?" Juanita asked.

To tell the truth, Cobey was worried about that very thing. Preacher was just the sort to try to figure out a way to rescue Juanita *and* save the treasure. But he could try all he wanted to, because in the end Cobey and his companions held all the aces in this game.

"He'd damned well better go along with it," Cobey said. "Otherwise, you're gonna be one dead señorita."

Preacher rode slowly down the canyon, guiding Horse with his knees because he had both hands on his rifle, ready to fire at the first sign of a threat. Dog walked in front of him, ears pricked forward. The big cur had wandered up after all the trouble was over, one of the few times since he'd been with Preacher that he had missed a fracas. Now, though, Preacher was mighty glad to have Dog with him. His senses were even sharper than Preacher's.

So when Dog suddenly stopped short and the fur around his neck bristled and he started to growl deep in his throat, Preacher knew trouble was waiting for him.

The fat man eased around the bend in front of Preacher. Not for a second, though, did Preacher believe that he was alone. One or more of the other hard cases would be with him. They might even have guns lined on Preacher at this very moment.

Dog would have lunged at the fat man and torn out his throat, but Preacher stopped him with a soft-voiced command.

"First thing I got to say to you," Preacher told the fat man, "is that if your pards try to bushwhack me, you won't never get your hands on that treasure."

"Why not?" the fat man asked with a wily smile. "Seems to me like it'd be smart to get rid of our most dangerous enemy while we've got the chance."

"Because if I don't come back, Esteban Alvarez will make sure nobody ever gets it. He's gonna blow it to kingdom come."

The fat man's eyebrows rose in surprise. "What? How in blazes is he gonna do that?"

"There are fumes down in the cave where the loot is. They seep up from somewhere deep in the earth, and if they build up enough, a spark will set 'em off and blow the whole side of that cliff off."

The fat man shook his head. "That's crazy."

"No, just a fact." Preacher paused and then added, "Ask the professor about it if you don't believe me. He ought to know enough about such things to know that I'm tellin' the truth."

"It couldn't be that bad," the fat man protested. "You and the Mex been climbin' up and down outta that hole all day."

"Yeah, but that shaft lets fresh air into the cave. It stunk a lot worse when we first opened it up and damned near knocked out one o' them Yaquis, and it had a small hole to let in fresh air even then. Now it's sealed up tight with rocks on top of the hole."

"You did that?" The fat man sounded like he couldn't believe it.

"Damn right we did," Preacher said. "But before we closed it up, we put a pistol down there, cocked and primed, with a string tied to the trigger. The string runs up the shaft to the surface. We left just enough room for it when we piled up the rocks to close the entrance. By now them fumes have probably built up to where they'd make a mighty big blast if somethin' set 'em off. And all it'll take is one pull o' that string."

The fat man was pale now, and worried-looking. "Whoever pulled on it would blow himself up, too."

Preacher smiled and shook his head. "Nope, because we tied several ropes to the end of the string. It can be pulled from a far enough distance so that whoever yanks on it will have a chance to get clear before the cliff comes down."

The fat man scrubbed a hand over his face. He turned and made a slight motion, and Preacher knew he was telling his companions not to shoot. He didn't want to take a chance that Preacher was telling the truth.

Which he wasn't—it was all a pack of lies—but the fat man didn't have to know that. The man glared at Preacher and said, "All right. Say what you came down here to say."

Preacher kept his face expressionless, but inside he was glad that the bluff had worked. He had thought of the whole rigmarole, and Esteban had agreed that it sounded plausible enough so that the men who had kidnapped Juanita might not want to risk a double cross.

Now Preacher said, "I reckon you want to trade the girl for the gold."

"Not just the gold. The whole treasure. All of it."

"That's what I meant. How do we know Señorita Juanita is still all right?"

"You'll have to take my word for it . . . but we can't very well expect to trade her if she ain't, now can we?"

"She better not be hurt in any way." Preacher's hard stare made it clear what he meant.

"Don't worry, ain't nobody bothered her. Cobey's seein' to that."

"He's your boss, is he?"

"He's the one runnin' things, yeah. And he's a mighty dangerous man, so you'd better not try any tricks."

Preacher shook his head. "No tricks, just a straight swap. You bring the girl back up and give her to us, and we'll ride away and leave the treasure in the hole for you."

"You'd already brought some of it up," the fat man protested.

"Yeah, we had," Preacher drawled, "but it's back in the hole now, along with that cocked pistol."

The fat man looked like he wanted to cuss, but he held it in. "How are we supposed to get the treasure if it's primed to blow up?"

"All you have to do is move the rocks coverin' up the top of the hole. Then the gas will come out and it'll be safe to climb down there and haul the stuff out. We did it without much trouble."

The fat man rubbed his jaw. "Yeah, I reckon."

"Just be careful not to pull that string until you've aired out the place," Preacher warned. "Might get more than you bargained for if you did."

After a moment, the fat man nodded. "All right. You got a deal, Preacher. The girl for the treasure, straight up. We'll bring her up here and give her to you, and you and the others ride off. We'll have you covered the whole time, though, in case you try anything."

"No tricks," Preacher said. "Juanita's life is worth more than a bunch o' old relics and some bars o' gold."

"I'm glad you feel that way," the fat man said with a grin. "How's that little priest feel about it?"

"He ain't happy," Preacher admitted, "but he'll go along with the plan."

"All right." The fat man backed toward the bend. "We'll be back in an hour with the girl. Don't try to sneak any o' them gold bars out, neither. You do and the deal's off."

"How many times do I have to tell you . . . there won't be any tricks."

"Remember that, or the girl's blood will be on your hands."

With that, the fat man ducked back around the bend and was gone. Preacher waited a minute to be sure, then said, "Come on, Dog." He turned Horse and started back up the canyon. The next hour was going to be a busy one.

TWENTY-ONE

Juanita's captors had stuck her in the back of one of the wagons and left the man they called Wick to guard her. Wick was probably the biggest man she had ever seen, close to seven feet tall and perhaps over three hundred pounds. The sleeves and shoulders of his buckskin shirt bulged with massive muscles. Juanita could tell when she looked at him, however, that he had the mind of a child. That gave her some hope. Perhaps she could convince him to let her go. She knew that she would have to befriend him first, though.

She wasn't sure where the other men were. The fat man and a couple of the others had gone back up the canyon. Professor Chambers and the one called Cobey, who seemed to be the real leader of the group, had disappeared somewhere, perhaps to plan their next move.

Juanita's hands were tied together in front of her. The rawhide thongs were tight enough so that her fingers had gone partially numb. She wasn't lying when she said through the open back of the wagon, "Señor Wick, my hands hurt. These bonds are too tight. Could you loosen them a little?"

He sat on a rock just outside the back of the wagon, with his knees sticking up because his legs were so long. He shook his head and said, "No, ma'am, I can't. Cobey told me to watch you and not do anything that you asked me to do, and I got to do what Cobey says."

"Why? Is he your father?"

Wick laughed. "My father? Cobey? No, ma'am, he ain't. I don't rightly remember my pa. I don't think my ma really knowed who he was."

"Your brother, then?"

"Nope. Ain't got no brother. Ain't had nobody since my ma died. Except for Cobey. He's my friend. He's my good friend. He looks out for me."

"How did you meet?" It was a strain for Juanita to keep her voice so affable and sound as if she were genuinely curious, but she had to do so.

"I don't know." Wick frowned in thought. "It's been a while. Cobey's been takin' care o' me for a long time." He scratched his jaw. "I think it was in St. Louie, or maybe Pittsburgh. Some town on a river. It's comin' back to me now. I was on a dock, unloadin' some boxes from a boat . . . an' I dropped one of 'em. I didn't mean to, but I dropped it and it busted open, and this fella laughed at me, and it made me mad so I hit him."

"You don't like for people to laugh at you?" Juanita asked gently.

"No, ma'am, I don't. It makes me mad. So when that fella laughed at me, I hit him in the head and he fell down, and a bunch o' blood come outta his ears and his nose, and some other fellas run up and looked at him and said he was dead. They said I had to go to jail." Wick shook his head. "I didn't want to go to jail. But they made me, after I hit some more fellas and made their heads bleed, too."

Juanita suppressed the shiver that ran through her as Wick recounted his gruesome tale. Obviously, he possessed enough strength to kill a man with a mere blow from his fist.

"They said they was gonna put a rope around my neck and string me up, whatever that means," Wick went on. "But that night, before they could do it, Cobey came and let me outta jail and said I was gonna go with him and he'd look after me from then on. He'd stuck a knife in the fella that was in charge o' the jail so he could get me out, so I knew he really liked me. Ever since then, I've stayed with Cobey and done whatever he told me to do. He's my friend."

Juanita knew that friendship had nothing to do with it. Cobey had recognized the opportunity to insure this giant's slavish devotion, and he had seized it. No doubt they had robbed and murdered their way all across the frontier, with Wick probably handling most of the violence while Cobey planned their crimes. Cobey had gathered other ruthless men around him, but Wick was his own personal tool, an implement of death as surely as a gun or a knife was.

Surprisingly, she found herself feeling some genuine sympathy for the huge man. There was no telling how many bloody-handed deeds he had carried out at his mentor's command, but Wick didn't really know he was doing wrong. He was just doing what his "friend" told him to do.

"I understand why you feel the way you do about him," she said. "I really don't think he would mind, though, if you loosened these bonds on my wrists."

Wick scowled. "He said you might try to trick me, so that you could run away. He don't want you to run away."

Juanita swallowed her frustration and kept her tone calm and gentle. "I cannot run away as long as I am in this wagon, and if I try to get out of the wagon, you can stop me. That has nothing to do with my hands hurting because my wrists are tied too tightly."

"Well . . . I reckon that's true."

"If you will loosen the thongs, I give you my word I will not try to run away." She felt bad about lying to him—no doubt he had been lied to a great deal in his life—but there were greater concerns here. She knew her captors were going to try to trade her for the lost treasure of Mission Santo Domingo. And Esteban would make such a trade, too, even though losing the treasure would be a terrible

blow to him. She could not let that happen if she could prevent it.

Wick put his hands on his knees and pushed himself to his
feet. "I guess I could look at your hands," he said grudgingly.
"Cobey didn't tell me I couldn't talk to you, or look at you,
or touch you. He just said for me to keep you here and for
me not to hurt you."

Juanita smiled at him and said, "If he told you not to hurt
me, then I think he would *want* you to loose my bonds so that
I am not in pain."

"You think?"

"It seems to me that it would be so."

His huge body almost filled up the opening at the rear of
the wagon. "Let me see."

She thrust her hands out toward him. He started to look
at them, but then he got distracted. His gaze strayed to her
breasts. His eyes widened and his breathing got faster.
Juanita felt a chill go through her, but tried not to show the
revulsion she felt as he stared at her.

"Them are mighty pretty bosoms, ma'am," he said.

"Th-thank you."

"Can I touch 'em? Cobey says I got to ask 'fore I touch
a lady's bosoms or do anything else like that with her."

"I . . . I don't think you should. It would not be proper."

"Oh." Wick's eyes fell. "All right, then."

"Wait," Juanita said hastily. She steeled herself and went
on. "I think it would be all right if you touched them, Wick.
Just a little, though."

His face lit up again. "Really?"

"Really," she assured him. "I do not think you should tell
Cobey about it, though."

"You reckon he'd mind?" Wick asked in a whisper.

"Oh, no," Juanita said. "He wouldn't mind. I would just
prefer that it was our secret. Don't you ever keep secrets,
Wick?"

"Not from Cobey."

"Well, this time you have to, otherwise you cannot do it. All right?"

He stared at her breasts for a long moment before he finally nodded his shaggy head. "All right."

"You promise?"

"I swear."

Juanita took a deep breath. "Go ahead, then."

He leaned closer and reached out with one huge hand. His fingertips touched the underside of her right breast through the fabric of her dress. He slid them forward gingerly until the whole thing was resting in the palm of his hand. His touch was gentle as he cupped that breast and then eased his hand over to the other one. Somehow, despite the riot of emotions going on inside her, Juanita kept a smile on her face and didn't shudder as he caressed her.

After a couple of minutes, she said, "That's enough, Wick," and he obediently took his hand away. She went on. "You said you would loosen these thongs around my wrists."

"Oh, yeah." He bent to that task, his sausagelike fingers fumbling as he worked with the knots. He poked the tip of his tongue out of his mouth as he frowned in concentration. Finally, the knots loosened, and Juanita tried not to grimace as feeling flowed painfully back into her hands.

"Is that better?" Wick asked.

"Much better," she told him, still smiling. "Thank you."

"I won't tell Cobey I loosened 'em. And I won't say anything to him about, uh, feelin' your bosoms."

She nodded and whispered conspiratorially, "Yes, I think that would be best."

"You're a really nice lady." He started to go back and sit down on his rock again, but he stopped and added, "I sure hope Cobey don't decide we got to kill you."

"It's agreed, then?" Chambers asked. "We don't let any of them live except the girl?"

"Of course not," Cobey said. "What sort o' dumb bastards would we have to be to do that?"

"I just don't want this coming back to haunt us later."

"It won't." Cobey rested a hand on the hilt of his knife. "And as soon as we've had our fill of the girl, she'll have to die, too."

With a regretful look on his face, the professor nodded. "That's all too true," he agreed. "No witnesses to testify against us."

"No witnesses," Cobey repeated.

Chambers didn't know it, but he wasn't going to survive this incident, either. Sure, he had been the one to find out about the treasure, through some friend of his in Mexico City, but that had been pure dumb luck. Chambers hadn't done anything to actually *earn* any of that loot. Cobey and his partners, on the other hand, had done the real work. They had risked their lives more than once for a shot at the treasure, and they were the ones who deserved to have it, not some fancy Easterner.

The two men stood under a tree near the mouth of the canyon. Cobey heard somebody coming, and wasn't surprised when Arnie Ross, Bert McDermott, George Worthy, and Chuck Stilson came into view, trudging out of the canyon. Cobey went to meet them.

"Somebody come down to parley?" he asked.

Arnie nodded. "Preacher his own self."

Cobey felt his pulse quicken. "Didn't the rest of you get a chance to bushwhack him? I didn't hear no shots."

"We couldn't shoot him," Arnie said disgustedly. "Before he came down to meet us, he put all the loot back in that cave and rigged the whole place to blow up if he didn't come back."

"What?" Cobey exploded. "How in hell did he do that?"

Quickly, Arnie explained about the gas building up in the cave and the pistol Preacher had set up to explode it if the string tied to its trigger was pulled.

Chambers listened to what Arnie had to say and then

nodded solemnly. "It could well be true," the professor said. "Such volcanic gas will explode if a sufficient concentration builds up. Plugging the shaft down into the cave might accomplish that. It's rather an ingenious thing to do, actually."

"Yeah, but he was bluffin'," Cobey growled.

Arnie asked, "How do you figure?"

"That Alvarez kid ain't gonna blow up the loot while we've still got his sister, no matter what happens to Preacher!"

Arnie frowned, took off his hat, and scratched his mostly bald head. "Damn it, you're right," he muttered.

"Preacher just wanted to throw you off balance long enough so that he could get out of there alive." Cobey snorted. "Looks like he did it, too."

"Yeah, but it don't matter," Arnie argued. "He agreed that they'd trade the treasure for the girl, and after we've made the swap we're gonna kill 'em all anyway, ain't we?"

"Yeah, but it would've been easier if Preacher was already dead."

There was no disputing that, so Arnie just shrugged.

"Well, what's done is done," Cobey went on. "What's the deal?"

"We bring the girl up to the top of the canyon and turn her over to Preacher and the others. They ride away, leavin' the treasure down in the hole so that we can take it out again."

"I thought you said the cave was full o' gas," Cobey said with a frown.

"We got to open up the shaft again and let it air out for a while. Then it'll be all right to go down and get the loot."

Cobey looked at Chambers, and the professor nodded and said, "Yes, it should be fine. They had a fire down there at one point, so the gas concentration must be very low when the shaft is open. We should probably wait an hour or two after it's opened up, just to make sure."

"All right," Cobey said. "We give 'em the girl, they start to ride away, and we shoot 'em. That's simple enough."

"Preacher's liable to be watchin' for a double cross," Arnie warned.

"I don't care. We'll have 'em outgunned."

"We're liable to have a fight on our hands."

"Think about all that gold and silver," Cobey said. "And think about that girl." His lips drew back from his teeth in a savage grin. "If all that ain't worth fightin'—and killin'—for, then I don't know what is."

TWENTY-TWO

Preacher had some figurin' to do, because he was damned if he was going to hand that treasure over to Chambers and those other bastards. He knew there was no way the thieves would let him and the others just ride away. The fat man had lied to him. A double cross was a certainty. Probably at the moment when Juanita was handed back over to them, or right after that, he decided.

There were steps he could take to make that less likely. For one thing, they would put all the treasure back down in the cave and make things look like the place was rigged to blow up, just as Preacher had told the fat man. The possibility of the cave and all the treasure being blown to kingdom come would certainly make the thieves think twice about trying anything.

In the end, though, Chambers and Cobey would feel like they couldn't afford to let Preacher and his companions live. They would have to do *something*. . . .

Preacher reached the top of the canyon and started across the shelf toward the cliff and the cave beneath it. Dog ran ahead of him. Before Preacher got to the cave, though, Dog was back, barking and running in circles like something was wrong. Preacher frowned at the big cur and said, "What the hell is it, Dog?"

With a nudge of his heels, Preacher sent Horse trotting forward at a faster pace. Within a few moments, he came in sight of the area around the cave. He noticed right away that Esteban's horse, and the other two horses, were gone. Alarm bells rang in his brain.

The horses could have pulled loose from where they were tethered and wandered off, although Preacher figured that was unlikely. But he didn't see anybody moving around the site, either. He expected Esteban would have come hurrying out to meet him, to see how the parley with Juanita's kidnappers had gone, and he should have been able to see Father Hortensio and the two Yaquis, as well.

"Esteban!" he shouted as he rode closer. "Padre!"

Where the hell had everybody gone?

That unanswered question made a bizarre thought flash through Preacher's brain. Father Hortensio had talked about the smell of brimstone and how that shaft leading down into the earth was like a portal to Hades itself. Maybe Lucifer and his imps had crawled up out of the hole and dragged Preacher's companions back down to Hell. . . .

He gave a little shake of his head. That was crazy. Preacher had no doubt Hell existed, but you couldn't get there by going down a hole in the Sangre de Cristo Mountains. Something had happened to the others, all right, but it wasn't the hand of Satan that had caused the trouble.

Spotting a limp figure sprawled on the ground near the opening of the shaft, Preacher reined in and flung himself out of the saddle before Horse had completely stopped moving. Preacher ran over to Esteban Alvarez and dropped to a knee beside the young man's motionless body. Esteban lay facedown. His sombrero had fallen off and lay next to him. Preacher saw blood welling from a swollen gash on the back of his head. Somebody had clouted the youngster a good one.

Carefully, Preacher turned Esteban over, wadding up the young man's sombrero and placing it under his injured head to cushion it. Preacher's fingers pressed against Esteban's neck, searching for a pulse. He found one beating strong and fairly regularly. Esteban's eyelids flickered and he stirred slightly as consciousness began to creep back into him.

"Esteban!" Preacher said urgently. "Wake up, hombre, and tell me what happened."

Preacher's gaze darted around the area, searching for any sign of Father Hortensio, Pablo, or Joaquin. The three men were gone, vanished just like the horses. Preacher's eyes narrowed as he noticed that the pile of sacks containing the holy relics from Mission Santo Domingo wasn't there anymore, either. Nor was the chest that had contained gold ingots. The suspicion that began to lurk in his head wasn't a pretty one.

Esteban groaned and opened his eyes. He stared uncomprehendingly up at Preacher. The mountain man leaned over him and said sharply, "Better get your wits back about you, son. We got all kinds o' trouble here."

"P-Preacher?"

"That's right. You remember me, but do you know what happened here whilst I was gone?"

Esteban lifted a hand toward his head, but stopped before he touched it. "Someone . . . hit me."

"I figured as much. Did you see who it was?"

Esteban hesitated. "Not . . . sure. I had been arguing . . . with Father Hortensio . . . when I saw one of the Yaquis . . . step behind me . . . Then . . . I was struck down . . . and I remember nothing more until . . . just now."

"One o' the Yaquis hit you?" That didn't come as a complete surprise to Preacher since he hadn't seen any sign that anyone else had been up here. Still, it was something of a shock, considering what devoted servants the Indians had seemed to be.

But they were actually Father Hortensio's servants, Preacher reminded himself. It was the priest they were devoted to, along with the Church itself.

"I . . . I cannot be sure," Esteban said. "But no one else was around." His voice strengthened a little and sounded certain as he went on. "It must have been Pablo or Joaquin. No one else was here except me and Father Hortensio, and he was in front of me. He motioned to whoever was behind me." Esteban paused and then said grimly, "He gave the order."

Preacher's jaw clenched in anger. "The padre betrayed you."

"*Sí.*" Esteban closed his eyes for a second, then opened them and said, "Though it pains me to admit it, Father Hortensio betrayed me. He told the Yaqui to strike me down."

"Why would he do that? What had the two o' you been arguin' about?"

"The treasure." That answer didn't come as a surprise to Preacher, either. "He said it belonged to the Holy Mother Church, and that he could not allow it to fall into the hands of heathens."

"What about your sister?"

"He said that he was sorry about Juanita, but that the needs of the Church came first." Esteban struggled to a sitting position, clawing at the sleeve of Preacher's buckskin shirt as he did so. Preacher put an arm around his shoulders to help him sit up. "He had one of the Yaquis knock me unconscious so that he could steal the treasure!"

"It sure looks that way," Preacher agreed. His face was set in bleak lines. "The padre wouldn't see it like that, though. To his way o' thinkin', he was savin' the treasure, not stealin' it."

"But how . . ." Esteban looked around wildly. "How did he get away? Where did he go?"

"I ain't sure about that," Preacher admitted, "but he sure as blazes went somewhere. Him and those Yaquis didn't just flap their arms and fly off like big ol' birds."

Esteban clutched at Preacher again. "What about Juanita? How can we trade the treasure for her if Father Hortensio has taken it?" His voice went up in a note of panic.

"Don't start worryin' about that yet," Preacher told him.

"Just lay back and rest for a minute whilst I take a look around."

Esteban didn't want to rest. He wanted to get up and rush around, looking for Father Hortensio and the Yaquis. But Preacher wouldn't let him, and Esteban was still too weak to stand. With a worried sigh, he lay down again.

Preacher stalked over to the spot where the bags of loot and the chest of gold had been left earlier. The rope was missing, too. Preacher stared at the hole for a moment, then grimaced and lowered himself into it, bracing himself against the walls and inching down the shaft as he had climbed up it earlier.

He reached the drop-off and let himself slide, catching the edge with his hands just long enough to break his fall before he let go and dropped the rest of the way to the floor of the cave. He was in darkness; the fire had gone out. But working by feel, he was able to gather up enough unburned brush to start a small fire with his flint and steel.

Looking around by the flickering glow, he saw that the other chests had been emptied of gold ingots as well, just as he expected. They were lying around haphazardly, wherever they had landed when they had been tossed back down the hole. Preacher counted the empty chests. There were eight of them, and he was pretty sure that was how many had been down here to start with. Father Hortensio and the Yaquis had been busy while he was gone. After knocking out Esteban, they had hauled up the rest of the chests, taken out the gold, and thrown the chests back down the hole. Preacher wondered about that for a moment, but then he realized it had been a shrewd move on Father Hortensio's part. Preacher had been forced to spend some time climbing down here, just to make sure the gold was gone. That was time he hadn't been able to use getting on the trail of the priest and the two Indians.

Moving quickly, well aware that minutes were ticking by, Preacher stacked up the looted chests so that he could climb on them and reach up to grasp the edge of the slanting shaft.

With a grunt of effort, he pulled himself into the shaft and started the laborious climb one more time. It would be the last time, because there was no longer any reason for him to come down here. The treasure chamber where Don Francisco Alvarez had cached the loot a century and a half earlier was now empty.

When Preacher reached the top and crawled out of the opening, he found Esteban sitting up again. The young man asked anxiously, "The gold?"

"All gone," Preacher told him bluntly.

Esteban's face fell. "But how?" he wondered. "How could they carry it all away? Where did they go?"

"They had three horses and some rope," Preacher said. "I reckon they tied the bags of relics together and slung them over the backs of the horses. Somehow they rigged some other bags for the gold and tied those to the horses so that they could drag 'em."

"But the weight would be tremendous!"

Preacher nodded. "Yeah, it would, and it would wear out the horses pretty quick, too. But I reckon Father Hortensio figured if he could get away from here, he could stop and let the horses rest as often as he needed to."

"They did not go down the canyon. You would have seen them."

"Yep, and they wouldn't go that way to start with, because Chambers and the others are down at the bottom. They went somewheres else." Preacher got hold of Horse's reins and swung up into the saddle. "I aim to go find out where."

Esteban started to get up. "What can I do to help?"

"Stay here," Preacher said. "You've still got a pistol and a rifle, in case Chambers and his bunch show up. Take cover and try to hold 'em off, and if I hear shootin' I'll light a shuck back here. With any luck, though, I'll find what I'm lookin' for and be back here before they show up to make the trade."

"Ah, Juanita!" Esteban said anxiously. He was muttering to himself in Spanish as Preacher rode off.

Horses didn't leave much sign on this dry, rocky ground, but it didn't take much for a man with eyes as keen as Preacher's. He found tracks that indicated three men on foot and three horses had started off toward the eastern end of the shelf. As he followed the tracks, he saw some scuff marks on the ground that confirmed his earlier guess: The horses were dragging something heavy behind them. Bags full of gold bars, no doubt.

Preacher hadn't been on this part of the shelf. His searching had been concentrated on the other end, and the actual location of the treasure cave was more toward the middle of the flat land that shouldered out from the side of the mountain. So it came as a surprise to him when he found a narrow trail leading off around the mountain. He wasn't *too* surprised, though. He had known that Father Hortensio and the Yaquis were heading *somewhere*, so there had to be another way off this shelf.

The trail was nothing more than a ledge that was just wide enough for a horse to negotiate it. The men had led the horses along it, with a sheer rock wall to their left and a drop of several hundred feet to their right. It must have been a harrowing trip, where one misstep would mean a long plunge to a crashing death. Preacher looked down the cliff, searching for any smashed bodies of man or horse. He didn't see any. Father Hortensio and the two servants had made it without falling at least farther than Preacher could see.

He wheeled Horse around and galloped back to where he had left Esteban. There was no sign of Chambers, Cobey, and the others. Without dismounting, Preacher held out a hand to Esteban and said, "Come on."

"Come on?" the young man repeated as he climbed unsteadily to his feet. "Where? Did you find out what happened to Father Hortensio and the Yaquis?"

"There's another trail over yonder." Preacher inclined his head toward the eastern end of the shelf. "It ain't much of one, but it was enough for them to be able to get out of here. We got to do the same thing."

"But what about Juanita? We . . . we cannot abandon her to being a prisoner of those men." Horror tinged his voice at the very idea.

"We ain't abandonin' her," Preacher said, "but we can't do her any good by stayin' here. There's only one way we can help her, and that's by gettin' that loot back and usin' it to bargain with the bastards who've got her."

"I . . . I suppose you are right, Preacher." Esteban passed a trembling hand over his face. Then he reached up, grasped the mountain man's wrist, and climbed onto Horse's back behind him. "But when they come up here, expecting to make the trade, and find us gone . . . what will they do then?"

"I ain't sure," Preacher said, "but they know the only chance they've got of swappin' for the treasure is to keep Juanita alive and unharmed. You hang onto that hope, Esteban, and I will, too."

They rode away, trailed by Dog, leaving the now-empty cave behind them.

TWENTY-THREE

Juanita saw the man called Cobey stalk toward the wagons. Wick got up from the rock where he had been sitting and greeted his friend by saying, "She's still in there, Cobey. She ain't tried to get away. I watched her real good, just like you told me."

Cobey brushed past the giant with a curt nod and didn't say anything to him. Perhaps stung by being ignored, Wick went on. "I didn't touch her bosoms or loosen them thongs around her wrists or nothin' like that."

Juanita closed her eyes for a second in despair. She had been working at her bonds for the past half hour, trying to loosen them even more, but so far she'd had little success. Now she wouldn't get a chance to continue the effort, because Cobey stopped short and swung around to glare at Wick.

"Damn it, Wick, what'd I tell you—"

Wick looked like he was going to cry. Cobey shook his head and went on. "I don't reckon it matters. We'll be tradin' her for that treasure in a little while, so she won't have time to try to get away. Get her out of the wagon."

"Sure, Cobey," Wick said eagerly, his expression happy again after having been given a job to do by his friend. He came over to the wagon and reached in toward Juanita. Instinctively, she shrank back from his grasping, hamlike hands. "Don't be scared," he told her. "I ain't a-gonna hurt you."

He slipped his hands under her arms and lifted her out of the wagon as if she had been nothing more than a child's doll. She couldn't help but gasp at the enormous power in his grip. As he had promised, though, he was gentle with her and didn't hurt her. He just set her feet on the ground and then let go of her.

Cobey stood in front of her and grinned. "Your brother must think a lot of you, Señorita. He's willin' to trade all that hidden loot for you." He brought his hand up and brushed his rough knuckles against the smooth skin of her cheek. "Too bad we ain't got time to get better acquainted before we make the swap."

Juanita wanted to spit in his leering face, but she suppressed the impulse. She didn't want to anger him or test the limits of his patience. She just wanted to be back with Esteban.

But could these men be trusted? The obvious answer was no. They would try some sort of trick, rather than sticking to whatever agreement they had made. Treachery would be second nature to them. But surely Esteban would realize that.

Even if he didn't, Preacher would. The mountain man would not be fooled, Juanita told herself.

She looked past Cobey as Professor Chambers walked up. Seeing a civilized man like him gave her hope, even though she knew it shouldn't. "Professor," she said, "are you sure you want to do this thing? There is no honor in it."

"No, perhaps not," he agreed. "But only a rich man can afford honor, my dear. Unfortunately, I've never fallen into that category."

Her hopes fell yet again. She couldn't look for any help from Chambers. Indeed, the look in his eyes when he gazed at her was just as lustful as that of any of the other men. Despite his background, he was just as evil as they were.

Cobey gestured curtly toward the mouth of the canyon. "Let's go," he ordered. "Wick, put the girl on my horse."

Again the giant sprang to obey. He lifted Juanita onto the back of one of their mounts, just in front of the saddle. She had to straddle the animal, which meant her dress was pulled up, revealing her boots and the stockings above them. She burned with shame at that indecent display, and her flush deepened as Cobey swung up behind her and slid an arm familiarly around her waist.

The other men mounted up as well, and the entire party started riding up the canyon toward the shelf where the cave was located. The rocking motion of the horse and the pressure of Cobey's arm around her waist meant that Juanita spent most of the time pressed tightly against her captor. "You're a sweet one, you are," he hissed in her ear. "I'll bet you're a real wildcat when it comes to lovin', too."

She ignored him as best she could and distracted herself from the humiliation he was putting her through by thinking about what Preacher might do to him. Preacher would find some way to prevent these men from getting away with their villainy, and then he would dispense frontier justice to them. That justice would be swift and ruthless. At least, Juanita hoped so.

It was late afternoon by the time the riders neared the top of the canyon. Despite the harrowing situation in which she found herself, Juanita was aware that she hadn't eaten since early that morning. Her stomach growled and complained. She ignored that, too.

Cobey called a halt while there was still one more bend between them and the top. "Remember, don't open fire until we've made the swap," he told the others.

Juanita stiffened at those words and tried to turn around to stare at him. He *was* going to betray the agreement, just as she had feared. That meant Esteban, Preacher, and Father Hortensio would be riding into a trap. Perhaps they were close by. She opened her mouth to scream a warning.

Before any sound could come out of her throat, Cobey looped a twisted bandanna around her head from behind. He jerked it tight, so that it closed off her mouth. All she could do was make incoherent noises. He tied the bandanna in a knot at the back of her head.

"Thought you was gettin' away from me, didn't you, gal?" He chuckled. "Well, you ain't. We're gonna have you, and the loot, too. You might as well get used to the idea."

Juanita made strangled noises.

"Don't worry about your brother and Preacher, though," Cobey went on. "They'll both be dead, along with the priest and them Indians of yours."

He was wrong about the Yaquis, of course. They were Father Hortensio's servants, not hers and Esteban's. Not that it mattered now. Pablo and Joaquin would be gunned down just like the others. Killed as Benedicto and Ismael had been. The slaughter would be complete. . . .

Unless Preacher had a few tricks of his own waiting for them. Juanita clung desperately to that hope.

Cobey nudged his horse ahead again, around the bend and up the last slope to the shelf. The others followed. They emerged from the canyon onto the shelf. Cobey reined in as Professor Chambers rode up beside him.

"Where are they?" the professor asked worriedly. "Weren't they supposed to meet us here?"

"I thought so," Cobey said. He looked around at the other men. "Arnie, didn't you say they'd be waitin' for us?"

The fat man edged his mount up on Cobey's other side. "That's what I thought we'd agreed to," he said. "Maybe Preacher took it different. Maybe they're waitin' for us over by that cave."

"And maybe they've set a damned trap for us!" Cobey snapped. "Spread out! Keep your eyes open!"

He rode forward slowly as the other men dispersed. All of them had guns drawn now, Juanita saw, except for Cobey. He held the reins in one hand and still had the other arm around her, holding her tightly. She was a human shield, she realized. Anyone taking a shot at Cobey would stand a greater likelihood of hitting her. Esteban and Preacher would not take that chance.

Even Professor Chambers had a pistol in his hand. The intent, avaricious expression on his lean face made him resemble a hawk searching for prey. Juanita asked herself how she could have ever considered him a civilized man. He was a brigand, just like the others.

They came in sight of the cave entrance, and Juanita stiffened as she realized that all the horses were gone. So were the five men who should have been there. Everyone was gone.

Cobey had seen the same thing. "Damn it," he grated. "Where'd they go?" Lifting his voice, he called to the others, "Watch out for an ambush!"

No shots shattered the late afternoon stillness, however. Gradually, the men all converged on the cave. "Take a look around!" Cobey snapped at them.

A few minutes later, Arnie reported, "There's nobody here, Cobey. They've lit a shuck."

"I can see that, damn it! What about the treasure?"

Arnie turned to one of the other men and said, "Get a rope and shinny down into that hole. See if they put it back down there before they left."

"Why me?" the man protested.

"Because you're the skinniest of us, Bert," Arnie said. "Now get movin'."

Grumbling, the man took a rope from his saddle and tied it to his horse. One of the other men fashioned a makeshift torch and lit it, then handed it to Bert as he got ready to lower himself into the shaft. Carefully, holding the rope in one hand and the torch in the other, he backed into the hole and let himself down.

"Weren't the bags with the old relics in 'em already up here when we snatched you?" Cobey asked Juanita.

She pointed with her bound hands, seeing no point in lying right now. "They were right there, along with one chest full of gold ingots."

"Well, what happened to all that loot?"

She shook her head. "I have no idea."

A few moments later, Bert called from down in the cave, his voice echoing hollowly up the shaft. "The chests are down here, but they're all empty! And there ain't no relics, neither!"

"It was all a lie," Cobey snarled. "They didn't rig the damn cave to blow up! They just loaded the loot and took off with it."

Juanita shook her head, unable to believe that Esteban would do such a thing. He would never abandon her like that, leaving her in the clutches of these cutthroats. . . .

"Looks like that brother o' yours is more attached to the treasure than he is to you, Señorita," Cobey said.

"No. No, it cannot be."

"What are we going to do now?" Professor Chambers asked.

"I don't know, but I ain't givin' up," Cobey said. "They didn't come down the canyon with that loot, so they must've gone somewheres else." His voice grew fierce with anger and frustration as he ordered, "Find 'em! Find out how they got outta here! I'm gonna have that treasure, by God!" He paused and then added, "And I'll have that bastard Preacher's head to go with it, too!"

TWENTY-FOUR

Preacher led the way along the ledge, with Horse right behind him. Esteban came next, followed by Dog. Preacher figured that if any pursuit started closing in on them, Dog would let him know.

Esteban was still a little unsteady on his feet, so he held onto Horse's tail. Horse didn't like it, but Preacher patted him on the shoulder and spoke to him in soothing tones until the big stallion accepted the indignity. The little party of two men and two animals made its way along the ledge at as fast a pace as Preacher dared to set.

Heights didn't bother him much, but just to make sure he didn't get dizzy, he kept his eyes on the trail in front of him or the wall of stone to his left, and advised Esteban to do the same thing. "I've seen fellas practically jump off the side of a mountain 'cause they got to lookin' down too much. All that empty space does somethin' to a man's brain."

"Don't worry," Esteban assured him. "I am not looking anywhere except at the tail end of this horse of yours."

Preacher chuckled. "Let's just hope you ain't followin' *two* horses' asses."

After a few minutes, Esteban asked, "What do you think is happening to Juanita?"

"I imagine she's scared, but I don't reckon she's been hurt. Like I said, those sons o' bitches stand a lot better chance of gettin' that loot if she stays unharmed."

"You would truly give the treasure to them in order to save her life?"

Preacher didn't hesitate before answering, "Sure I would. I'd hate like the devil to just turn that much loot over to them, but to save Juanita's life I'd do it. I don't reckon it'll ever come down to that, though."

Esteban sounded alarmed as he said, "You do not think we will recover the treasure from Father Hortensio?"

"Oh, we'll get it back, all right," Preacher said confidently. "But no matter what Cobey and Chambers say, they ain't gonna abide by any deal they make. They'll try their damnedest to kill us, even if we swap the loot for Juanita."

"Then why would we even try?"

"Because we don't have any other choice. We got to make them think we're playin' along with 'em, and to do that we got to have the treasure. Then, when they try to betray us, we'll turn the tables on them some way."

Esteban shook his head. "It all sounds hopeless to me."

"As long as we're drawin' breath, we got reason to hope," Preacher told him. "I've gotten out of plenty of worse scrapes than this."

"I pray you are right, Preacher. And I pray for Juanita's safety."

"That's a good idea. You keep it up, and I'll say a prayer myself."

The ledge curved on around the mountain. Shadows began to gather. Preacher felt like they had been following the narrow trail for hours, but he knew that was because his nerves were drawn taut. It really hadn't been that long. He began to wonder, though, what they would do if darkness caught them up here in this precarious position.

A short time later, the ledge began to slope downward. That was what Preacher had been hoping for. The ledge had to provide a way down off the mountain, otherwise it wouldn't have done Father Hortensio and the Yaquis any good to take it. But how had they known the ledge was truly an escape route? It could have just as easily petered out and left the fugitives stranded on the side of the mountain.

It had been a matter of blind faith, Preacher realized. Father Hortensio had trusted in the Lord to get them out of here.

The ledge curved sharply to the left, around a blind corner. Preacher stepped around it and then came to an abrupt halt. He couldn't go any farther. The way was blocked by a wall of rock.

"Damn it!" The sight of the unexpected obstacle jarred the curse out of him.

"What is it?" Esteban asked anxiously. "Why have we stopped?"

"Because we can't go any farther," Preacher explained. "There's been a rock slide. The ledge is covered up."

"No! We must get through! Juanita's life could depend on it."

That was true enough, but it didn't change things. Preacher studied the rocks that blocked the trail, then turned his head to look up at the cliff where a whole section had broken off and slid down here. The scars left behind by the rock slide looked very recent.

"The padre did this," he said. "That's the only explanation, because they came this way and we sure ain't run across 'em. They got past this spot with the horses and the treasure, and then the padre started a slide somehow and blocked the trail."

"How could he do that?"

"Sometimes all it takes is pullin' one piece of rock loose. That unsettles everything enough for more to come down. Maybe he used the rope and threw a loop over some outcroppin', then hitched it to one o' the horses and yanked it outta place. That might have been enough."

"But what do we do now?" Esteban asked. "We cannot go back."

"No, that'd be a big chore, all right. There ain't room for Horse to turn around, so he'd have to back all the way, and I don't reckon he'd take kindly to that." Preacher rubbed his bearded jaw and frowned in thought. "I reckon the only thing we can do is clear away the rocks so we can keep on goin'. And that's gonna be a job, too."

"I will slip past the horse and help you."

"Not just yet," Preacher said. "Stay where you are for now. You may have to come up and spell me later on, but we'll wait and see about that."

He hung his hat on the saddle and went to work, picking up the smaller rocks and tossing them over the edge. Some of the chunks of stone were too big for him to lift, but if he cleared away most of the smaller ones he thought he could roll the larger ones off the ledge.

It was hard work, but Preacher's corded muscles were accustomed to such labor. The air was cool at this altitude, too, which helped. Once the sun set, it would be downright cold, but Preacher didn't plan on stopping for long enough to let the chill stiffen up his muscles.

He lifted and shoved and rolled and threw, and slowly the barrier of stone began to diminish. The sun went down and the sky turned from blue to purple to black, with the stars winking into life one by one overhead. Preacher continued working as the moon rose and cast a pale silvery glow over the rugged landscape. He wedged his way behind one of the larger boulders and got his hands and feet on it, bracing his back against the cliff as he pushed. The boulder rocked a little, and Preacher pushed harder. It began to move even more, and then gravity and the boulder's own weight took over. It toppled over the edge, leaving Preacher sprawled dangerously close to the brink. He crabbed backward as a booming crash came floating up from far below. The boulder had landed.

"A couple more o' those out of the way, and I think we'll be able to pick our way past," Preacher said.

"Yes, but this delay has given Father Hortensio enough time to get far ahead of us," Esteban said. "I fear we may never catch him."

Preacher snorted. "You're givin' up too easy, amigo. One thing I've learned out here on the frontier is that if a fella keeps on goin' after what he wants, he finally gets it more often than not. You just got to be stubborn as a mule, and don't never give up."

"All right, Preacher. Perhaps you should have been a real preacher, since you are eloquent in your own rough way."

"Thanks . . . I think," Preacher said with a chuckle. "I'll leave it to other folks to spread the Gospel, though. They're better at it than I am." He pushed himself to his feet, this brief breather over. "Right now I got to get back to work on these rocks."

Cobey stalked back and forth, waiting for his men to come back and report whatever their search of the area had turned up. Chambers sat under a tree watching him, and not far away, Juanita sat on a log with Wick perched beside her. The giant was still charged with keeping an eye on the prisoner, as Cobey had ordered.

After a while, Wick spoke up tentatively when Cobey's pacing brought him close to the log. "Cobey, you reckon it'd be all right to take this gag off the lady now?"

Cobey stopped and glared at him. "What?"

"I said, you reckon we could take this gag off—"

Cobey gestured curtly and said, "Yeah, sure. Those bastards have already flown the coop with the treasure. She can yell her head off and it won't hurt anything now."

"Thanks, Cobey." Wick turned to Juanita and began fumbling with the knotted bandanna at the back of her head.

"Oh!" she said in relief as the bandanna came loose, allowing her to close her mouth and easing the ache in her jaws.

"I'm sorry, ma'am," Wick said. "I know that must've hurt."

Juanita worked her jaws from side to side. She couldn't even speak for a moment. When she could, she said, "Thank you, Wick."

He blushed and looked down at the ground. "Why, you're sure welcome."

Cobey ignored them and said, "Damn it, the boys oughtta be back by now."

A few minutes later, in fact, the searchers did return, led by Arnie Ross. The fat man swung down from his saddle and said, "Well, we found out where they went." He jerked a thumb toward the eastern end of the shelf. "There's another trail over yonder that leads off around the mountain. Just a little ledge, really, about wide enough for a horse to walk on."

"How do you know they went that way?" Cobey demanded.

Arnie shrugged. "Found a few tracks. And where else could they have gone? We've covered the whole shelf. There ain't no other way down, at least that a horse could take, except the canyon. And we know they didn't leave that way. Since they ain't here anymore . . ."

"Yeah, yeah, I guess you're right," Cobey muttered. He took off his hat and ran his fingers through his tangled hair. "Lemme do some figurin'."

Arnie went on. "The trail's got to go somewhere. I think we ought to send a couple o' men along it to see where it comes out. The rest can go back down the canyon to the wagons. Once we know where that ledge leads, we can pick up the trail, and one of the fellas can come back to get the rest of the bunch. It may take some time, but we'll track 'em down one way or the other."

"Damn right we will," Cobey said. "Are you volunteerin' to follow the ledge?"

Arnie shrugged again. "I reckon I can. Ain't that fond o' heights, but they don't bother me that awful much."

"Take Worthy with you."

Arnie nodded. "All right. Come on, George."

The two men rode off. That left Cobey, Chambers, Wick, Bert McDermott, and Chuck Stilson, along with Juanita, to return down the canyon to the wagons. Cobey got them moving quickly, since it was already late enough in the day so that it would be dark by the time they returned to the valley of the Purgatoire River.

Once again, Juanita was set on the back of Cobey's horse, and he climbed on behind her. This time, when he put his arm around her, he pressed it up against the undersides of her breasts. "Looks like we're gonna have plenty of time to get to know each other, Señorita, thanks to your brother desertin' you like this."

Juanita sat stiffly in silence and stared straight ahead, ignoring Cobey's touch and his leering comment. She was thinking about Esteban, and she was filled with fear for him. She knew that he would not have abandoned her to her captivity by choice. Something had happened to him. It must have. She hoped that his disappearance meant that he was still alive. If he were dead, his body surely would have been left behind when the others departed on the narrow ledge. But was he a prisoner, too? Who could have captured him? Were there hostile Indians in this region? Preacher had not seemed worried about such a threat.

Of course, it might take a lot to worry a man like Preacher.

The questions kept Juanita's mind occupied so that she was able to ignore the vile things Cobey whispered in her ear as they rode down the canyon. She knew that before she escaped from this man—as she was sure she would do eventually—her honor might be forever compromised. Time would tell. If this ordeal left her indelibly stained, she would enter a convent when she returned to Mexico City. She had already given much thought to spending the rest of her life inside the walls of a nunnery. Right now that prospect seemed almost appealing.

Darkness settled down as the group of riders followed the twists and turns of the canyon. At one point, Cobey reined in sharply as the sound of a distant crash came to them. "What was that?" Chambers asked.

"Sounded like a big rock fallin'," Cobey replied. "Hope it didn't fall on Arnie and George."

They pushed on, and a short time later they neared the bottom of the canyon. The moon was up now, flooding the valley with pale illumination. Between that lunar glow and the light from the stars, it was almost as bright as day.

Plenty bright enough, in fact, for them to see that the wagons were gone.

TWENTY-FIVE

It took Preacher another half hour to clear away enough of the rock slide so that he and Esteban, along with Horse and Dog, could pick their way along the ledge past the obstruction. It was tricky working the big stallion along an even narrower path than the ledge had provided so far, but Horse was almost as sure-footed as a mountain goat and made it just fine.

Other than a lingering headache, Esteban claimed to feel much better now, too. Once they were past the rock slide, he moved along the ledge easily, keeping one hand against the cliff to the left.

The trail dropped at an even steeper angle now. Preacher checked the stars now and then and could estimate the time fairly closely by their position as they wheeled through the sky. He figured it was close to midnight when he and Esteban reached the bottom of the ledge and found themselves in some knobby foothills.

Preacher pointed and said, "I don't reckon the river is more than half a mile over yonderways. That's probably the way Father Hortensio and them Yaquis went, but it'll be hard to know for sure until mornin', when we can see better."

"We are not going to try to keep on following them tonight?" Esteban asked, sounding surprised.

"There are some situations where you can track somebody at night, especially if there's plenty o' moonlight, like tonight," Preacher explained. "But that don't hold true where there are so many stretches o' rocky ground, like there are in these parts. Unless we want to risk losin' the trail completely, we got to wait for the sun to come up."

Esteban heaved a sigh. "I suppose if we must . . . but it is hard to wait, knowing that Juanita is still in the hands of those . . . those . . ."

"Yeah, I can't hardly think of a name bad enough for 'em, neither," Preacher said. "Why don't you hunt you a soft place to lay down under them trees, and you can get some sleep. I'll stand watch."

"I should take a turn, too," Esteban protested. "You must be exhausted after all the work you did moving those rocks."

"I'll be a mite sore in the mornin', I reckon, but you're the one who got walloped in the head. You prob'ly need the rest more'n I do."

"We will trade," Esteban said stubbornly. "Wake me in a few hours."

"We'll see."

Esteban stretched out on a patch of grass. Horse grazed a little on the same grass, and Dog lay down there, too. Taking his rifle from its sling attached to the saddle, Preacher walked over to a rock that was in a dense shadow cast by a tree and sat down. He wouldn't be very noticeable here if anybody tried to slip up on them. Resting the rifle across his legs, he drew several deep breaths and willed his muscles to relax. His brain stayed keenly alert, though, and his eyes never stopped moving as his gaze roved over the surrounding countryside.

He thought about Juanita Alvarez and hoped that things weren't going too rough for her. Earlier, he had been fairly confident that her kidnappers wouldn't molest her while they were still planning to swap her for the treasure. Now, with all that loot maybe gone for good, they might decide they didn't have to treat her so gently. She could be in for a hard time of it at their hands. Preacher wasn't sure how well she would be able to cope with something like that. Frontier women had always known there was a real danger of such things happening to them if they were captured by Indians. Juanita hadn't been raised on the frontier, though. She had lived, for the most part, a pampered and sheltered life in Mexico City.

But while he had been around her, Preacher had sensed that she had a core of strength in her, the same sort of inner steel that was present in women who had spent their lives in much harsher surroundings. He hoped for Juanita's sake that she really did possess such strength.

Because before all this was over, she was liable to need it.

Cobey was livid. He leaped down from his horse and ran back and forth. "We left them wagons right here, damn it!" he shouted. "I know we did!"

Chambers looked around and said, "I believe you're right." He pointed. "That clump of brush right over there is where we hid when we ambushed those first two Indians. And I remember those trees as well, not to mention the fact that the mouth of the canyon is right over there. This is the place, certainly."

Cobey stared up at him. "Then where are the damn wagons?"

Chambers could only shake his head and say, "I don't know."

Bert spoke up. "What about that other Yaqui? If the one lived who jumped you later on, Cobey, and ruined ever'thing, maybe the other'un did, too. He could've run off with the wagons."

"Only if he sewed up his own throat where Arnie cut it!" Cobey shook his head in disgust. "No, that Injun's dead, no two ways about it. Poke around over there in the brush where we slung the body and you'll probably find it. Somebody else had to come along and steal the wagons."

On the back of Cobey's horse, Juanita sat, still silent, and thought that from the way he was carrying on, anyone would have thought that the wagons belonged to *him*. In truth, of course, Cobey had stolen them from Juanita and her brother.

She was puzzled by what had happened to the vehicles and their teams, too. All sorts of odd things were happening here in these mountains named after the Blood of Christ. Father Hortensio had talked about how the cave where the treasure was hidden smelled like brimstone. Perhaps the area was cursed. Perhaps the treasure itself now had a curse on it. Juanita didn't know. All she could be certain of was that she was cold and frightened and so very, very tired. Even though she couldn't forget that she was a prisoner, all she wanted to do right now was lie down and rest.

She turned to the giant and asked quietly, "Wick, would you help me down?"

"Just a minute," he rumbled. "Cobey, is it all right if I take the señorita off your horse?"

Cobey flapped a hand dismissively. "I don't care what you do with her. Just don't let her run off."

"She won't. I promise." Wick dismounted and stepped over to Cobey's horse. He reached up and scooped Juanita into his arms. He carried her like she was a baby, limping a little on his still-healing leg as he walked over and sat her down on a large, flat rock. It still held a little of the heat it had absorbed from the sun during the day.

"You sit right there," he told her.

"I will," she promised.

"You want a drink?"

Juanita nodded. "That would be very nice. I'm thirsty."

Wick stepped over to his horse and got a canteen from the saddle. He uncorked it and handed it to Juanita, who had to take it in both of her hands because her wrists were still tied together.

She lifted the canteen to her mouth and took a long drink. When she lowered it, she said, "Thank you. I'm hungry, too."

He dug a strip of jerky out of his pocket and handed that to her, taking back the canteen. "There you go. Are your teeth good enough to gnaw on jerky?"

"Of course." She smiled up at him, and as usual, almost immediately he became too embarrassed to look at her.

Meanwhile, Cobey had resumed pacing around in anger. Chambers watched him for a few minutes and then asked, "What are we going to do now?"

Cobey paused. "This don't change anything. We're still goin' after that treasure, as soon as Arnie or George get back and tell us which way those bastards went."

"Has it occurred to you that it may well have been our quarry who took the wagons?"

Cobey turned sharply toward the professor. "You mean Preacher and his bunch?"

"They had to transport that treasure out of there in some way," Chambers pointed out. "Once they escaped, however, it would be much easier to carry the relics and the gold, especially the gold, in wagons. Perhaps some of them circled back here, took the wagons, and then rejoined the others."

Cobey balled his right hand into a fist and smacked it into his left palm with a sound like a gunshot. "By God, you're right! That's the only explanation that makes sense. It's all Preacher's doin'!"

Chambers just smiled.

Cobey resumed his stalking back and forth. "That's just one more reason to want the son of a bitch dead! He's got to learn to stop messin' with me, and the best way to teach him is to kill him!"

Juanita shuddered a little as she listened to Cobey ranting. She knew that Preacher could take care of himself, but Cobey's hatred was so strong, so fierce, that it was almost like a thing alive, a powerful force that would not be denied.

Beside her, Wick said quietly, "You know, I done heard

some o' them things Cobey said to you whilst we was ridin' back down here. I didn't like 'em."

"Neither did I," she told him gravely.

"Cobey's my friend, but he shouldn't talk that way to a lady. Especially not a pretty lady like you, Miss Juanita."

"Thank you, Wick." She smiled at him again, and this time he didn't look away.

"It sorta hurts my head, but I reckon I'm gonna have to do some thinkin'," he mused. "This whole thing, it's startin' to seem more and more like it ain't right."

For the first time in a while, Juanita began to feel hope growing inside her again. She still believed that Preacher and Esteban would come for her, but if she could work Wick around to being on her side, as well . . .

There was a chance she might come out of this alive after all, she told herself. But in the end, her fate might depend on a giant of a man with the mind of a child.

Dog had settled down on the ground beside the rock where Preacher sat. It was still a good while before dawn when the big cur suddenly lifted his head and growled low in his throat. Preacher reached down and rested a hand on the ruff of fur around Dog's neck, silencing the angry rumble from the dog. He felt the tension in Dog's muscles.

Preacher was a mite tense himself. Dog could have smelled some animal close by, but it was doubtful the scent of a varmint would have caused him to react like that. It was much more likely Dog had smelled a human.

And the chances of anybody wandering around out here who wasn't an enemy were pretty darned small.

Preacher listened intently, and a moment later he heard the sound of hoofbeats. Two riders, he thought. They were coming from the direction of the ledge.

Two of Cobey's men, or maybe the boss hard case himself. Nobody else would be on that ledge. Preacher came to his

feet and cat-footed through the darkness to Esteban's side
He went to a knee next to the young man and reached out to
clap a hand over Esteban's mouth. Esteban woke up, startled
by the unexpected touch, and began to thrash around. Preacher
stilled him by leaning over and hissing in his ear, "Shhh! It's
just me. We got company."

After a moment, when he was sure Esteban wouldn't yell
out, Preacher took his hand away. Esteban whispered, "Who
is it?"

"Don't know. Couple of riders. Bound to be some o'
Cobey's men. They followed us along the ledge."

"What are we going to do?"

"Just sit still and be quiet," Preacher told him. "We'll see
what they do and where they go."

He stood up and motioned for Dog to follow him as he
slipped deeper into the darkness under the trees. The sound
of hoofbeats came closer.

Preacher debated whether to jump the two men or let them
go and hope that they didn't discover him and Esteban. It was
always tempting to cut down the odds by disposing of a couple
of enemies. But that might involve shooting, and the sound of
gunfire could travel a long way. That might just announce
to the others where Preacher and Esteban were and pull more
trouble down on them before they had a chance to catch up to
Father Hortensio and recover the treasure.

It was likely that the two men would rejoin the rest of their
bunch sooner or later. Preacher considered letting them go,
following them, and trying to get Juanita away from her
captors. More than once in the past, he had stolen into an
Indian camp and rescued prisoners. This situation was much
the same, except Cobey's bunch was smaller and likely not
as alert as a war party.

If he attempted that, however, Father Hortensio was going
to have more time to get away with the treasure. But which
was more important, the treasure or Juanita's life? Preacher
didn't even have to think about the answer to that question.

Juanita was more important, of course—except to a fanatic like Father Hortensio.

The two men on horseback were close now. Preacher heard them talking. One of them said, "How we gonna tell where they went while it's dark, Arnie?"

"We'll have to wait for sunup," the other man replied. Preacher recognized his voice. It belonged to the fat man with whom he had parleyed in the canyon. "We might as well get down and rest the horses for a spell." Both men reined in and dismounted.

Preacher stood tensely in the darkness, no more than twenty feet from them. So the two thieves were going to wait for dawn, too, and they were going to do it in the same spot as Preacher and Esteban.

That was a mighty interesting development.

TWENTY-SIX

Juanita lay down on the big rock, curling on her side and pillowing her head on her arms as best she could. Her ankles were tied now, too, so that she couldn't run away. She was exhausted, but the uncomfortable position and the fright she felt made it almost impossible to sleep. Every sound in the night made her jump and catch her breath, fearful that something was about to happen.

Wick sat nearby with his back against a tree, but he had not had any trouble dozing off and now was sound asleep, with loud snores emanating from him. Juanita didn't know what it would take to wake him up. Nor did she know how he would react if one of the other men tried to bother her.

A footstep somewhere close by made her sit up sharply. She gasped and looked around wildly.

"Easy, Señorita," Professor Chambers said quietly. "I mean you no harm. I just thought perhaps we could talk for a moment."

"Professor. You frightened me."

"My apologies. I wish there was some way this entire situation could be made better for you, Señorita."

Juanita glanced toward the sleeping Wick. Quietly, she said

to Chambers, "You could untie me. I would be very grateful."

Chambers laughed softly. "I'm afraid that's not possible. You'd try to escape, and then Larson would kill me for allowing that to happen. He already plans to get rid of me."

She frowned at him in the darkness and said, "You know this, and yet you still aid him?"

"Of course. I'm not a fool. The man despises me, simply because I'm not an unlettered lout like he is. He has no intention of sharing the treasure with me, even though without me he would have no idea of its existence."

"What are you going to do?"

"Wait for the proper time, and then show Mr. Larson that he isn't the only one who can double-cross his allies." Chambers leaned closer to her. "I'm telling you this for only one reason, Señorita. I want your help."

"Why would I help you? You hold me prisoner as surely as the others do."

"I can protect you," he said. "The fact that Cobey wants to trade you for the treasure is the only reason you're still unharmed. Join forces with me and I'll do my best to see that you stay that way."

Juanita didn't believe him. She had seen the way he looked at her. He wanted her just as much as the others did. But if she played along with him, that might increase her chances of coming out of this alive.

"What would I need to do?" she asked.

Chambers's voice was barely a whisper now. "When the time comes, I'll slip you a weapon and cut you loose. Help me kill the others, and I'll let you go."

"How can we do that? There are too many of them! A woman and . . . a civilized man such as yourself . . . against half-a-dozen barbarians . . ."

"Who won't be expecting anything," Chambers said. "The element of surprise will be entirely on our side. Besides, we should have one other ally."

"Who?"

Chambers inclined his head toward the sleeping giant. "Wick. Everyone can see that he follows you around like a puppy, and he adores you like a puppy adores its mistress, too."

"He follows me because the one called Cobey has ordered him to guard me. Wick would never turn against him."

"I think you're wrong. In fact, you could say that I'm gambling my life on it."

Perhaps he was right. Juanita had to admit that having Wick on their side would go a long way toward evening up the odds. He could probably knock at least two men out of a fight before they knew what was going on.

"There's something else to consider, too," Chambers went on. "By the time we're ready to make our move, the odds against us may not be so high. I'm sure we can handle Preacher when we recover the treasure, but some of Cobey's men may be killed or hurt in the process." He shrugged. "What it comes down to, Señorita, is that the only chance either one of us really has is to work together. Can you deny that?"

Juanita hesitated before answering, but finally, she had to whisper, "No. I cannot deny it."

"You'll see," Chambers said. "Everything will be—"

"Who's that?" Cobey Larson's harsh voice came from somewhere nearby. Wick snorted and snuffled as he woke up. Cobey stalked out of the darkness before Professor Chambers could slip away and demanded, "What the hell are you doin' here?"

"Just checking on the prisoner," Chambers said easily. "Your so-called guard was sound asleep. The señorita might have gotten away if not for me."

Cobey grabbed Juanita's wrists and shook them, then did the same with her ankles. "She's still tied up good. She ain't goin' anywhere, not unless she wants to crawl on her belly. And I don't reckon she'd get very far that way." He chuckled. "But I got to admit, the idea of a high-toned señorita like her crawlin' on her belly is a mite appealin'."

Juanita shuddered at the man's coarseness.

"Better move on, Professor," Cobey went on. "You ain't needed here."

"What do you intend to do?" Chambers asked.

"None o' your damn business." Cobey cupped Juanita's chin. "Whatever happens, it's just between me an' the pretty little señorita."

She wanted to jerk her head away from his touch, but she forced herself to remain still as she said, "Señor, I ask of you . . . do not dishonor me."

"It's a little late for you to be worryin' about honor, ain't it? Your brother ran off and left you with us. He don't give a damn what happens to you, so why should I?"

"Please . . ."

Cobey's hand closed roughly on one of her breasts. "Beg some more," he hissed between clenched teeth. "I like it."

"Larson—" the professor began.

Cobey turned on him, letting go of Juanita and moving his hand to the butt of the pistol stuck behind his belt. "Are you still here, damn it?"

Juanita waited tensely to see if Chambers would defend her. She wasn't surprised when he said, "All right, Cobey. I'm leaving."

"Damn right you are."

Chambers shuffled off into the darkness. Cobey turned back to Juanita and reached for her again. "You and me gonna have some fun, Señorita," he said.

"Cobey."

The voice came from behind him. When he glanced over his shoulder, he saw Wick rising from the ground like a mountain in miniature erupting from the earth.

"Go back to sleep, Wick," Cobey ordered. "This don't concern you."

"I don't think you should be botherin' the señorita, Cobey," Wick said stubbornly.

With a savage snarl, Cobey said, "I told you, this don't concern you."

"Yeah, but it does. You said for me to keep Miss Juanita safe."

"I told you not to let her run off."

"You said to keep her safe," Wick insisted. "That's what I figure on doin'."

Impatient and frustrated, Cobey stepped over to confront Wick. "Well, now I'm tellin' you to leave me the hell alone! Can you understand that, or are you too damn dumb?"

Wick drew back as if Cobey had slapped him. "You never called me dumb before," he said. "Ever'body else did, but you never did, Cobey."

"Then stop actin' dumb. What I'm gonna do to the gal ain't gonna hurt her—"

"It will, Wick," Juanita cut in. "It will hurt me very badly."

Cobey twisted toward her. His hand flashed up and cracked across her face, knocking her sprawling back on the rock. "Shut up, you greaser bitch!" he roared. Juanita whimpered in pain and shock.

And then, as Cobey swung back around toward Wick, the giant rumbled in rage and fell on him like the mountain he so resembled.

Preacher glided noiselessly through the shadows and knelt beside Esteban again. "It's two o' Cobey's men, like I thought," he whispered to the young man. "And they're gonna camp here until sunup, so they can see which way the padre went."

"They're staying *here*?" Esteban whispered back.

Preacher grimaced in the darkness. "Yep. They're about twenty yards over yonder."

"But will they not discover us?"

"Maybe, maybe not. It all depends—"

That was when one of the men's mounts must have caught Horse's scent, because a shrill whinny ripped through the night. Preacher came up from his crouch and clapped a hand over Horse's nose to prevent the stallion from answering.

Even without that, though, Arnie and the other hard case realized something was wrong. Preacher heard Arnie's exclamation. "Must be somebody else around here, George! Come on! Hit 'em hard!"

The two men flung themselves back on their horses and charged toward Preacher and Esteban. "Split up!" Preacher snapped at Esteban as he darted to the right. Esteban rolled over, came to his feet, and went to the left.

The two hard cases on horseback charged between them. Preacher saw a stray beam of moonlight reflect off a gun barrel.

"Dog!" he said.

With a growl, the big cur launched himself off the ground and grabbed one of the riders by the arm. The man screamed as Dog's teeth tore into his flesh. The impact of the heavy beast knocked him out of the saddle. He fell to the ground with a heavy thud. Dog landed on top of him and continued savaging his arm, snarling and snapping. The man screamed and tried to scuttle away.

At the same time, Preacher leaped toward the second man, who was trying to wheel his horse around. Reversing his rifle, Preacher drove the weapon's butt into the man's stomach. The man slewed sideways but managed to remain mounted. Preacher had to jump out of the way to avoid being trampled by the man's horse. He saw the pistol swinging toward him and rolled to the side as the gun roared. The heavy lead ball smacked into the ground where Preacher had been an instant earlier.

Preacher yanked one of his pistols from behind his belt and cocked it as he raised it. Aiming in bad light like this was always a chancy proposition, but he tried for the man's shoulder. He didn't want to kill the hard case, but wanted to wound him instead, taking him alive so that he could be questioned.

Unfortunately, just as Preacher pulled the trigger, the man's horse, spooked by the previous shot, danced skittishly to the side. Preacher saw the man's hat leap into the air as the shot caught him squarely in the face and blew off a large chunk of his head.

"Damn it!" Preacher growled as the man's limp body hit the ground like a sack of potatoes. Preacher stood up and turned toward Dog and the other man.

Only they weren't there anymore. The big cur's snarling had stopped, and Preacher didn't see any sign of him or the man he had gone after.

"Dog!"

There was no response.

"Esteban! You here?"

Nothing. The night was quiet except for a few faintly fading echoes of the two shots.

Preacher hurried toward the spot where he had last seen Dog. His foot hit something soft and yielding in the darkness, and he almost fell. Catching his balance, he lowered himself to a knee and reached out. His hand touched thick fur. With worry stretching his nerves taut, Preacher explored along the bundle of fur and muscles until he came to Dog's head. His fingers encountered a sticky, swollen lump. A moment later he found a strong pulse beating in the animal's neck. Dog was all right, just knocked out. The man he had been fighting with must have clouted him with a gun barrel. Even as Preacher prodded around on him, searching for other, more serious wounds, Dog began to stir. He whimpered, lifted his head, and moved his legs. Preacher helped him roll onto his belly.

"You all right, Dog?" he asked.

Dog raised his head even more and licked Preacher in the face. Relief flooded through the mountain man. Dog had been his friend as long as any human had been, and a better friend than most, at that.

But there was still the question of Esteban's disappearance. Preacher told Dog to stay where he was and stood up. Calling Esteban's name a couple of times still produced no results. He looked around. The moon was lower in the sky by now, with the approach of dawn, but there was still enough light for Preacher to see. He quickly came to the conclusion that Esteban was gone.

And that led to another conclusion that was pretty troublesome. Preacher checked the body of the man he had killed. He thought maybe it had belonged to one of the men who had been with Professor Chambers at the old mission, the two so-called guides. It was hard to be sure because of the damage the pistol ball had done to his face. But he wasn't fat, which meant that it was Arnie who had gotten away.

Preacher recalled how deceptively dangerous Arnie was in a fight. The fat man must have stumbled into Esteban in the darkness after knocking Dog out, and even injured, he had been able to take the young man with him as he fled, either knocking Esteban unconscious, too, or simply forcing him to go along at gunpoint. The dead man's horse was still here, but Arnie's mount wasn't. Chances were, the fat man was on his way back to join Cobey and the others right now.

Only he wasn't alone. Preacher's enemies now had two hostages instead of one, as both of the Alvarez siblings were now their prisoners.

TWENTY-SEVEN

Juanita cried out again as Wick's rush knocked Cobey back onto the rock against her. "I said leave her alone!" Wick roared, sounding like a grizzly bear. He looked sort of like a grizzly bear, too, as he loomed over Cobey for a second and then lunged down on him, wrapping his big hands around Cobey's throat.

Cobey fought back desperately, bringing a knee up into Wick's groin and hammering punches to his head. Wick didn't seem to feel the punches, but the knee made him grunt in pain and relax his grip on Cobey's throat. Though Cobey was considerably smaller than the giant, he was still a big, powerful man, and when he clubbed his hands together and drove them hard against Wick's jaw, he was able to knock the larger man to the side.

Wick shook off that blow in a hurry, though, and a back-handed cuff to Cobey's head packed enough of an impact to knock Cobey into Juanita again. Both of them slid off the rock and fell to the ground beside it. Cobey landed on top of Juanita. His weight knocked the breath out of her and made it difficult for her to drag more air into her lungs. Panic went through her at the thought that she might suffocate underneath him.

He wasn't there long enough for that, however. Still yelling incoherently, Wick reached down, grabbed the front of Cobey's buckskin shirt, and jerked him upright again. Gratefully, Juanita gasped for breath. Several smaller rocks dug painfully into her body where she had fallen on them, but she ignored that.

Wick shook Cobey like a terrier shaking a rat. "You shouldn't'a hit her!" he bellowed. "You shouldn't'a done it!"

"H-help!" Cobey shouted. "He's g-gone crazy!"

Juanita rolled over and became aware that Bert McDermott and Chuck Stilson had rushed up, drawn by Wick's yelling and the sounds of the fight. Professor Chambers was there, too, but he hung back, obviously reluctant to take a hand in the struggle.

Bert and Stilson were not so hesitant. They both leaped at Wick from behind, Bert grabbing him around the shoulders while Stilson tackled him around the waist. Again reminiscent of a bear, Wick simply shrugged them off and sent them flying through the air while he continued shaking Cobey.

Juanita found herself hoping that in his rage, Wick would kill the gang's leader. Without Cobey around, it would be that much easier for Preacher and Esteban to rescue her later on. And if Wick killed Cobey for trying to molest her, it would insure that the others would all be too afraid to bother her as long as she was under the giant's protection. As she watched Cobey's head loll violently back and forth, she hoped that his neck snapped.

That wasn't to be. Bert surged back to his feet, drew his pistol, and slammed the weapon against Wick's head with all the strength in his wiry body. Stilson followed suit, crashing a blow on Wick's head with his pistol. The two men took turns hammering on Wick's skull with their weapons, and after a moment, Wick's grip on Cobey's shirt relaxed and Cobey slipped free. He dropped to the ground, half-conscious at best.

Wick tried to turn toward Bert and Stilson. He stumbled as they hit him again. Juanita's heart went out to him as he fell to his knees. Bert kicked him in the face, but that just made him lean backward. As he straightened, Stilson hit him again, on top of the head this time. Wick pawed feebly at the two men. He let out a rumble of pain and confusion, and then he pitched forward on his face. After twitching a couple of times, he lay still. For a second Juanita was afraid that he was dead, and she knew that if he was gone, her chances of surviving had just dropped dramatically. But then she heard the harsh sound of his breathing and knew that he was still alive. Even though he had been dealt an incredible amount of damage, his massive frame and thick skull had been able to absorb it.

Juanita turned her head toward Chambers, thinking that this might be the perfect time for the professor to strike. He could kill Cobey while the man was helpless and probably cow Bert and Stilson into cooperating with him.

Chambers, however, wasn't making a move to do any such thing, and Juanita thought she knew why. Chambers didn't want to turn on his supposed allies until they had their hands on the treasure. It might take all of them to get the gold and silver and the old relics away from Preacher. Everyone was waiting, using the others and stringing them along, until they had obtained what they had come here to the Sangre de Cristos to steal. Then it might well be every man for himself.

"Son of a bitch!" Bert said. "It was like tryin' to knock down a damn mountain!"

Stilson cocked his pistol and pointed it at Wick's head. "I'll blow his damn brains out!"

Bert grabbed the gun barrel and forced it to the side. "Don't be a fool!" he snapped. "Once Wick wakes up, he'll be calmed down again. We may need him 'fore this is all over."

"Are you crazy?" Stilson argued. "If I don't kill him, Cobey's gonna as soon as he wakes up."

"Don't be so sure about that. Gimme a hand." Bert knelt next to Cobey and started to lift him to a sitting position. He glanced at Chambers and went on. "Professor, see about gettin' the señorita off the ground."

"Of course," Chambers said, stepping forward at last. He got hold of Juanita and lifted her onto her feet. She couldn't walk because her ankles were bound, but with Chambers's help she was able to get back onto the flat rock where she had been lying earlier. She sat on it now and watched as Bert and Stilson lifted Cobey and held him up, kneeling on either side of him as he sat on the ground.

Bert slapped Cobey's face lightly and said, "Hey. Hey, Cobey. You all right?"

Groggily, Cobey shook his head and groaned. He pawed at his face and said thickly, "Wha . . . wha . . . happened?"

"Wick tore into you," Bert said. "I ain't quite sure why. Chuck and me didn't know what was goin' on until Wick had hold of you and was treatin' you like a mama grizz goin' after somebody who'd bothered her cubs."

"Yeah . . . yeah, I remember. . . ." Cobey looked around. "Where is he?"

"Layin' over there on the ground. He's knocked out, but I don't reckon he's hurt too bad. Chuck and me walloped him a bunch of times with our pistols, but you know how thick that big bastard's skull is. Prob'ly didn't even put a dent in it."

"Want me to kill him, Cobey?" Stilson asked.

"What?" Cobey said. "Kill who? Wick? Hell, no!"

Stilson was a little taken aback. "I figured after what he did—"

"He lost his head," Cobey cut in harshly, "and I'll have a talk with him about it. But he's too valuable to us to just kill him."

Bert looked at Stilson as if he were saying that he'd told him as much.

"Help me up," Cobey went on. "I just want to get back to my bedroll and lay down for a while. Then one of you stand guard over the señorita, since Wick's out cold."

"Sure, Cobey," Bert said. Together, the two men helped Cobey to his feet.

Juanita heaved a sigh of relief. Cobey was too shaken up to bother her again, at least for the rest of this night.

But there was no way of knowing what new ordeals morning would bring.

Preacher saddled Horse and got ready to ride. Then he hunkered on his heels and gnawed on a strip of jerky from his possibles bag while he waited for the gray of dawn to advance across the sky. As soon as it was light enough to see even a little bit, he stood up and started looking around, his keen eyes examining the ground intently.

It didn't take him long to find what he was looking for. The wheels of a pair of wagons had left definite marks on the ground, heading east, while a single horse had pounded off to the west.

He stood there for a long moment staring at the wagon tracks. It seemed unlikely that there would be a pair of wagons in the Sangre de Cristos other than the ones brought up here by the Alvarez party. Not impossible, of course, but certainly unlikely. The day before, those wagons had been in the hands of Cobey Larson, Professor Chambers, and the rest of that bunch. Preacher didn't think that Cobey and the others would have brought the wagons back along here. The fact that Arnie had taken off in the opposite direction with Esteban added to the strength of that theory.

That left only one good explanation. Once Father Hortensio and the two Yaquis had reached the bottom of the ledge, Pablo and Joaquin had left the padre here with the treasure and gone to steal back the wagons. It had probably still been daylight then, and Father Hortensio would have known that Cobey, Chambers, and the others were likely to be up on the shelf, trying to trade Juanita for the treasure. They might have left someone down below to guard the wagons, but chances were they hadn't.

That priest was tricky enough to have thought of all that, Preacher decided. And it was the only thing that really made sense. The Yaquis had brought the wagons back here, loaded the treasure on them, and then they and Father Hortensio had lit a shuck back the way the party had come in the first place, heading out of the mountains as fast as they could push the teams.

Father Hortensio was taking the treasure back where it belonged, to Mission Santo Domingo.

But that still left Juanita Alvarez and now her brother Esteban as prisoners.

Preacher wasn't given to agonizing over decisions. He looked at a situation, weighed all the angles quickly but carefully, and then made up his mind. Now, he swung up into his saddle and rode west, following the tracks left by the fleeing Arnie Ross. He knew where to find Father Hortensio and the treasure when the time came; for now he had to see about getting Esteban and Juanita out of the hands of the hard cases who had captured them.

While the sun was still just peeking over the eastern horizon, Preacher reached the Purgatoire River. Not surprisingly, the tracks he had been following turned to parallel the river. The fat man was running back to his comrades as fast as he could. Preacher rode along the river, too, but he veered away from it until he was a couple of hundred yards away from the stream. He didn't want to run head-on into Cobey's bunch. Chances were, as soon as they heard about Arnie's encounter with Preacher and Esteban, they would backtrack the fat man and try to pick up the trail of the treasure where the fight had taken place. By now they would know that the wagons were gone, and both Cobey and Chambers were cunning enough to figure out what had happened to them.

Preacher had only gone a mile or so when the skin on the back of his neck began to prickle. It was an instinctive reaction, and one that he had experienced many times in the past. He considered it a sort of alarm system.

Somebody was watching him.

Without slowing Horse or being too obvious about it, Preacher looked around, searching for any signs of whoever was following him. He didn't see anything, which didn't mean they weren't there. It just meant that they were good at what they were doing.

The valley of the Purgatoire was about half a mile wide along here. Steep bluffs rose on both sides, and the mountains climbed above them. A few miles ahead, the valley narrowed down more, and that was where the twisting canyon leading up to the shelf where the treasure had been hidden was located. The landscape where Preacher rode was hilly and dotted with thick stands of pine. Plenty of places to hide, in other words. He might be riding right into an ambush.

Somehow, though, he didn't believe that was the case. It felt more like he was being trailed.

He didn't have any friends up here except Esteban, and if the young man had gotten away from Arnie somehow, he wouldn't follow Preacher and not announce himself. Preacher had to assume that whoever was dogging his trail wished him harm.

He was going to have to do something about that, before he got around to dealing with Cobey and the others.

He rode up a hill into some pines with Dog padding along beside him and Horse. At the top of the slope the land flattened out into a long level stretch, but the trees still grew thickly. Preacher said quietly, "Keep goin', Horse. You, too, Dog." Then he reached up, grasped a branch, and pulled himself out of the saddle. He hung there for only an instant before climbing agilely into the tree where the dense foliage shielded him from view. The pine needles pricked him, but he ignored the discomfort. Down below, Horse and Dog moved on through the trees just as Preacher had ordered.

He waited with the patience of a true frontiersman, who knew that the ability to stay still and quiet was sometimes all that saved a man's life. He could still hear Horse's hoofbeats, which was good. That meant whoever was following him could hear them, too.

Sure enough, a couple of minutes later, Preacher heard another horse coming through the trees. He waited, motionless, until the horse came into view. It was an Indian pony, and that was somewhat surprising. So was the man who rode it. He was a strong-faced warrior with thick black hair pulled back in a couple of braids, and the distinctive markings on the buckskins he wore identified him as a Crow. He was a long way from home. The Crow hunting grounds were hundreds of miles to the north of here. Preacher had had run-ins with members of that tribe in the past, but unlike the Blackfoot, who were almost universally hostile to white men, some Crows got along with the whites. It was impossible to know how this one felt, but the fact that he had been trailing Preacher in such a stealthy manner didn't bode well.

When in doubt, ask, Preacher told himself. The next moment, as the Indian rode beneath the tree where Preacher was perched, the mountain man dropped suddenly on him, tackling him and driving him off the back of the pony.

Both men crashed to the ground. Preacher landed on top, knocking the breath out of the Crow warrior. He planted a knee in the Indian's belly, locked his left forearm across the Crow's throat like a bar of iron, and used his right hand to pull the heavy-bladed hunting knife from the sheath at his belt. Preacher held the tip of the keen blade against the Crow's throat and grated, "Move and I'll slice you open, mister. Now, how come you're followin' me?"

Under the circumstances, the Crow was going to have a hard time answering the question. But before Preacher could relax the pressure of his forearm and let his prisoner speak, a gun barrel prodded the back of the mountain man's neck and a deep voice said, "Let him go. The last thing I want to do is kill you."

TWENTY-EIGHT

It was not yet dawn when Juanita heard the horse coming. The swift rataplan of hoofbeats was loud in the night and roused her from the uneasy half sleep into which she had drifted as she lay on the big, flat rock.

The noise alerted the rest of the party, too, except for Wick, who had not regained consciousness. From the way he was snoring again, however, Juanita thought the giant had passed from being knocked out to simply being asleep.

Cobey, Chambers, Bert McDermott, and Chuck Stilson all sprang up and reached for their guns. McDermott had been sitting on a log close to the rock where Juanita lay, standing guard over her as Cobey had ordered. He said quietly to her, "Take it easy, Señorita. Don't yell out or anything until we know who's comin'."

All four of the men were ready to fight if they found themselves under attack. But a moment later a loud hail came to them, and they knew that wasn't the case.

"Cobey! Cobey, it's me! Don't shoot!"

"That's Arnie!" Cobey exclaimed. "Hold your fire!"

Although it was awkward because of the way she was tied, Juanita managed to push herself up onto an elbow so that she could see better. The running horse slowed. Arnie Ross rode into the camp. There was just enough light in the graying sky so that Juanita could see he had someone with him, riding double on the same horse. The man was in front of Arnie, leaning forward over the neck of the horse, and seemed to be either hurt or unconscious. Juanita supposed it was George Worthy, who had gone with Arnie to find out where that ledge led.

From the way Arnie shoved the man off the horse, though, and let him fall limply to the ground, it didn't seem likely the man was an ally. That was confirmed a second later when Arnie said, "Better tie him up. It's the Alvarez kid."

Fear shot through Juanita. She twisted herself into a sitting position and cried out, "No! Esteban!"

"Bert, keep an eye on her," Cobey snapped as he bent over the man Arnie had dumped on the ground. "It's Alvarez, all right. Chuck, help me tie him up."

Juanita's heart pounded so hard in her chest, it seemed as if it were about to burst out of her body. She wondered wildly what had happened, how Esteban had gotten captured by Arnie Ross. What was going to happen to them now?

And where was Preacher?

Cobey and Stilson quickly lashed Esteban's ankles and wrists together. Then Cobey dragged him over to the rock where Juanita sat and dumped him in front of her. Even though she couldn't see the sneer on Cobey's face, she could hear it in his voice as he said, "I reckon your lovin' brother just couldn't stay away from you, Señorita."

"Please," she begged. "Do not hurt him."

"Long as he behaves himself, he'll keep on livin' . . . for a while." With that chilling statement, Cobey swung toward Arnie and demanded, "What the hell happened? Where's Worthy?"

"Preacher killed him," Arnie said bluntly. "Blew half his head off with a pistol. And that damn dog of his about chewed my arm off." Arnie held up his left arm. The sleeve of his shirt was shredded and dark with dried blood. "If I hadn't got lucky and walloped the critter with my gun, he'd have worked his way up to tearin' my throat out."

"Where'd you run into Preacher and the Alvarez kid?"

"At the other end of that ledge. We followed the trail along it until it sloped down into the valley again. One place looked like it had been blocked by a rock slide, but we were able to get through. I reckon Preacher must have cleared the slide away."

"What about the priest and those Yaquis? And the treasure?"

Arnie shook his head. "Didn't see hide nor hair of the priest or them Injuns. I think Preacher and Alvarez were by themselves." He looked around. "Hey! Where in blazes are the wagons?"

Cobey gave a disgusted grunt. "They were gone when we got back down here. Best guess is that the Yaquis slipped back here and stole 'em."

Arnie nodded slowly and said, "Yeah, I reckon that makes sense. As much sense as anything, anyway."

"I don't understand how come Preacher and the kid weren't with the others, though."

Chambers spoke up. "It's quite evident that the good padre prevailed on his swarthy sycophants to assist him in appropriating the treasure."

"What?" Cobey asked. He sounded irritated.

Chambers sighed. "Father Hortensio and the Yaquis betrayed Preacher and young Alvarez and stole the loot. I suppose Father Hortensio knew that Preacher intended to trade the treasure for Señorita Alvarez, and he wanted to prevent that at all costs."

Juanita frowned as she listened to the exchange. Could Father Hortensio have really done such a thing? It would explain a great deal. The priest and his Yaqui servants could have taken the treasure and left before Preacher reached the shelf again after negotiating the exchange with Arnie Ross. Esteban would have tried to stop them, and it was possible that one of the Yaquis, acting on Father Hortensio's command, might have knocked him unconscious or incapacitated him in some other way. Then, when Preacher found Esteban and discovered that Father Hortensio and the Yaquis were gone and had taken the treasure with them, Preacher and Esteban would have gone after them. . . .

It all fit, but Juanita took no satisfaction in piecing the puzzle together. All that really mattered was that she and Esteban were both now the prisoners of these desperate men, and the treasure they sought was gone, spirited away by Father Hortensio. That left her and Esteban to whatever fate awaited them at the hands of their captors.

Except for the fact that Preacher was still out there somewhere, loose and able to cause trouble.

Juanita sensed that there was no more dangerous wild card in this deadly game than the man called Preacher.

"What do we do now, Cobey?" Arnie asked.

"It'll be gettin' light soon," Cobey said. "Can you find your way back to the place where you ran into Preacher and Alvarez?"

Arnie nodded. "I reckon I can."

"If we've got everything figured right, that'll be the same spot the priest and the Injuns started from after they loaded the treasure in the wagons. We'll pick up their trail there."

"So we're still goin' after 'em?"

Cobey gave a harsh, humorless laugh. "Damn right we're goin' after 'em. You didn't think I was gonna give up on that treasure, did you?" He raised a hand and clenched it into a fist. "That loot's gonna be ours, and I don't care who has to die along the way."

Preacher didn't move when the gun barrel poked the back of his neck. He kept the knife at the Crow's throat and said to the unseen man who had threatened him, "I don't want you to kill me, neither. But I reckon even if you pull the trigger, I'll still have time to shove this knife right through the Injun's neck."

The man with the gun hesitated a second before saying, "I suppose you might, at that. There's a heartbeat of time between the firing of the priming charge and the ignition of the main charge in the barrel. That might be enough of an interval for a man with sufficiently swift reflexes to carry out such a threat."

"So we've got us a standoff," Preacher said. "You could call it a Nuevo Mexican standoff."

"If you wanted to make a play on words," the other agreed. "I think we can bring it to a satisfactory conclusion, however. You *are* the man called Preacher, aren't you?"

It surprised Preacher that this fella, whoever he was, knew his name. But he said, "That's right."

"Then I don't see any reason why we can't be friends. To prove it, I'll take my rifle away from your neck. You can reciprocate by removing your knife from my companion's neck."

"You're askin' me to trust you," Preacher pointed out. "You can move that rifle and still shoot me with it."

"The alternative is to wait here all day and see who tires first. I doubt if you want that."

"Damn right I don't," Preacher said. He took a deep breath and then nodded. "All right. It's a deal."

The rifle barrel went away from the back of his neck. Preacher lowered his knife and pushed himself up off the Crow. So far, the Indian hadn't made a sound, and no expression had crossed his impassive face. But now he reached up and touched the tiny spot of blood where the tip of Preacher's blade had pricked his neck. He looked at the smear of crimson on his fingertip and said, "Ummm."

Keeping the knife in his hand, Preacher turned toward the man with the rifle. He planned to flip the knife underhand if he thought the fella intended to shoot him. Preacher's eyes narrowed, though, and he stiffened in surprise as he got his first good look at the man.

The gent wore buckskins and a coonskin cap, marking him as a typical frontiersman. There was nothing else typical about him. He was only about three and a half feet tall, the size of a child. His heavily muscled torso, short legs, and bearded face told Preacher that he wasn't a child. He was full-growed, as much as he ever would be.

"Son of a bitch," Preacher said.

"Indeed." The man tucked his rifle under his arm. The barrel had been cut down some so that it would be easier for him to handle, but the pistol tucked behind the man's belt was full size, and so was the sheathed hunting knife at his waist and the tomahawk that he carried behind his belt as well.

Preacher heard the Crow getting up, and moved a little so that he could keep an eye on both of them. "Who are you boys?" he asked.

"My name is Audie," the little man said. He nodded toward the Crow. "This is Nighthawk."

"Ummm," the Crow said.

"We've seen you around at Rendezvous," Audie went on, "but we've never been introduced."

"You're fur trappers?" Preacher asked.

"That's right. If Jeb Law or Dupre were here, they would vouch for us, I assure you."

Those names carried some weight with Preacher. Jeb Law and Dupre were good friends of his. But anybody could throw out their names as Audie had just done. That didn't really mean anything.

"I wish ol' Jeb *was* here," Preacher said. "I could use a hand right about now."

"If you have a problem, Nighthawk and I would be glad to assist you. I realize we got off on the wrong foot, so to speak—"

"You mean the way the two of you were trailin' me like you meant to cause trouble for me?"

"We were simply curious," Audie explained. "We saw you riding along, and Nighthawk said that he thought he recognized you. Isn't that right, Nighthawk?"

"Ummm."

"So it's true that we followed you," Audie continued, "but we meant you no harm, Preacher."

Preacher was still dubious. "If the two of you are trappers, what're you doin' off down here instead o' bein' further north where the pelts are better?"

Audie smiled and said, "Wanderlust, pure and simple. We'd heard about this country and wanted to see it for ourselves. I must say, it's rather enchanting."

Something jogged in Preacher's memory, and he said, "I recollect hearin' about a fella named Audie. Story went that he was some sort o' teacher back East before he came to the mountains."

"That would be me. I was an instructor at a school in Pennsylvania before I decided to follow my restless nature."

"Fella who told me about you didn't say nothin' about . . . well . . ."

"About me being a midget, you mean?" Audie grinned. "Well, that was certainly an important element of the story to leave out, wasn't it? But I assure you, I *am* the man you've heard about."

Preacher was beginning to believe him. His instincts were telling him, too, that Audie spoke the truth about wanting to help him. Preacher had lived as long as he had by relying on his hunches, as well as his ability to judge a man's character. In the case of Audie and Nighthawk, he sensed that both of them would do to ride the river with.

He slipped his knife back in its sheath and then held out his hand. "All right," he said. "I'm pleased to meet you boys, and if you ain't got somewheres else you need to be right now, I could sure use your help."

Audie reached up to clasp Preacher's hand. His grip was

sure and strong. So was Nighthawk's when Preacher shook hands with the Crow.

"Tell us about it," Audie suggested.

Preacher quickly sketched in everything that had happened over the past week or so. Audie's eyes lit up at the mention of the treasure, but not with greed or avarice.

"Fascinating," he murmured. "Such artifacts must have great historical value, in addition to their intrinsic worth."

"They mean a whole heap to Father Hortensio, that's for sure," Preacher said. "He was willin' to leave the señorita in the hands of those no-good bastards rather than try to trade the loot for her."

"Ummm," Nighthawk said, and he managed to convey a considerable amount of disapproval with the grunt.

"The one who really angers me is this Professor Chambers you mentioned," Audie said. "Imagine, a scholar, a man who should be devoted to learning, a man who once inhabited the ivy-covered halls of Harvard, stooping to such ruthless behavior. He sounds like a disgrace to the entire teaching profession."

"He's pretty disgraceful, all right," Preacher agreed.

"So what we have to do is extricate the young señor and señorita from their captivity and then perhaps give some thought to recovering the treasure."

"The treasure's already recovered," Preacher pointed out. "It was goin' back to the Church anyway, except for what Esteban and Juanita had comin' to 'em for helpin' out. Since Father Hortensio's got the loot and seems to be headin' back to the old mission, I don't reckon we have to do anything about that." Preacher paused and then added, "Much as I'd like to pay him back for what he did to those kids."

"Even with the lead he's established, won't it take the father several days to get back to Mission Santo Domingo?"

Preacher nodded. "I reckon it will. Loaded down like they will be, those wagons can't move too fast."

"So it's possible that this gang of thieves, once they figure out what's going on, will pursue the wagons and make another effort to steal the treasure?"

"I'd say it's mighty likely," Preacher agreed grimly.

Audie frowned. "And they'll bring the two young people with them, to use as hostages if necessary."

"That's what I'm hopin'. That'll give us a chance to snatch 'em back."

"And of course there's a good likelihood we'll also have to protect the treasure along the way."

"Yep." Preacher chuckled. "That's all."

Audie rubbed his hands together and said, "Well, we've certainly got our work cut out for us. Perhaps we should give some thought to—"

"Ummm," Nighthawk said.

"Yeah, I hear it, too," Preacher said. "Hoofbeats. Here they come now."

TWENTY-NINE

As soon as it was light enough to see where they were going, Cobey ordered McDermott and Stilson to saddle the horses. Stilson muttered something about not getting any breakfast, and Cobey snapped at him, "Gnaw some jerky while you ride."

Then Cobey strode over to where Wick Jimpson still lay snoring. He prodded the big man in the side with his foot and said sharply, "Wick. Time to get up."

Wick didn't budge, and his stentorian snores continued. Cobey nudged him again, harder this time. "Wake up, damn it."

"He could be suffering from some sort of concussive cranial damage, considering how your men struck him repeatedly over the head with their weapons."

Cobey turned to glare at Professor Chambers, who had made the comment as he leaned casually against a tree trunk.

"If they hadn't, he'd have probably killed me. That wouldn't'a broke your heart, though, now would it, Professor?"

"I've been a faithful ally, Cobey," Chambers insisted. "I've done everything you've suggested."

"Yeah, but takin' orders from a gent like me sticks in your craw, don't it?"

"You haven't been giving me orders," Chambers said quietly. "We're partners, remember?"

Cobey's scornful grunt made it clear how he felt about that. He turned back to Wick and prodded his shoulder again. "Dadblast it, you big ox! Wake up!"

From where she sat on the rock, Juanita watched the brief confrontation between Cobey and Chambers and didn't know what to hope for. If the two men had a falling-out, one of them might kill the other, meaning that there would be one less man for her and Esteban to escape from. But if that happened, the chances were it would be Chambers who died and Cobey who lived, and Chambers might represent their best chance of getting away. She would help him when he tried his double cross of the others—she had nothing to lose by doing so, as far as she could see—but she certainly didn't trust him when he said that he would let them go. He was just as big a danger, in his own way.

The exchange of words between Cobey and Chambers didn't go any farther, because Cobey was now ignoring the professor and continuing his efforts to rouse Wick from slumber. The giant finally stirred. After moving around a little, he lifted his shaggy head and peered around, blinking in confusion. Then he looked up and said, "Oh. Mornin', Cobey. Is it time to get up?"

"Yeah, it is," Cobey growled, making an obvious effort not to lose his temper with Wick. "We got places to go and things to do."

"All right." Wick pushed himself to his feet, stretched, and then shook his head. He winced and reached up to touch his skull. "Huh. My head hurts a mite, and I got lumps all over it. What you reckon happened to me, Cobey?"

"I don't know. You be able to ride?"

"Oh, yeah, sure. It don't matter if my head hurts a little."

Chambers drifted over closer to Juanita and Esteban and

said quietly, "Fascinating. He doesn't even remember what happened last night. Perhaps the blows to the head caused that. Or perhaps he's simply too mentally deficient to retain an unpleasant memory."

Juanita knew that wasn't true. Wick had told her about the incident that had led to him being thrown in jail for killing a man with one punch. She didn't bother correcting Chambers, though. She was more concerned with Esteban, who had not yet regained consciousness himself.

"Professor," she said, "could you check on my brother?"

"What? Oh, certainly. Your brother." Chambers knelt beside Esteban, felt in his neck for a pulse, and then rolled both eyelids back to look at his eyes. Esteban stirred slightly. Chambers looked up at Juanita and said, "His pulse is strong, and his eyes look all right. I think he should be waking up soon."

Juanita had heard Cobey and Arnie talking and knew that the fat man had literally run into Esteban when he was trying to flee from Preacher's dog. Arnie had struck the young man with his pistol just as he had the big cur, grabbed his horse, and thrown Esteban over the animal's back before vaulting into the saddle and galloping away. It had been sheer bad luck that had allowed Esteban to be taken prisoner.

True to the professor's prediction, Esteban opened his eyes a few minutes later, while the men were still saddling the horses. Bound hand and foot like Juanita, he had to struggle to sit up. When he did, he saw her sitting there on the rock and his eyes widened in surprise.

"Juanita!" he exclaimed. He looked around, and his face grew grim as he recognized the men moving around the camp and realized that he was a captive. Instinctively, he strained against his bonds for a moment before giving up. The rawhide thongs weren't going to loosen enough for him to get free.

"What happened?" he asked, so quietly that only she could hear. "The last thing I remember, I was with Preacher. . . ."

She leaned closer to him and equally quietly answered,

"The fat man, the one called Arnie, and another man attacked you and Preacher. Preacher killed the other man, but Arnie captured you and got away."

Esteban nodded, wincing a little from the pain in his head caused by the movement. "I remember now. . . . Juanita, *mi hermana,* are you all right?"

"They have not harmed me," she assured him, adding to herself, *Though not for lack of trying.*

"What happened to Preacher?"

She shook her head. "I do not know. He is still out there somewhere."

"Then there is still hope," Esteban breathed.

"Esteban . . . what about the treasure, and Father Hortensio?"

His face hardened even more. "Father Hortensio betrayed me. When I said that I was going to trade the treasure for your safety, he ordered one of the Yaquis to strike me down. Then they took the treasure and escaped. Preacher came back and found me, and we went after them."

Juanita nodded and said, "That is what these men decided must have happened. The wagons are gone, and they think the Yaquis came and took them while we were all up at the top of the canyon."

"I can believe that," Esteban said. "Father Hortensio has been one step ahead of all of us, doing everything he can to protect the treasure for the Church."

"Esteban," she said softly, "what else would you have him do? It is his calling. We decided ourselves, before we ever came up here to Nuevo Mexico, that the treasure must go back to the Church."

"Not at the cost of your life. That changed everything."

"Not to Father Hortensio."

He didn't say anything for a moment. He was sitting close enough to her so that he could lean over and rest his head against her knee for a second. She reached out with her bound hands and stroked his dark hair, which was now sticky with dried blood where Arnie had pistol-whipped him.

"Oh, Esteban," she murmured as Cobey ordered the men to put the prisoners on a couple of horses and then mount up. "What are we going to do?"

"Have faith," he grated. "It is all that is left to us."

"Faith in El Señor Dios?"

"In El Señor Dios . . . and in Preacher."

Lying at the top of a hill, screened by heavy brush, Preacher, Audie, and Nighthawk peered down at the Purgatoire River and the trail that ran beside it. Dog lay next to Preacher, tongue lolling from his mouth and his eyes alert. The mountain man had an arm looped around the big cur's neck. Waiting farther back were Horse, Nighthawk's spotted pony, and the sturdy, short-legged mount that Audie rode.

The three men watched intently as the party of riders came into sight. Beside Preacher, Dog let out a growl as he recognized the men. Preacher felt a mite like growling, too. Cobey and his bunch of thieves and killers provoked such a reaction in him.

Cobey was in the lead, as usual, and he had Juanita Alvarez on the back of his horse with him, riding in front of the saddle with Cobey's left arm around her waist. Just slightly behind them came Arnie, riding double with Esteban. Preacher was relieved to see that the youngster looked all right. He had been banged up and probably knocked out a couple of times, but he was tough, especially considering his privileged upbringing in Mexico City.

Professor Chambers rode next to the massive Wick Jimpson, and the other two men brought up the rear. All of them were looking around as they rode, watchful for any sign of trouble.

"Six of them and three of us," Audie said. "That's only two

to one odds, and there's a good chance we could even them up with one volley from our rifles."

"We probably could," Preacher agreed, "but with those Alvarez youngsters ridin' with Cobey and Arnie, we couldn't risk shootin' them. We'd have to go for three o' the others, and that'd leave Esteban and Juanita at the mercy o' those two bastards. I wouldn't put it past Cobey and Arnie to kill 'em right away if any shootin' was to start."

"Ummm," Nighthawk said.

Audie nodded. "I agree. If they did that, they'd be throwing away their own shields. Surely they wouldn't do such a thing."

Preacher's eyes narrowed as he said, "You're askin' a couple o' kill-crazy, gold-hungry skunks to act reasonable-like. That's a chance I ain't willin' to take, not when the lives o' those two kids are on the line, too."

"Of course," Audie said without hesitation. "It's your decision to make, Preacher. You've dealt with those men, and you know them. Nighthawk and I don't."

Preacher watched the group of riders as they trotted along the river and went around a bend out of sight. "We'll follow 'em," he said. "Wait for a better chance to grab Esteban and Juanita."

He backed down the hill, waiting until he was sure he was out of sight of the river before standing up. Audie and Nighthawk did likewise. They faded back into the trees, got their horses, and mounted up.

One thing about it—they all knew where they were going. The treasure was bound for Mission Santo Domingo, and so were the two groups of men following it. Nobody was likely to get lost.

Preacher and his two companions stayed well out of sight of the party they were trailing. The sun rose higher in the sky and the air grew warmer. Audie looked around at the wooded hills and the majestic mountains and the arching blue sky and the clear, bubbling creeks that flowed down to join the river, and the little man exclaimed, "My God, this is a beautiful country!"

"What's it like where you come from?" Preacher asked.

"Oh, it has its beauties, too," Audie replied. "But nothing really to compare with this. I enjoyed my life back there, I suppose, but I've never been happier than I am out here on the frontier, in the midst of all this magnificence." He paused, and when he went on a moment later, his tone was more reflective. "It's not just the landscape, of course. It's the freedom, and the knowledge that I'll be judged on what I do, not what I look like or how tall I am."

Preacher grunted. "How else would anybody be judged, except on what they do with their life?"

"Oh, ho, my newfound friend, you've been away from civilization too long."

"I been to St. Louis," Preacher said. "I even been to Philadelphia."

"Then you should be aware that back East, people are usually judged on everything *but* their own character and accomplishments. At one end of the spectrum, they're judged on how much money they have, and who their parents and grandparents were. At the other end, people are judged by how poor they are or sometimes by what color their skin is."

"Well, that's a damn-fool way to be," Preacher said. "A rich man ain't always worked for what he's got, and a poor man ain't always to blame for bein' born poor. Now, if he don't mind stayin' poor and don't want to work to make himself better, that's a different story. I got no use for a fella like that. As for the color of a man's skin, he ain't got no control over that."

"Speaking as one whose best friend is of a definite reddish hue, I wholeheartedly agree," Audie said.

"It ain't just redskins, though," Preacher went on. "When I was down in Louisiana, back when I was a young fella, I saw a bunch o' slaves, and they was a miserable lot, lemme tell you. But I never thought much about it until I rode a few rivers with Jim Beckwourth. Him and me went on more'n one trappin' expedition for Major Ashley."

Audie nodded. "Yes, I know Jim. He's a mulatto."

"That's a fancy way o' sayin' he's part black, ain't it? Well, to folks who keep slaves, part black's the same as all black, and once I got to know what a fine fella Jim was, it got me to wonderin' how many o' them slaves would've been just as smart and strong and full o' grit if they'd ever had the chance." Preacher shook his head. "That's why I don't hold with it."

"Some people up North are starting to feel the same way. They call themselves abolitionists, because they want to force the people in the South to give up their slaves."

"Well, one part o' the country forcin' another part o' the country to do somethin' ain't right, neither," Preacher said with a frown. He shook his head again and then chuckled dryly. "I'm mighty glad it ain't up to me to figure out what the country ought to do. I got enough on my mind right now, what with rescuin' them two youngsters and seein' that the lost treasure o' Santo Domingo don't fall into the hands o' Cobey Larson and his bunch o' murderin' desperadoes."

"Yes, as you put it earlier," Audie said, "that's all."

THIRTY

Preacher, Audie, and Nighthawk followed Cobey's bunch all day, staying well back so that they wouldn't be seen. To men such as these, getting around unseen in the wilderness was little more than child's play. They avoided the high ground, so they wouldn't be skylined if any of the men they pursued happened to look back at just the wrong moment, and they used ridges and gullies and thick stands of trees to keep themselves from being spotted when they were closer to their quarry. Preacher and Audie each had a spyglass in their possibles bag, so from time to time they stopped and the two men took turns climbing up in a tree so that they could check on the progress of the other group. Cobey kept his men moving at a brisk pace all day. Preacher hoped that wasn't too hard on the two prisoners. He and Audie and Nighthawk could have caught up just about any time they wanted to, but after talking about it they had decided that it would be better to wait until nightfall to make their attempt to rescue Esteban and Juanita.

So far there hadn't been any sign of Father Hortensio, the two Yaquis, and the treasure-laden wagons. But they had to be up ahead somewhere, Preacher knew, and the two groups following them had to be cutting into the lead that Father

Hortensio and his companions held. It was just a matter of time. . . .

Spending all day in the saddle was nothing to hardened mountain men. They paused occasionally to let the horses rest, but otherwise they kept moving. Preacher shared his jerky with Audie and Nighthawk, and the Crow warrior passed around strips of pemmican from his supplies. Audie contributed some chunks of pone he had cooked a few days earlier. They washed the food down with swigs of water from their canteens.

Even though the strain of the long day wasn't felt much in Preacher's iron-hard frame, he knew it had to be telling on Esteban and Juanita. They weren't used to such things. Chances were they'd be mighty sore when Cobey finally called a halt for the night.

If he called a halt for the night, Preacher amended. It was possible the gang would press on even though darkness fell. They knew where they were going, and they had to be getting mighty anxious to get their hands on that gold and those gold and silver gem-encrusted relics.

As the sun dipped below the western peaks behind them, Audie said, "What do we do now, Preacher? If we keep moving after dark, and those men stop for the night, we're liable to stumble right into their camp."

"And if we stop and they don't, they'll have a big lead on us by mornin'," Preacher said.

Nighthawk said, "Ummm."

"You're right, it is a dilemma," Audie agreed.

Preacher considered for a moment and then said, "Way I see it, we can't risk stoppin' as long as we don't know what the others are doin'. We'll slow down a mite and hope that if they do make camp, we'll know it before we ride in on 'em. If they don't, they may gain on us a little, but we can make up that ground tomorrow."

Audie nodded. "That sounds like a workable plan to me. It's our best option, at any rate."

Shadows began to gather thickly. Preacher, Audie, and Nighthawk reined their horses back to a walk. They were close enough to the river now so that Preacher could hear the chuckling and bubbling of the stream as it flowed over its rocky bed. He said quietly, "Dog, go take a look around."

The big cur loped off ahead of the three men. Audie said, "He seems to have understood you, Preacher."

"Yeah, Dog's pretty smart. And we been together a long time, so that helps us understand each other."

"You don't think he'll give away our presence if he catches up to the others?"

Preacher shook his head. "He won't let them see him, and he won't attack or do anything else unless I give him the word. He'll just come back and let me know what he found."

"Amazing," Audie murmured. He sounded as if he didn't quite believe Preacher's claim.

A short time later, though, Dog came bounding back. He ran up to Preacher, who reined Horse to a stop. When Preacher reached down, Dog nuzzled his hand and then growled. Preacher nodded.

"I figured as much."

"Oh, come now," Audie said. "What could the creature have communicated with such simple gestures?"

"That the bunch we're after ain't far ahead of us. He wasn't gone long enough for it to mean anything else."

"Perhaps you're right. I just find it difficult to believe, that's all."

Preacher jerked a thumb toward the Crow. "I ain't heard Nighthawk do more'n grunt all day, but you seem to know what he means when he does it."

"Well, of course. We've been partners for a good while. . . . Oh, I see."

"Ummm," Nighthawk said, and Preacher thought he saw a faint suggestion of a grin on the warrior's hawklike face.

"Let's get down and walk a ways," Preacher suggested. He swung out of the saddle and Audie and Nighthawk did likewise. With rifles in one hand and their reins in the other, the men started forward. Dusk had settled down over the rugged terrain, and the stars were coming out overhead. The moon was not yet up, though, and wouldn't be for a while. This was actually one of the worst times of the day for seeing clearly. Often a man could make out more even by starlight than he could in such a thick dusk.

But even if he couldn't see very well at the moment, Preacher's nose worked just fine. He stopped abruptly, and so did his two companions. Preacher sniffed and then looked at Audie and Nighthawk, both of whom nodded. All three men had smelled the same thing: wood smoke. Dog growled, indicating that he had caught the scent, too.

"They've made camp," Audie whispered.

"Yeah, I reckon," Preacher agreed, "and not too far off. Let's leave the horses here and see how close we can get."

They tied the reins to some saplings and cat-footed forward through the gathering darkness. Nighthawk was the best at moving silently, but Preacher was almost as good and Audie was no slouch. It would have taken a mighty keen set of eyes and ears to notice the trio of grim-faced men moving through the woods.

Evidently sensing that they were close to their quarry, all three stopped at the same time and crouched behind some brush on a bluff overlooking the river. Down below was a stretch of level, relatively treeless ground next to the stream, and that was where Cobey and his men had made camp. Preacher could hear their voices as they talked among themselves. Stretching out on the ground, he crawled forward, pushing the brush aside until he could see down the steep slope in front of him. Audie and Nighthawk followed his example. Even Dog got down on his belly and crawled up next to Preacher.

Preacher parted the brush again and studied the camp through the narrow gap. The men had placed rocks in a circle and built a small fire within it. Preacher smelled food cooking and coffee brewing. The tantalizing aromas made his belly contract a little. He was more interested in checking on the welfare of the prisoners, though, than he was in being hungry.

Esteban and Juanita sat side by side on a log, looking tired and miserable. Their faces were drawn and haggard in the dim, reddish firelight. Juanita leaned exhaustedly against her brother's shoulder. One of the men, a tall, lanky gent in buckskin trousers, homespun shirt, and coonskin cap, stood near them with a rifle tucked under his arm. He was guarding them, that much was obvious. Across the camp, Cobey, Arnie, and Professor Chambers stood together, talking quietly. The stocky man called Stilson who had been with Chambers at the mission was at the fire, tending to the food.

Preacher wondered where the giant was. From his vantage point, he could see the entire camp, and there was no sign of Wick Jimpson. Had something happened to him? Had the others left him behind for some reason?

A sudden crashing of brush from behind Preacher, Audie, and Nighthawk, much like the sound a grizzly bear would make tramping through the underbrush, seemed to answer that question.

Wick was behind them, and he was coming their way.

Juanita hadn't known that muscles could hurt so bad. In fact, she ached where she hadn't even known it was possible for a person to ache. Esteban had ridden more than she ever had in the past, so he wasn't in quite as bad a shape as she was, but he was utterly exhausted, too.

The one good thing about the way Cobey had pushed them all day was that there hadn't been time during any of their brief rest stops for him to make advances toward her. It was bad enough that she had felt his hands on her body as they rode and had been forced to listen to his occasional crude comments. However, he now seemed less interested in her as a woman. Thoughts of the treasure consumed him, and most of the time he regarded her more as a potential hostage and bargaining chip than he did as an attractive young female.

Surely he had figured out by now that Father Hortensio didn't care what happened to her and Esteban. If the priest had cared, he never would have gone off and left them behind the way he had. While she wasn't really surprised, and while they couldn't have expected Father Hortensio to do anything else under the circumstances, as she had pointed out to Esteban, still his betrayal hurt her. She had thought that the good padre felt more affection for them than that. After all, was it not the two of them who had made it possible for the treasure to be recovered in the first place?

But that meant nothing when weighed against the needs of the Church. Juanita just had to accept that.

Bert McDermott was guarding them now. Evidently Cobey no longer trusted Wick to do that job. That might make things more difficult later on. Juanita hadn't given up on the idea of turning Wick against his companions. He might not remember what had happened the night before, but he was still vulnerable to her charms. More than once during the day, she had caught the big man gazing at her in open adoration. Surely there would be a way to make use of that when the proper time came. At the moment, though, Wick had wandered off somewhere, perhaps to relieve himself in the woods.

Stilson brought over some fried salt pork and a couple of tortillas. He handed the plate to Juanita and said, "Here you go. You'll have to share with your brother. We ain't got a lot of supplies."

"These are tortillas you took from the provisions in the wagons, before you lost them," Esteban said.

Stilson sneered. "So what? You're lucky to be gettin' anything to eat at all. If'n it was up to me, I'd put a pistol ball through your head and then have me some fun with that sister o' yours, greaser."

Esteban stiffened and might have tried to get up, but Juanita told him quietly in Spanish to let it go. They had more to worry about than coarse insults. Reluctantly, Esteban nodded.

Bert jerked a thumb toward the fire. "Go on about your business, Chuck," he said to Stilson. "You ain't accomplishin' anything by harassin' these folks."

"Who appointed you their protector?" Stilson shot back.

"Cobey told me to guard 'em. I reckon that's sort of the same thing."

"The hell it is. He just don't want 'em to get away. That's all you're supposed to stop."

"I just don't want to listen to it," Bert said with a sigh.

"Fine, fine, I'm goin'." Stilson couldn't resist adding a parting shot. "You just want that señorita's pepper pot for yourself, Bert. I know what's goin' on."

Bert snorted in disgust but didn't say anything else.

On the log, Esteban tore off a small strip of the tortilla Juanita had given him. He put it in his mouth and chewed deliberately for a long moment before swallowing. When he had, he said quietly, "I am sorry, Juanita."

"For what?" she asked.

"For bringing you along with me on this accursed journey. You should be safely in our home in Mexico City."

"Do you not remember, Esteban, that it was I who insisted on accompanying you?"

He shrugged. "I am your brother, your protector. I should have said no, regardless of any argument you made." He tore off another bit of tortilla and ate it.

"I do not blame you," Juanita said. "I knew there might be danger. I knew it was likely there would be."

An uneasy silence settled over the siblings. Neither of them really knew what Cobey intended to do when he caught up with Father Hortensio and the Yaquis. If it was possible, he would probably just slaughter them and take the treasure. In that case, Esteban would probably die a quick death, as he would no longer be of any possible use to the thieves.

Juanita, on the other hand, would take much longer to die, and she knew it.

They were just finishing their skimpy meal when Cobey sauntered toward them. Juanita saw the look in his eyes and caught her breath. She was in for trouble again.

And this time, Wick wasn't here to protect her.

THIRTY-ONE

"Don't move," Preacher hissed at Audie and Nighthawk as Wick came toward them. "Maybe he won't see us."

The three men lay utterly still and silent as Wick approached. His footsteps were heavy, and he thrust brush aside with a great deal of crackling and snapping. But as he came closer, it grew apparent that he was going to miss them. He was about twenty feet to their left as he walked to the edge of the bluff and looked down at the camp.

Preacher glanced in that direction, too, and saw that Cobey had walked over to stand in front of Esteban and Juanita. Preacher wasn't sure what was going on, but as he watched, Wick began to wave an arm above his head and called down to those in the camp below, "Hey, Cobey! Hey, Arnie! Look at me! I'm gonna jump off this cliff and see if I can fly!"

If he jumped, he sure wouldn't fly. He would drop like a rock instead, and the bluff was about thirty feet tall. Such a fall might not kill him, but he would probably wind up with a busted leg or arm, at best. If he landed wrong, the drop might even prove fatal. Preacher didn't really care what happened to Wick—he still remembered the way the giant had wanted to molest Lupita Ojeida back at the trading post—but he didn't much like the idea of watching the be-

hemoth throw himself off the bluff, either, simply because
he was too dim-witted to know what he was doing.

But of course, he and Audie and Nighthawk couldn't try
to stop Wick, either. That would mean revealing their presence and giving up any element of surprise.

Wick spread his arms like they were wings and perched
on the edge of the bluff. Down below, Cobey ripped out a
curse and shouted, "Damn it, Wick, stop! Don't jump!"

Wick hesitated. "But Cobey," he said, "I seen a eagle earlier, and it looked so nice, the way he was flyin' around. I done
tried flappin' my arms, but I can't get off the ground. I figured I ought to jump off some high place to get in the air first,
and then flap my arms."

Cobey thrust out a hand toward him, motioning him back
away from the edge. "Just stay there!" he yelled. "I'll come
up and get you!"

Preacher wasn't worried about Wick noticing them, but
Cobey was a different story. He was a lot smarter and a lot
more alert than the big man. Preacher whispered to Audie and
Nighthawk, "We'd best fade away 'fore Cobey gets up here."

"Ummm," Nighthawk said, and damned if it didn't sound
like a grunt of agreement, Preacher thought.

Staying on their bellies, they crawled backward until they
were well away from the edge of the bluff. They could hear
Cobey cussing as he made his way into the woods and circled around toward the spot where Wick waited for him.
When Preacher and his two companions got to their feet, they
slipped back in the other direction, working away from
Cobey and Wick. Preacher had to hold onto Dog's ruff and
practically drag the big cur along with them. No growls
came from Dog's throat now, but Preacher could tell how
eager he was to get at Cobey and rip him to pieces. Ol' Dog
had always been a good judge of character.

When they could risk talking again, Audie whispered,
"That was a near thing."

"It sure was," Preacher agreed. They had taken a circuitous route, but they were back at the spot where they had left their horses.

"What are we going to do now?"

"There's not enough cover around that camp to let us slip in and get close enough to grab Esteban and Juanita. I reckon we'd best just bide our time and wait for a better chance." Preacher frowned and rubbed his bearded jaw. "Waitin' sure as hell gnaws at my innards, but I don't see as we've got a choice."

Audie nodded. "Perhaps tomorrow will bring a better opportunity."

"I hope so," Preacher said. "Dog here is itchin' to tear into them sons o' bitches, and I know just how he feels."

Juanita felt like she had been given a reprieve. Cobey had not had time to do much more than walk up to her and Esteban when the giant had appeared at the top of the bluff, shouting about jumping off and flying. Cobey had been forced to go up there and bring him down, and once again—although inadvertently this time—Wick had saved her from the man's unwanted attentions.

By the time Cobey had talked Wick into giving up the idea of flying and brought him back down to the camp, Juanita had been stretched out on the ground with Esteban lying next to her, and they had both pretended to be sound asleep. Through one eye opened a mere slit, Juanita saw Cobey looking at them for a moment, and then he had turned away with an irritated shrug. The ruse had worked, and once again she was safe.

But how long, she wondered, could she keep dodging that particular fate?

Morning came much too early. It seemed to Juanita that she had just closed her eyes and gone to sleep for real when Bert McDermott said, "Time to get up, Señorita." At the same time, Bert prodded Esteban's shoulder with his boot.

Juanita let out an unladylike groan as she sat up. Her muscles were almost too stiff and sore to let her move. Esteban sat up without quite as much trouble, but he still looked tired, too. He managed to stand up and then said to Bert, "Help my sister to her feet, please."

Bert smiled. "Sure. I never mind helpin' a pretty lady." He bent to take hold of Juanita's arms.

As he did so, Esteban reached out quickly with his bound hands and plucked the pistol from behind Bert's belt. Stepping back quickly, he raised the gun and cocked the hammer.

"Esteban, no!" Juanita gasped.

Bert let go of her. He had lifted her about a foot from the ground, and when he released her she sat down hard, the impact jarring her. Wide-eyed with fear, Bert stared at Esteban and said quickly, "Be careful with that pistol, kid. The trigger's mighty touchy."

"Then *you* are the one who should be careful, Señor," Esteban grated. "I have nothing to lose."

"What about your sister?"

"I would rather she die quickly than suffer at the hands of you and your friends."

Bert licked his lips. "Listen, kid, I ain't done nothin' to you or her. Fact is, I been tryin' to look out for the two o' you—"

"Damn it!" The exclamation came from the other side of the camp, where Arnie Ross had just rolled out of his blankets. "The kid's got a gun!"

That got the attention of everyone else. Cobey came running out of the trees where he had gone to empty his bladder. He had his rifle with him, and he pointed it at Esteban as he slid to a stop.

"Drop the pistol," he ordered tersely, "or I'll blow your brains out."

"Not before I pull the trigger and kill your man," Esteban said.

"Better listen to him, Cobey," Bert said. "I think he's crazy enough to do it."

"Yeah, I reckon you're right." Cobey shifted his aim a little. "I'll give you to the count of three, Alvarez, and then I'm puttin' a ball through your sister's head."

"Esteban . . ." Juanita said.

"One."

"Give it up, kid," Bert said. "There's no way you can win this one."

"Two," Cobey said.

Esteban swallowed hard. His eyes flicked toward Juanita and took in her drawn, pale features. He sighed.

Cobey had just opened his mouth for the count of three when Esteban lowered the pistol. With the barrel pointing at the ground, he eased the hammer off cock. Bert reached out with a hand that shook just slightly and took the gun out of Esteban's grip.

As soon as Esteban was disarmed, Cobey stepped forward, reversing the rifle in his hands. He drove the butt of the weapon into Esteban's stomach in a brutal blow that made the young man cry out and double over. Cobey lifted the rifle and brought the butt down on the back of Esteban's neck, sending him to the ground. Juanita screamed.

Then, with his face contorted with hate, Cobey loomed over Esteban's fallen figure and turned the rifle again so that the barrel pointed at Esteban's head.

"You little greaser bastard," Cobey said. "I think I'll go ahead and kill you right now."

Preacher, Audie, and Nighthawk had withdrawn about half a mile the night before and made a cold camp high on the side of a hill. They had taken turns standing watch, just to make sure no one discovered them. They'd drawn lots to determine the order, and Preacher wound up with the third watch. So Audie and Nighthawk were still asleep when the sky turned gray with the approach of dawn, but Preacher was wide awake. Telling Dog to stay there, he started down toward the river, curious to see what was going on in the enemy camp.

He was about a hundred yards away from the edge of the bluff, about to belly down and crawl the rest of the way as he and his newfound friends had done the night before, when he heard Juanita scream.

The terrified sound shot through Preacher's brain, and in that instant, he knew what he had been doing wrong for days now—he had been thinking too damned much. Trying to outguess, outfigure, and outtrick his enemies hadn't accomplished anything except to get those two young'uns captured. There was a time for thought and a time for action, and as Juanita's scream died away, Preacher knew the time for action had come.

He lunged forward, gliding through the brush like the great gray wolf he sometimes resembled. His long legs covered the ground in a hurry, and as he reached the edge of the bluff, he looked down and saw that Esteban was on the ground, with Cobey standing over him and pointing a rifle at his head. Preacher snapped his own rifle to his shoulder, drew a bead in less than the blink of an eye, and pressed the trigger.

The rifle roared and kicked against his shoulder, and the heavy ball that it launched should have smashed right through Cobey Larson's evil brain. Instead, just as Preacher pressed the trigger, Arnie spotted him on the bluff and yelled, "Cobey! Look out!"

Cobey twisted instinctively in response to the shout, turning so that the rifle ball on its downward trajectory barely clipped the top of his left shoulder. The impact was still enough to knock him to his knees and make him drop his rifle. He jerked his head up and saw the tall, buckskin-clad figure at the top of the bluff. "Preacher!" he shrieked. "Kill him!"

Preacher dropped the empty rifle, yanked both pistols from behind his belt, and cocked them as he stepped off the edge and started sliding down the slope. The drop-off wasn't sheer right here, but it was steep enough so that Preacher could barely stay upright as he slid down on his heels. He saw Chambers, Stilson, and Wick off to his right, so he swung his right-hand pistol toward them and fired. The weapon was double-shotted, with a heavy charge of powder. One of the balls whined past Chambers's head and made him cry out and duck for cover. The other smashed Stilson's left thighbone and knocked his leg out from under him. Stilson went down with a hoarse cry of agony.

Preacher had time to wonder if the pendulum had swung too far and he had gone to the other extreme, from thinking too much to being a damn fool, and then he reached the base of the bluff and somehow kept his footing instead of sprawling on his face. He used his momentum to send him racing forward, toward Esteban and Juanita. Bert McDermott wheeled toward him and brought up a pistol. Preacher ducked as smoke and flame geysered from the barrel. The ball passed over his head. He threw his empty pistol, sending it spinning through the air to slam across Bert's face and knock him backward, off his feet and out of the fight, at least for a little while.

Cobey was still down, too, but Arnie was on his feet and dangerous, with a pistol in each hand. Preacher weaved to the side as Arnie fired the first one. He felt something pluck at his shirt and knew he had come that close to dying. Arnie fired the other pistol, but he rushed the shot and it missed Preacher's head by a good three inches.

Preacher kicked Cobey in the back as he went by, knocking him sprawling. Esteban seemed to be unconscious. Juanita had crawled over to her brother and thrown herself half on top of him in an obvious effort to protect him. Preacher reached their side and dropped to a knee beside her, lining his left-hand gun on Arnie as he did so. Arnie had emptied both his pistols without any luck, and now grabbed at his powder horn in an attempt to reload, but he froze as Preacher barked, "Hold it!" By striking so swiftly, he had gained a momentary advantage.

Three of his enemies were down, Arnie was momentarily un-armed, Chambers looked confused, unsure of what to do. . . .

That left Wick.

And suddenly, the rising sun was blotted out and a deafen-ing shout assaulted Preacher's ears, and when he twisted his head and brought the pistol around, the dark mass looming above him looked like an avalanche about to fall on him.

But it wasn't an avalanche, just Wick Jimpson, and he crashed down on top of Preacher with stunning force before the mountain man could pull the trigger.

THIRTY-TWO

Wick's crushing weight drove all the breath out of Preacher's lungs and made skyrockets explode through his brain. He gasped for air but couldn't get any. The pistol had been knocked out of his hand, and he couldn't reach his knife because he was pinned down so effectively by the giant. All he could get free was his right arm. It shot up, and he clamped his right hand on Wick's throat. His fingers wouldn't reach all the way around Wick's bull-like neck, but he got the best grip he could and hung on for dear life.

Wick was too close to use his long arms and immense strength effectively. He cuffed Preacher, but even though the mountain man's head was rocked from side to side by the blows, they lacked the killing power of one of Wick's normal punches. The muscles in Preacher's arm and shoulder bunched and corded as he poured all the power he could into his strangling grip. Wick's face began to turn a dark red.

Preacher didn't know what else was going on in the camp. All his attention was focused on Wick. In the back of his brain, he knew that even if he was able to escape from the big man, by now Cobey, Arnie, and the others would be ready to kill him. His only real hope was that Audie and Nighthawk had heard the shots and would come a-runnin' to join the fray.

Wick suddenly jerked and stiffened, and Preacher heaved to the side as hard as he could. Wick rolled off him, leaving Preacher free to gulp down a huge lungful of life-giving air. Preacher rolled, too, and saw an arrow protruding from Wick's back. The feathers and the markings on the shaft identified it as a Crow arrow, so Preacher knew that Nighthawk had shown up. As he scrambled to his feet, a rifle roared on top of the bluff. The shot drove Arnie back, even though it didn't hit him. A few feet away, Preacher saw Cobey crawling toward the rifle he had dropped earlier when Preacher's shot grazed him.

Spotting the pistol that *he* had dropped, Preacher rolled toward it and snatched it off the ground. He twisted toward Cobey, expecting to trade shots, but to his surprise he saw Cobey surge onto his feet and run toward the river. Arrows whistled around his head as he ran.

Preacher pushed himself up and looked around. Arnie and Cobey were fleeing from the barrage of arrows and rifle fire laid down from the top of the bluff by Nighthawk and Audie. Chambers and Bert McDermott had hold of the wounded Stilson, one on either side of him, and they were hustling away from here as fast as they could, too. Wick still lay facedown, the arrow sticking up from his back.

The thieves reached their tethered horses and ducked behind the nervous animals, using them for cover. Cobey and Arnie jerked the reins of their mounts loose from the trees where they were tied and sprang into the saddle, ducking as lead sang around their heads. McDermott and Chambers hoisted Stilson onto another of the horses and pressed the reins into his hands, then lunged for their own mounts. Bert grunted in pain as a rifle ball clipped his arm, but he managed to make it into the saddle. He kicked his horse into a run, following Cobey and Arnie. Chambers and Stilson did likewise.

Preacher lowered his pistol, unfired. The fleeing hard cases had quickly drawn out of range. Dog chased them for a short distance, barking furiously, before turning around and trotting back to Preacher, who now knelt beside Esteban and Juanita.

The young woman was conscious and seemed to be all right. Preacher helped her up and then rolled Esteban onto his back. Pressing a couple of fingers into the young man's neck, Preacher found a strong pulse.

"I reckon he'll make it," he said reassuringly to Juanita. "Looks like he took a hard wallop."

"Si, and he would be dead now if not for you, Señor Preacher." Impulsively, Juanita threw her arms around the mountain man. *"Gracias, señor, mil gracias!"*

Even as he clumsily patted her on the back, Preacher heard hoofbeats and looked over Juanita's shoulder to see Audie and Nighthawk riding along the riverbank toward them. Nighthawk was leading Horse. The two trappers had circled around to a point where they could descend the bluff with the horses.

Preacher glanced in the other direction, where Cobey, Arnie, and the others had disappeared around a bend in the Purgatoire, back the way they had come from the day before. Although they had been forced to flee by the deadly accurate rifle and arrow fire from Audie and Nighthawk, Preacher didn't believe for a second that the hard cases had given up and would not come back. Cobey wouldn't abandon his goal of getting his hands on that treasure, and now he would be even hungrier for vengeance on Preacher and the Alvarez siblings, not to mention Preacher's newfound allies.

Gently, Preacher disengaged himself from Juanita's hug and turned to Esteban. He lightly slapped the young man's face until Esteban began to come around. "Sorry, amigo," Preacher said, "but we got to get movin', 'fore that bunch o' thieves and killers regroups and comes after us."

With Preacher's help, Esteban sat up and shook his head groggily. When his gaze focused on Preacher, he exclaimed in surprise. "Preacher! Where did you come from?"

Juanita said, "He came down that bluff like an angel descending from Heaven."

"First time I recollect that anybody compared me to an angel," Preacher said with a grin. He helped Esteban to his feet. "I been followin' Cobey's bunch with a couple o' fellas I ran into yesterday. That's Audie and Nighthawk." He nodded to the little man and the Crow warrior in turn.

"I'm pleased and honored to meet you, Señorita," Audie said, taking off his coonskin cap and bending low in a bow without leaving the saddle. He straightened, replaced his cap on his head, and went on. "Preacher, we'd better light a shuck out of here while we still can."

"Ummm," Nighthawk concurred.

Juanita said worriedly, "We don't have enough horses."

"I reckon Nighthawk's pony can carry double," Preacher said, "especially if you ride with him, since you're lighter. Horse is plenty strong enough to carry me and Esteban for a ways."

"Where are we going?"

Preacher looked east along the river, opposite the direction in which the hard cases had fled. "The padre and the Yaquis and them wagons are still up ahead somewheres. They'll be bound for the old mission. I reckon we ought to head for there, too."

Esteban said, "You do not intend to try to take back the treasure from Father Hortensio, do you? I am angry with him for what he did, but still, the gold and the relics belong to the Church. . . ."

"The Church is welcome to 'em," Preacher said. "What I was thinkin' was that Mission Santo Domingo might make a pretty good place to fort up when Cobey and his bunch come after us. We got to get there first, though."

Without any more delay, they mounted up, Preacher and Esteban on Horse, Juanita climbing onto Nighthawk's spotted pony in front of the stoic Crow. The riders set off at a ground-eating lope, not pushing the mounts too hard since two of them were carrying double, but not wasting any time, either. They left behind the fire, which was now dying out in its circle of stones, and the arrow-pierced body of Wick Jimpson.

Preacher and his friends were out of sight when Wick suddenly stirred. The giant groaned and tried to push himself up on hands and knees, only to fail and sprawl out again. He lay there for a while, gathering his strength. When he was ready to try to move again, he let out a yell and climbed unsteadily all the way to his feet. His broad face contorted in a grimace at the pain in his back. He reached behind him and found the arrow. His thick fingers closed around the shaft and snapped it off, which left the head buried inside his back, just under his shoulder blade. A few inches of the shaft remained attached to the arrowhead, sticking out through the blood-stained hole in the back of Wick's shirt.

He looked at the arrow, wondering where it had come from, and then threw it aside, not really caring. All that mattered was that when he looked around, he didn't see the señorita anywhere. He saw tracks, though, hoofprints that led off to the east. That must be where the señorita had gone, Wick's muddled brain decided.

He shuffled off in that direction and then broke into a shambling run. He didn't know where Juanita had gone, but he was going to find her. He didn't care if he had to run all day and all night and all the next day.

One way or another, he was going to find the señorita.

Chambers had never seen Cobey so angry. The man looked like he was going to explode with rage. Cobey had lost his hat somewhere, and as he paced back and forth he raked his fingers through his long, tangled hair.

"I'll skin him alive!" Cobey ranted, and Chambers knew who he was talking about. There was no doubt that Cobey referred to Preacher. "He's got more lives than a damned cat, but we'll see how long he makes it once I start peelin' the hide off him, one strip at a time!"

"Why don't you gimme a hand here?" Arnie suggested from where he knelt beside Chuck Stilson. He had been working on Stilson's wounded leg ever since they had stopped and Stilson had lost consciousness and toppled out of the saddle, maybe hurting himself even worse.

Arnie had used a tourniquet to get the bleeding stopped and cleaned away enough of the crimson gore to see what he was dealing with. He stretched Stilson's leg out and heard the ends of the shattered bone grating against each other. Even though he was out cold, Stilson groaned loudly and shifted around, instinctively trying to get away from the pain that engulfed him.

"We need to get this leg splinted," Arnie muttered as Cobey continued to pace and rave.

"Perhaps I can help," Chambers offered. "What do you need me to do?"

Arnie looked up at the professor. "See if you can find a couple of fairly straight pieces of tree limb, about twice as big around as your thumb and maybe two feet long. I can use them as splints if you can find some like that."

"I'll see what I can do." Chambers hurried off on that errand.

"What about me?" Cobey demanded. "I'm hit, too. This shoulder hurts like blazes. Damn it, my arm ain't completely healed up from where Preacher shot me before, and now the bastard's shot me again!"

Without looking up from Stilson, Arnie said, "I'll look at you when I get a chance, Cobey. Bert got nicked, too, you know."

Bert McDermott stood to one side, calmly tying a strip of cloth around his bullet-burned upper arm, using his teeth to hold the makeshift bandage as he knotted it tight. When he was finished, he said, "Don't worry about me, Arnie. I'll be all right."

Cobey threw his hands in the air. "Ever'thing's shot to hell! It's all fallin' apart around me!"

It was true they'd had a run of bad luck . . . but some of it was Cobey's fault. They shouldn't have brought the girl and her brother with them. Either kill them or let them go, Arnie thought. Either of those things would have been better. The youngsters wouldn't have represented much of a threat, and having a pretty girl around where gents could fight over her always led to trouble sooner or later. And if they had released Esteban and Juanita unharmed, Preacher might not have come after them. . . .

That was pretty unlikely, of course. Once a man like Preacher got his dander up, he wasn't going to just go away. He would have felt like he had a score to settle, and nothing short of death would stop him.

That was still the case. Preacher had those kids back now—although there was no way of knowing what sort of shape Esteban was in after having been attacked by Cobey—but he was still a threat. For one thing, he was between Cobey and that gold, so they would have to deal with him sooner or later. Cobey wasn't going to give up the treasure.

Chambers came up carrying a couple of pine branches. "Will these do?" he asked as he held them out to Arnie.

The fat man took them and nodded. "Yeah, they look fine, Professor. Good job."

He ripped up a homespun shirt from his own possibles bag and used it as bandages, tying them as tightly as possible around the holes in Stilson's leg where the pistol ball had gone in and out. When he loosened the tourniquet, the bandages reddened a little from fresh blood, but not too much. Arnie thought there was a good chance Stilson wouldn't bleed to death, anyway.

Carefully, he laid the branches on either side of the wounded leg and tied them in place with rawhide thongs. He thought the bone was back together as best he could get it, although it was possible the ball had pulverized enough of the bone so that it would never heal properly. This leg might wind up shorter than the other, and Stilson would always have a bad limp. Better to be crippled for life, though, than dead.

Chambers watched with interest as Arnie patched up the wound, and after a few minutes he said, "Am I imagining things, or have you had some medical training, Mr. Ross?"

Arnie shrugged. "When I was younger, I thought I might be a sawbones. I apprenticed to one for a while. It never worked out, though."

"A pity. You have some definite skills in that area."

Impatiently, Cobey demanded, "You got Stilson ready to ride yet?"

Still on his knees beside the unconscious man, Arnie looked up and said, "He ain't gonna be doin' any ridin' for a while, Cobey. Not for a day or two, at least. If he does, it'll hurt like hell—"

Cobey snorted. "I don't care if he's in pain."

"And that wound will open up again and he'll bleed to death," Arnie went on doggedly.

"We're all hurt," Cobey said with a shrug. "You got your arm half gnawed off by that damn dog. The only one who ain't been hurt is the professor, for God's sake!"

"Just fortunate, I suppose," Chambers said with a smile.

Cobey ignored him and said, "So Stilson has got to ride. We have to get movin'. We can still catch up to the priest and get that treasure."

"Preacher will likely be joined up with him by then," Arnie pointed out.

"Fine with me. I want another shot at that son of a bitch."

"I know you do, but Stilson can't ride." Arnie sighed. "You and Bert and the professor can go after them, I reckon. I'll stay and take care of Chuck."

Cobey looked at him intently and asked, "You sure about that?"

"Yeah. We can't just leave him alone."

Cobey pulled his pistol, cocked it, and fired. The action

was so swift and unexpected that Arnie had no chance to stop him. The ball struck Stilson in the middle of the forehead and made him jerk and arch his back off the ground as it bored on through his brain and exploded his skull. His body sagged back to the ground in death.

Cobey lowered the smoking pistol and said, "I reckon we can leave him and get after Preacher and that treasure now."

Arnie, Bert, and Chambers stared at Stilson's lifeless body and his shattered head. Finally, Arnie nodded and said in a resigned voice, "I reckon we can."

THIRTY-THREE

Horse, Nighthawk's pony, and Audie's stubby-legged mount had all had a night's rest, so they were fresh and strong. Preacher set a brisk pace that day, although he did call a halt more often than he might have otherwise, since two of the animals were carrying double and he didn't want them to get too tired.

They were low on supplies, too, and everyone was hungry as the day wore on. There was no time to stop and hunt for fresh meat, though. Preacher was certain that Cobey and the others would have regrouped by now and would be coming after them.

For a change, though, the odds were even. With Jimpson dead and Stilson badly wounded, that left just Cobey, Arnie, Chambers, and McDermott to go after the treasure. Preacher figured that he, Audie, Nighthawk, and Esteban were a match for them. Add Juanita into the mix—she had proved that she had plenty of pluck, and Preacher knew she could be counted on—and they actually outnumbered their pursuers. There were the two Yaquis to consider, too, if Preacher and his friends could catch up to the wagons before the next fracas. Preacher knew better than to be overly optimistic, but he was starting to feel like they now had a good chance of coming through this alive.

That afternoon they left the mountains behind and found themselves once again in the foothills, heading east toward the vast rolling plains. And as they descended from the mountains, Preacher's keen eyes spotted the wagons miles ahead of them, so far in the distance they were little more than dots. He called a halt to let the horses rest, and while they were doing that he got out his spyglass and trained it on the far-off vehicles.

Those were definitely the wagons from the Alvarez expedition. He couldn't see the drivers from this angle, but he was confident they were Pablo and Joaquin. Nor did he see Father Hortensio. But the padre would be there, Preacher knew. After everything that had happened, the priest wouldn't let that treasure out of his sight.

None of the others seemed to have noticed, so Preacher lowered the spyglass and pointed. "There are the wagons," he announced.

Esteban and Juanita were standing next to Nighthawk's pony. They looked up sharply at the sound of Preacher's voice and followed his pointing finger. Esteban took a step forward, excitement animating his body. "I see them," he said. "Are you sure they are the ones we seek, Preacher?"

"Certain sure," Preacher responded. "For one thing, it ain't likely there'd be another pair o' wagons out here right now. We're well west o' the Santa Fe Trail. For another thing, I recognize 'em, as well as the teams pullin' 'em."

Esteban crossed himself and murmured a prayer. "Can we catch up to them before they reach the mission?"

"Probably. Loaded down the way they are, they ain't movin' very fast."

Juanita looked around at him. "Even if we do not catch up to them before then, we know that is where they are going, do we not?"

Preacher nodded. "I reckon."

"But that bunch of brigands and highwaymen will be

coming on quickly, too," Audie pointed out. "If they catch up while the wagons are still out in the open, they can pick off the mules, pin the wagons down, and make things very difficult for all of us."

"Dang right," Preacher agreed. "That's why we need to catch up and hurry the padre along with those wagons as much as we can."

A short time later, they mounted up again and rode on, and now there was an even greater urgency goading them through the foothills after the wagons.

Wick ran until he couldn't run anymore, and then he collapsed facedown on the ground. He wasn't sure where he was, wasn't even sure if he was still going the right direction. He couldn't see the tracks left by the horses.

But he heard the river and knew he had to follow it. He had trouble remembering exactly *why* he was supposed to follow the river, but he knew he was. After a while, enough of his strength came back to him so that he was able to push himself to his feet and stumble on.

Juanita. Her face filled his thoughts, and his vision of her kept him moving.

He was thinking about her when he passed out again, and this time he didn't even feel himself hit the ground.

Arnie thought it was odd when they reached the spot where Preacher had jumped them that morning and he didn't see any sign of Wick. The last time he had seen the giant before they'd been forced to flee before the withering fire of whoever Preacher had with him, Wick had been lying on the ground with an arrow protruding from his back. He had certainly looked dead, and that was how Arnie expected to find him.

The footprints told an obvious story, though. Wick's feet

were huge, like the rest of him, and the tracks he had left showed him heading off to the east, the same way Preacher and the others had gone.

"Wick's a good boy," Cobey said when Arnie pointed out what he had discovered. "He's gone after those bastards."

More than likely Wick was just thinking about the señorita, Arnie mused. Regardless of that, though, he was glad that Wick wasn't dead after all.

They pushed on, with Bert leading Chuck Stilson's horse, since, of course, Stilson didn't need the mount anymore. It was past the middle of the afternoon when Cobey exclaimed, "What the hell!" and pointed to a large, shaggy shape lying on the ground up ahead.

"That's Wick!" Arnie said as he urged his horse forward. When he reached the massive form, he swung quickly out of the saddle and dropped to a knee at Wick's side.

Wick's back rose and fell as he breathed, so he was still alive. The arrow below his shoulder blade was broken off so that only a few inches of the shaft remained. A large blood-stain soaked his shirt around the wound. Arnie knew that he couldn't pull the arrowhead out; that would just do more damage. It would have to be cut out, and that would be a tricky job, requiring plenty of light and a good place to work and a lot of bandages and hot water—none of which he had here and now.

"Is he alive?" Cobey asked from horseback.

"Yeah. He's lost quite a bit of blood, though."

"Can you wake him up and get him on a horse? We've got an extra one, you know."

They had an extra mount because Cobey had murdered Chuck Stilson. But, all in all, Arnie was willing to trade Wick's life for Stilson's. He had known Wick a lot longer, and Stilson hadn't been very friendly, when you got right down to it.

"I'll try," Arnie said. "Somebody gimme a hand. I need to roll him onto his side."

"We can't take too long at this," Cobey cautioned.

"Just give me a few minutes."

"I'll help you," Chambers offered as he dismounted. Together, he and Arnie rolled Wick onto his right side. Then Arnie took out a small silver flask and uncorked it. There wasn't much in the flask, and it was the last of his whiskey, carefully horded over the past couple of weeks, but Wick needed it now. Arnie pried the big man's mouth open and poured a little of the fiery liquor in it.

Wick sputtered and snorted and opened his eyes. He tried to roll onto his back, but Chambers was there to stop him. That would have just driven the arrowhead even deeper into his body. Blinking in confusion, Wick said, "A-Arnie . . . ? Where's Cobey?"

"He's here, don't worry," Arnie assured him. "You'll be all right, Wick, but you got to get up and get on a horse we've got for you."

"I was . . . goin' after . . . the señorita . . ."

"So are we," Arnie told him. "Come with us and we'll find her."

"Oh. All right." Wick tried to push himself upright, but he gasped and slumped down again. "The world sure is . . . spinnin' around all funny . . ."

"Just take it slow and easy."

"Not slow," Cobey snapped.

The sound of his voice made Wick look at him. "Hey . . . Cobey," he said. "I'm sorry . . . I got hurt."

"Just get up and get on Stilson's horse," Cobey ordered.

"Where is . . . ol' Chuck?"

"Dead," Arnie said quietly.

"Oh. I'm sorry."

"You didn't have nothin' to do with it, Wick." Arnie glanced toward Cobey, who was clearly growing more impatient by the second. He was damned if he was going to ride off and leave Wick here to die by himself. He said, "Come on, Wick, you can do it. Help us, Professor."

Together, he and Chambers got Wick on his feet and

helped him climb into the saddle on Stilson's horse. Wick's horse had run off during the fighting that morning, and they hadn't seen it since. Stilson's mount was almost as big and strong, though. It could carry Wick, at least for a while.

"Come on, let's go, let's go," Cobey urged. They set off, riding beside a long, thick clump of brush.

They hadn't yet passed the brush when the air was filled with the sound of rifles being cocked, and a strident voice ordered, "*Alto, señores!* Hands up, *por favor,* or my men will fire!"

It was almost sundown when Preacher and his companions rode down a hill, through a screen of trees, and out into a broad, open park. On the far side of the park were the two wagons. Preacher said, "Come on, Dog!" and heeled Horse into a run that carried him and Esteban swiftly across the open ground. He swung out a little to the side so that as he approached he could see Pablo and Joaquin whipping the teams mercilessly, doing their best to get more speed out of the mules and horses pulling the vehicles.

But even though Horse had to be a little tired, the big stallion seemed to enjoy stretching his legs. He ran easily, eating up the gap between him and the wagons.

Esteban rode behind Preacher, holding on to the mountain man. Over the thundering hoofbeats, he called out, "What are we going to do?"

"Stop them wagons until your sister and the others catch up!" Preacher replied. They had almost reached the rear wagon.

"Look out!" Esteban suddenly cried.

Preacher had already seen Father Hortensio poke his head out the back of the wagon. The priest had some sort of weapon in his hands. As Preacher galloped closer, he saw that it was an old blunderbuss. Smoke spurted from the barrel of the ancient gun. A touch of Preacher's heels sent Horse swerving sharply to the side. He heard a humming in the air as the heavy, slow-moving ball went past them.

Father Hortensio had claimed that he was a man of peace and could not resort to violent measures. Obviously that didn't hold true when he believed he was doing the Lord's work. But the important thing was that he didn't have time to reload before Preacher caught up to him.

"Get ready to take the saddle!" the mountain man told Esteban.

"All right, but what—"

They drew even with the rear of the wagon. Preacher vaulted out of the saddle, leaping the short distance to the wagon. He caught hold of the tailgate, and his lean muscles bunched as he pulled himself inside the vehicle. Father Hortensio was fumbling with the blunderbuss, trying to reload it, when Preacher crashed into him, knocking the gun out of his hands and driving him backward onto a stack of gold ingots. Those heavy bars with their dull sheen might look pretty, but they didn't provide a sort place to land. Father Hortensio groaned and lay there, half-stunned.

Preacher looked through the opening in the canvas cover at the front of the wagon and saw Joaquin looking back at him over his shoulder, wide-eyed with fear and surprise. Preacher pulled a pistol from behind his belt, leveled it, and ordered, "Stop this wagon—now!"

Joaquin hauled back on the reins. The wagon began to slow. Father Hortensio regained his wits and came up off the pile of gold bars to lunge at Preacher with his hands outstretched. "No!" he shouted. "You cannot have the treasure! It belongs to the Holy Mother Church!"

Preacher put his free hand on the priest's chest and held him off even as Father Hortensio flailed punches at him. A shove sent Father Hortensio stumbling back against the ingots again. As he tried to catch his balance, the wagon lurched to a halt.

Looking past Joaquin, Preacher saw that Esteban had

caught up to the other wagon on Horse and managed to get Pablo to stop, too, probably at gunpoint.

"Damn it, settle down!" he snapped at Father Hortensio. "We ain't come to steal the treasure. You'd know better if you'd just stop and think about it."

"You must not take the holy relics," Father Hortensio babbled. "And the gold will rebuild the Mission Santo Domingo and do many good works—"

"That's fine," Preacher cut in. "But that won't happen unless you listen to me, Padre. Larson and his bunch are still behind us somewhere, and they still want to get their hands on that loot."

"You cannot trade it to those men for Señorita Juanita's safety. I am sorry, but—"

"They don't have the señorita anymore, blast it! She's with us now."

That finally got through to Father Hortensio. Preacher pointed, and the priest looked across the park to where Juanita, Audie, and Nighthawk were riding quickly toward them.

"A savage!" Father Hortensio exclaimed. "And . . . a child?"

"Nope. He may be little, but he's all man. That's Audie, and the redskin with him is called Nighthawk. They're friends o' mine. They helped me get Esteban and Juanita back from Larson's bunch."

Father Hortensio looked confused. "But . . . Esteban was at the cave where the treasure was stored. . . ."

"A whole heap has happened since then," Preacher said curtly, "and I ain't got time to explain it all. Come on out for a minute, and then we'll get goin' again."

They couldn't afford much of a delay, but he wanted to be sure Father Hortensio and the two Yaquis understood the situation. When everyone was gathered beside the wagons, Preacher spoke swiftly.

"I think Larson's only got three men left who are fit to

fight," he said. "So that's four o' them against seven of us, eight if you count the señorita. We got the upper hand, but not if they catch us out in the open. That's why we got to get back to the mission as fast as we can. If we can get the wagons inside what's left of the sanctuary, those old walls will give us good cover."

"You think we will have to fight those men?" Father Hortensio asked.

"I'd count on it, if I was you," Preacher replied with a grim nod. "Cobey ain't gonna give up as long as there's breath in his body. He's crazy-mad now, not just for the gold but for our scalps as well. That's why we got to fort up."

"But . . . Santo Domingo is a mission, not a fort," the priest protested. "It is a holy place. There should not be a battle fought there."

"But, Father," Esteban said, "what better place for good men to struggle with evil?"

"True, true," Father Hortensio murmured. After a moment, he nodded. "Very well. We will reach the mission as swiftly as possible and make our stand there."

"Now you're talkin'," Preacher said. "Let's get these wagons movin'. We're all on the same side again."

"The side of the angels," Father Hortensio said.

Preacher just hoped that before it was all over, the angels wouldn't be singing for *them*.

THIRTY-FOUR

Cobey, Arnie, and the others sat rigidly in their saddles as a dozen men in white trousers, blue uniform jackets, and stiff black hats emerged from the brush carrying rifles. They were Mexican soldiers, members of the army of the dictator, General Santa Anna. Their leader was a slim young officer who carried a saber.

"I am Lieutenant Fernando Escobar," he announced. "We are looking for a young señor and señorita who are supposed to be in this area. Have you seen any wagons recently, Señores?"

Cobey didn't answer the question. Instead he asked one of his own. "Why are you lookin' for 'em?"

"It was reported that they might be in danger, and since they are from an old family with influence in the capital, we were sent to search for them. It was lucky my patrol was close by when the report was made by the man who owns the trading post near the pass into the Sangre de Cristos. We have been riding around here for several days, searching for Señor and Señorita Alvarez."

It was pure luck that had kept Preacher and the others from running into these Mex soldiers, Cobey knew. If they had, any hopes he had of latching onto that treasure would be gone now. As it was, though, he might be able to take advantage of this chance encounter. He remembered hearing that nearly all of the troops in Santa Anna's army were conscripts. Many of them had, in fact, been taken out of prisons in Mexico City and elsewhere and forced into service as soldiers. As he looked at them now, Cobey saw that with the exception of Lieutenant Escobar, the patrol was composed of men who might as well have been cutthroats and brigands.

Men with whom he had something in common, in other words.

"Arnie, you speak pretty good Mex," Cobey said quietly to his second in command. "Tell those soldiers that if they come to work for me, I'll make 'em all rich men. *Ricos.*"

His use of that word perked up some interest among the stolid-faced troops. Escobar flushed and said, "Señor, what is this you say? These men are under my command—"

"Tell 'em, Arnie," Cobey cut in.

In a torrent of rapid Spanish, Arnie blurted out Cobey's offer. The Mexican soldiers instantly looked interested. Cobey was a gringo, which meant he was not to be trusted, but he was promising wealth, and besides, they were hundreds of miles from Mexico City and Santa Anna, as feared as he might be, could do nothing to them over a distance such as that. Cobey could practically see those thoughts going through their heads, and he saw the greed that sparked in their eyes.

"Tell you what," he said. "I'm gonna kill the lieutenant, and then they won't have to worry about him no more."

The young officer yelped in panic and began to claw at the pistol holstered at his waist.

Cobey drew, cocked, and fired before Escobar could come close to getting his own weapon out. The ball slammed into the lieutenant's chest and picked him up off his feet, driving him backward into the brush. His legs twitched a few times where they stuck out, and then he lay still.

A few of the soldiers looked surprised, but none of them

seemed overly concerned about the unexpected fate of their commanding officer. Cobey smiled at them and said, "You boys work for me now. *Ricos,* each and every one of you."

Arnie translated. One of the soldiers thrust his rifle into the air above his head and shouted, *"Viva el gringo!"*

Cobey grinned. In a matter of a few minutes, this twist of fate meant that he had gone from potentially being outnumbered to having his own little army.

Preacher was sure enough in for a surprise when Cobey and his newfound troops showed up to take that treasure.

Even though the foothills were still rugged in places, the trail the wagons were following was easy enough so that Preacher decided to keep them moving, even after night fell. There was enough moonlight for him to be able to recognize the place where they were supposed to cut off away from the river and head straight across a stretch of relatively flat land toward the old mission.

He knew the chances were that Cobey and the rest of the gang of thieves would keep moving, too. It was a race now, to see if they could reach Santo Domingo before the killers caught up to them.

Juanita had climbed into one of the wagons to get some much-needed rest, and she had persuaded Esteban to come with her. The young man had been through a lot in the past few days, and Preacher told him that he needed to recuperate while he could. Nighthawk was scouting ahead, and Audie had fallen behind to keep an eye on their back trail, so that he could warn them if the pursuit approached. That left Preacher to ride alongside the wagons.

He was moving along easily beside the lead wagon when Father Hortensio climbed onto the driver's seat next to Pablo. "I must speak to you, Señor Preacher," the priest said stiffly.

"What about, Padre?"

"About what happened back there in the mountains, when I took the treasure away from Esteban."

"Yeah, I been wonderin' a mite about that," Preacher mused. "How'd you get that gold outta there?"

"We made bags out of our clothing and dragged them with the horses. It was difficult."

"I expect it was."

"But that is not what I wish to discuss," Father Hortensio said. "I want to explain to you why I did what I did."

Preacher looked over at him and said, "You don't owe me no explanations, Padre. You knew we were gonna try to trade that loot for Juanita's life, and you didn't want to risk losin' it."

"It is not *loot*. Those relics are holy—"

"Yeah, so I've heard."

"And the gold belongs to the Church," Father Hortensio went on stubbornly.

"You agreed that Esteban and Juanita ought to have a share of it for what they did to help."

"The archbishop agreed. I would not have. Devotion to the Church should not require a . . . a payoff, as you gringos say."

"Well, maybe not," Preacher said. "But there ain't anything wrong with bein' fair about things, neither. That ain't really any o' my business, though. I'm just here because I don't want to see a low-down polecat like that fella Cobey get what he's after. I want those young'uns to make it back home all right, too."

"As do I. I simply want to make it clear that I offer no apologies for anything I have done. I followed my conscience, that is all."

"Fine. I reckon we understand each other. Even a heathen like me can have a conscience, you know."

Father Hortensio hesitated and then said, "Perhaps I was wrong about that."

"About what?"

"About you being a heathen, Señor Preacher."

Preacher grinned. "Well, thanks . . . I reckon."

The party moved on through the night, stopping only occasionally to let the animals rest. Audie came up and reported no signs of their pursuers . . . yet. Preacher remained convinced that Cobey and the others were still back there somewhere, though.

Along toward morning, when the moon was low in the sky and the stars were losing their twinkle against the graying of the sky, Nighthawk rode back to the wagons and gave Preacher an emphatic nod as he said, "Ummm."

"You spotted the old mission?" Preacher said. Nighthawk nodded again.

That was good news, but Preacher hadn't really had time to appreciate it when the swift rataplan of hoofbeats from behind the wagons warned that Audie was approaching. The little man wouldn't be riding that fast, Preacher sensed, unless trouble was riding right behind him.

Preacher wheeled Horse around as Audie raced up out of the night's tail end. "They're back there, Preacher," he said, "and coming up fast! I thought you said there were only four or five of them."

"That's all I know about," Preacher replied as he tensed at the implications of Audie's words.

"Well, there are more than that now. There at least a dozen riders, probably more."

"Maybe it ain't Cobey's bunch. . . ." Preacher began.

But who else could it be, he asked himself as his words came to an abrupt stop. Somehow, Cobey had gone and found himself some more men, just when Preacher had started to feel good about the odds for a change.

"How far back you reckon they are?"

"Not much more than a mile."

Preacher turned to Nighthawk. "How far are we from those ruins?"

"Half mile," the Crow said, the first time Preacher had heard him utter actual words.

"Esteban! Juanita! Padre!"

Preacher's voice rang out, summoning the three he had called from the interior of the wagons. As they looked out from the covered beds of the vehicles, Preacher waved Pablo and Joaquin on.

"Keep them teams movin'!" he ordered. "Get all the speed out of 'em you can!" To the priest and the Alvarez siblings, he went on. "Those hard cases are closin' in behind us, comin' up in a hurry. We'll make a run for the old mission and try to get there before they catch up to us, but I want all the guns loaded and ready, because one way or another there's bound to be a fight! Audie and Nighthawk and me will drop back a ways and see if we can slow them down some, but don't count on that. Padre, keep them Yaquis o' yours pushin' the teams. Esteban, you and Juanita get ready to fight if you have to."

Esteban nodded, an eager look on his face in the graying light. "*Sí*, Preacher. We will be ready."

"Be careful!" Juanita called to them as they turned their horses to ride back in the direction they had come from. Preacher told Dog to stay with the wagons and waved a hand in farewell.

As they rode back along the path they had been following, Audie said to Preacher, "The señorita is quite fond of you, my friend."

"What?" Preacher said, genuinely surprised.

"I'd say she's rather smitten, in fact."

"Aw, hell, you're crazy. She's just a kid."

"On the contrary, she's a full-grown woman, and you're not more than six or seven years older than she is."

"Well, that ain't the way it seems," Preacher said. "The way she growed up, and the way I've lived since I come to the frontier, makes for a whole lot more difference than a few years."

"I'm just saying that there was more to her admonition than a simple wish for you to be careful."

Preacher had a hard time believing that, but maybe Audie was right. It didn't really matter, though, because first they all had to live through the next few hours. If they accomplished that, then he could worry about how Juanita really felt about him, Preacher told himself.

"There they are," he said suddenly as he spotted a large group of riders coming toward them across a stretch of open ground about five hundred yards wide. Audie had been right about the number. There were about a dozen-and-a-half men in the party. The dawn light was strong enough now so that Preacher could see the white trousers and blue jackets on some of the riders. He exclaimed, "Damn it, some o' them are Mexican soldiers!"

Audie whipped out his spyglass and studied the oncoming horsemen. "You're correct about that," he said, "but I also see the one you called Cobey and several of his companions from our earlier clash, including that gigantic fellow."

"Wick's still alive?" That was as surprising as the fact that Cobey's bunch had been joined by what seemed to be a patrol of Mexican cavalry.

"He's with them," Audie confirmed. "There's no mistaking an individual of that size."

Preacher thought quickly. "Way back when all this started, I told the fella who owns the tradin' post to get word to Santa Fe and send the army up here to look for those youngsters. Maybe Cobey and the others are prisoners."

The sound of several shots rolled over the foothills, and Preacher saw distant spurts of smoke from rifle muzzles.

"That doesn't appear to be the case," Audie said dryly as he put away his spyglass. "As a matter of fact, it looks more like Cobey is in command."

"Damn it!" Preacher grated. As if the situation hadn't been bad enough already, now they had to fight the Mex army, too. If word of that ever got back to Mexico City, he'd sure be in Dutch with ol' Santa Anna. Of course, if he lived through this mess, it was entirely possible he'd never drift down this way again. . . .

He lifted his rifle and cocked it. "We'll let 'em get a little closer and then give 'em a volley. They ain't in range yet, but if they want to waste powder and shot, that's fine with me."

Audie and Nighthawk got their rifles ready to fire, too, and the three men waited patiently as their enemies galloped closer and closer. More shots blasted out from Cobey's group, and some of the balls came close enough for Preacher to hear them. Finally, he said, "I reckon that'll do," and calmly lifted his rifle to his shoulder.

He could see Cobey, so naturally he drew his bead on the leader, announcing it so that Audie and Nighthawk could choose different targets. No more words were necessary. Preacher took a deep breath and stroked the trigger.

The rifle boomed and kicked and geysered smoke. When the gray cloud cleared, Preacher saw that two saddles had been emptied. Unfortunately, neither of them belonged to Cobey. Two of the Mexican soldiers were down. Either Preacher's shot had missed entirely, or the ball had gone past Cobey and struck one of the soldiers. Didn't really matter. Preacher was glad to have inflicted some damage on the enemy but disappointed that Cobey was still drawing breath.

He said, "Let's go," and wheeled Horse around. Audie and Nighthawk turned their mounts as well, and the three men galloped after the wagons, reloading as they rode. That was a tricky business, but they all had plenty of experience at it.

When they were ready, Preacher reined in and turned Horse again. Three more shots rang out, and another Mexican soldier hit the dirt. A second one reeled in the saddle and clutched a wounded shoulder, but he didn't fall.

"It's me, I'm afraid," Audie said with a sigh. "With its shorter barrel, this rifle of mine doesn't have quite the carrying power it needs for this fight."

"Don't worry about that," Preacher told him. "I reckon the range will be closer later."

"Undoubtedly correct. Well, we've accounted for three of them, at least."

"Yeah, and they're slowin' down. Cobey may have got those

Mex troopers to work with him somehow, but right about now they're startin' to wonder if they've made a mistake."

"Ummm," Nighthawk said.

"Yeah, you're right. Let's light a shuck outta here."

They raced on toward the mission. As they came in sight of the old, tumbled-down walls, they saw the wagons rolling into the shelter of the ruined sanctuary. Remembering what had happened here before, Preacher muttered, "I hope they remember to keep their eyes open for snakes."

"The ruins are populated by serpents?" Audie asked.

"Diamondbacks. Big fat ones."

A shudder went through the little man. "I hate snakes."

"You and me, both," Preacher said.

They rode on, and minutes later entered the ruins themselves. Preacher noted with approval that the Yaquis had pulled the wagons behind the wall that had the most of it remaining. It was high enough to completely shield the vehicles.

He and Audie and Nighthawk dismounted and led their horses into a corner where they would be protected from two directions. Then Preacher walked quickly over to the wagons and found Esteban, Juanita, and Father Hortensio waiting for him. "Good job gettin' here fast like you did," he told them. "We got a chance now."

"Yes, but how much of one?" Father Hortensio said. "We're outnumbered again, are we not?"

"Yeah, but we got the fort," Preacher replied with a grin. "They got to bring the fight to us on our ground."

"On the Lord's ground," the priest corrected.

"Yeah," Preacher agreed with a glance toward the riders, who had come to a stop about three hundred yards away. "But it's liable to be a dark and bloody ground before the sun gets much higher in the sky."

THIRTY-FIVE

"Damn it, don't you want to be rich, you spineless bastards?" Cobey shouted at the Mexican soldiers as they hesitated.

Arnie translated, couching the question in more diplomatic terms. One of the soldiers, a corporal named Ruiz who seemed to be their spokesman, said, "We will fight, but the gringos are dead shots, Señor."

Professor Chambers edged his horse forward. "Perhaps I can be of assistance here," he said.

Cobey glanced sharply at him. "What'd you have in mind?"

"Why don't I ride out there under a flag of truce and talk to them? Preacher struck me as being a reasonable man."

Cobey snorted in contempt. "There ain't nothin' reasonable about that mountain man! You ride out there under a white flag and he's liable to shoot you right off your horse!"

"I don't think so," Chambers replied coolly. "At any rate, it's my own life I'm risking, and since I know you don't have a very high opinion of my fighting ability, it doesn't seem to me that you'd be risking very much."

"Ain't that the truth! All right, Professor, if that's what you want to do, have at it. The rest of us will sit back here until you've got yourself killed, and then we'll go get that treasure."

"Very well." Chambers pulled out a handkerchief and tied it onto the barrel of the rifle he had been carrying, which had originally belonged to Chuck Stilson. He propped the butt of the weapon on the saddle so that the barrel stuck up in the air and heeled his horse into a walk.

Cobey watched him go and then said to Arnie, "What's he gonna say to 'em? You think this is gonna do us any good?"

Arnie shrugged. "Like the professor said, we ain't riskin' much to find out, are we?"

"One of them is coming," Audie called to Preacher, who walked over to the wall to have a look.

"Only one?"

"Yes, and he's under a flag of truce." Audie looked at Preacher. "I assume you intend to honor it?"

"I reckon," Preacher said grudgingly. He had recognized the rider by now. "Although there's a part o' me wants to blow the son of a bitch out of the saddle. That's Professor Chambers, the fella who roped Cobey and his bunch into this business in the first place."

"I see. A scholar. I'd probably enjoy a conversation with him, under different circumstances."

Chambers was about fifty feet from the ruins now. Without stepping out into view, because he didn't trust Cobey not to take a potshot at him if he did, Preacher called around the edge of the collapsed wall, "That's far enough, Professor. What do you want?"

"Just a few minutes of your time, Preacher," Chambers lifted his voice to reply. "Could you step out where I can see you better?"

"Nope."

Chambers was close enough so that Preacher heard his low laugh. "I can't say as I blame you, my friend."

"I ain't your friend," Preacher pointed out. "Now speak your piece."

"Very well. Cobey thinks that I'm here to negotiate with you, that I'll promise you something like freedom for you and your companions if you'll give us the treasure, or some such patently false proposal."

"You're sayin' Cobey don't intend to let us go no matter what we do?"

"Exactly. Nor does he intend to let me live." Chambers took a deep breath. "So I'm not negotiating, Preacher. I'm asking if you'll allow me to come in and join you."

The others had come over to the wall to listen to the conversation between Preacher and Chambers, and when the professor made his plea, Esteban exclaimed, "No!"

Juanita laid a hand on her brother's arm. "Perhaps we should consider it, Esteban. He would be one more to fight on our side."

When Preacher didn't reply immediately, Chambers went on. "I don't blame you for not trusting me. But you can ask the señorita. When she was a prisoner, she and I had begun to work out the details of an agreement. I was going to turn on Cobey and the others and help her. Ask her if that's not the case."

Juanita nodded. "*Es verdad*. The professor did promise to help me."

"Never had to see whether or not he'd have gone through with it," Preacher pointed out in a growling voice. "But I reckon it's true enough Cobey plans to double-cross him, and Chambers is smart enough to know that. And he'd be one more gun on our side, all right."

"It's up to you, Preacher," Audie said.

"Ummm," Nighthawk said.

Preacher turned back to the wall and called over it, "You realize that even if you join us, Professor, we'll still be outnumbered by two to one."

"I know," Chambers said. "But if I stay with Cobey, my

chances of surviving the day are nil. At least with you, I'd have a slim chance of living through this."

"Reckon you could look at it like that." Preacher made up his mind. "All right, Professor. Come on in. Best be quick about it, though. Once Cobey realizes you've betrayed him, he's liable to try to shoot you out o' the saddle."

"Yes, I know." Chambers eased his horse closer to the wall, aiming for an area that was only about two feet tall. "Here I come."

He jammed his heels into his horse's flanks and sent the animal lunging forward. At the same time he leaned far forward over the horse's neck, making himself as small a target as possible. Sure enough, Preacher saw several spurts of smoke as Cobey and some of the others fired at Chambers. The distant reports boomed and echoed over the rugged landscape. Rifle balls kicked up dirt around the hooves of Chambers's horse as the professor hauled back on the reins and sent his mount soaring up and over the remains of the wall.

The horse landed cleanly, and Chambers pulled him into a tight turn that carried them both behind the shelter of the higher portion of the wall. Preacher and Audie had been peering around the edge of that part, and they pulled back as rifle balls began to smack into the thick stone wall, chipping off splinters and throwing out dust, but doing no more damage than that.

With a tight grin, Preacher said, "I reckon Cobey's figured out you ain't on his side no more, Professor."

"No doubt. All I can say is that I'm glad to be here."

"Ummm!" Nighthawk warned.

"He's right, Preacher!" Audie said. "Here they come!"

"Pick your spots and pick your shots!" Preacher called in a ringing voice.

Everyone ran to positions they had picked out along the wall, even Father Hortensio. Preacher was a little surprised to see that the priest was going to join the fight, but he remembered how Father Hortensio had blazed away at him with that blunderbuss earlier. Clearly, the padre had decided that he was willing to fight for his faith, and that it was all right with El Señor Dios for him to do so.

Cobey and his men were making an all-out charge, galloping straight at the old mission. Preacher ordered, "Hold your fire! Let 'em get closer!" Chambers was a few yards to his right. Preacher said to him, "How'd Cobey wind up with the Mexican army fightin' on his side?"

"We ran into a patrol searching for the Alvarezes," the professor replied. "Cobey killed their lieutenant and appealed to the baser instincts of the soldiers. He promised to make them all rich."

"That'd likely do it all right," Preacher said, "with the sort o' scum Santa Anna forces into his army." He raised his voice again. "Little bit closer . . . *Let 'em have it!*"

Shots rang out along the ruined wall as all nine of the defenders fired. The storm of lead scythed into the onrushing attackers and swept several of them out of their saddles. Four or five of the Mexican soldiers went down, and so did a couple of their horses in a tangle of thrashing legs and hooves. Bert McDermott flipped backward off his horse, flinging his arms out to the sides as blood spurted from his chest. He hit the ground and bounced and rolled in the limp sprawl that signified death.

But Cobey and Arnie were still coming, along with five of the soldiers. Wick was far behind them, slumped over his mount's neck but trying to keep up.

With Cobey in the lead, the remaining attackers reached the wall and leaped their mounts over it, and with a mad swirl of dust and hooves and noise that made a mockery of what should have been a peaceful early morning, they were among the defenders and the battle was suddenly hand to hand, *mano a mano*.

Preacher dropped his empty rifle and yanked the two pistols from behind his belt. He fired the left-hand gun at one of the soldiers, and at close range like this, both balls from the double-shotted weapon blew fist-sized holes through the luckless man's torso, making him fly off the back of his horse. Preacher drew a bead on Cobey with the right-hand gun, but just as he pulled the trigger one of the horses rammed him with its shoulder, throwing off his aim. The balls missed and went harmlessly into the air.

Cobey's pistol spurted flame and Joaquin went down, blood fountaining from his neck where Cobey's shot had torn it open. Pablo lunged at Arnie, reaching up to try to pull him from the saddle, but the fat man planted a foot in the Yaqui's chest and kicked him back. Pablo stumbled and fell and then screamed as Arnie rode over him, a steel-shod hoof landing in the middle of his face and shattering his skull.

Esteban reversed his rifle and clubbed one of the soldiers off his horse, breaking the weapon's stock as he did so. As the soldier landed on the ground, Esteban leaped on him and drove the shattered stock into his face again and again, smashing the life out of him.

A few yards away, one of the soldiers leaned over and grabbed Juanita, jerking her feet off the ground as she cried out in anger and fear. With a leer on his face he tried to lift her to his horse's back in front of his saddle, but he stiffened suddenly as an arrow erupted from his throat. The wound spewed blood. Nighthawk's bow had driven the shaft all the way through the man's neck from the back. He went limp and let go of Juanita. She tumbled to the ground and rolled desperately to avoid the slashing hooves of the dead man's horse.

Another soldier raced his mount after Audie, who scampered toward a pile of rocks with grass growing up between them. The Mexican slashed at the little man's head with the saber that had belonged to the patrol's lieutenant before Cobey murdered him. Audie ducked under the swipe, stopped short, and reached up to grab the man's arm. With a heave of broad, muscular shoulders, Audie pulled the man from the saddle and used his own momentum to flip him into the rocks. That was enough to stun the man momentarily, but he sprang up a second later, shrieking in horror. Several long, fat rattlesnakes hung from his arms and torso, their fangs sunk deep in his flesh. Audie had inadvertently tossed him right into a den of the rattlers. One of the diamondbacks was even attached to the soldier's neck. The man did a grotesque jig that just pumped the load of venom through his veins that much faster, and then he collapsed.

The lone surviving soldier wheeled his horse toward Esteban and Juanita. Before he could reach them, however, Chambers leaped in front of him. The professor's pocket pistol cracked wickedly. The soldier jerked back a little, but Chambers's shot had just grazed his arm. He had plenty of strength left to thrust out the rifle in his hand. The bayonet attached to the end of the barrel drove deeply into Chambers's chest. He staggered back, pawing at the blade that was still buried in his body. His eyes opened wide in horror and the realization that he was dying. He fell to his knees and then slumped forward. The butt of the rifle struck the ground and held him propped up that way, almost as if he were praying.

The soldier kept going, aiming his horse directly at Esteban and Juanita, who were now huddled together. In another moment he would have trampled them, but suddenly another rider was beside him, a huge arm lashing out in a smashing blow. At the same instant, Wick rammed his horse into the soldier's horse. The two men and their mounts went down in a welter of dust. Wick was the only one who came out of the billowing cloud, dragging a broken leg behind him. He hobbled toward Juanita, croaking, "Señorita!"

Cobey whirled his horse and charged toward them, shouting, "Wick! Get out of the way!"

Wick turned and held up his hands. "Cobey! Stop!"

The pistol in Cobey's hand exploded. Wick staggered back as the ball struck him in the chest. "Cobey . . . ?" he whispered as blood welled from the wound.

Then he fell to the side like a massive tree toppling.

On the other side of the ruined sanctuary, Arnie left his saddle in a diving tackle that slammed into Preacher and knocked them both sprawling to the ground. Preacher rolled and came to his feet first, knife in hand, but Arnie was up only an instant later, also brandishing steel. The two men came together in a blur of thrust and parry and counterthrust, their blades ringing together loudly and throwing off sparks as they clashed. Preacher had been in knife fights before, but never had he faced such a whirlwind of steel. Arnie's knife bit and slashed him in several places, but Preacher dealt out some damage of his own, leaving bloodstains spreading in several places on Arnie's homespun shirt. Both men knew they were just about evenly matched, and the first slip, the first mistake, would likely decide this deadly match.

That slip was Preacher's, as a rock turned under his foot and threw him off balance for an instant. In that shaving of time, Arnie's blade licked out, aiming true for Preacher's throat. It took every bit of speed and instinct Preacher possessed to pull his head to the side just in time, so that Arnie's knife just ripped an ugly gash in the side of Preacher's neck.

But that missed thrust brought Arnie in too close to protect himself from Preacher's counterthrust. Preacher slammed his knife into Arnie's chest, the keen blade slicing deeper and deeper until it was buried all the way, right up to the "Green River" stamped on the hilt. Arnie stiffened and said, "Damn," and then blood trickled from his mouth and the life went out of his eyes. He sagged against Preacher, who ripped the knife free and shoved Arnie's body away from him. Preacher turned. . . .

And saw Cobey standing in front of Esteban and Juanita, both hands filled with pistols. The only thing between him and the two young people was Father Hortensio, who stood there unarmed and said, "In the name of God, I call on you to lay down your arms, henchman of Satan!"

An ugly grin stretched across Cobey's face. "God left

this place a long time ago, old man. Now there's just me, and I got one pistol for you, one for the kid, and then it'll be just me and the señorita." The left-hand pistol came up toward Father Hortensio.

Preacher drew back his knife hand. It would be a long throw, but he had to make it.

Before he could let fly with the blade, a hamlike hand rose behind Cobey, grabbed the back of his shirt, and jerked him down. Cobey yelled in surprise and twisted frantically, but he couldn't escape Wick's grip. The giant closed his other hand around Cobey's throat and slammed him on the ground. Pale and bleeding heavily, Wick loomed over his former friend. Both hands were around Cobey's neck now, squeezing for all they were worth. Cobey jabbed both pistols into Wick's midsection and pulled the triggers. Wick's body muffled the twin explosions as the balls blew a huge hole all the way through him. His back arched under the impact of the shots.

But he didn't let go. His hands remained locked around Cobey's neck, and with his dying breath he lurched and heaved. Preacher was running toward them, and he heard the sharp crack as Cobey's neck broke. The muscles in Wick's arms and shoulders bunched one last time, and he tore Cobey's head right off his shoulders. As Wick slumped forward over his former friend's body, the grisly trophy slipped from his fingers and rolled to the side so that Cobey's eyes stared sightlessly toward the wagons.

Toward the lost treasure of Mission Santo Domingo, now home again at last.

THIRTY-SIX

"Well," Preacher said to Father Hortensio, "I reckon you got a good start on somethin' every church needs—a graveyard."

"Unfortunately, you are right about that, my son," the priest replied.

Along with Audie and Nighthawk, the two men stood beside the last of the numerous graves they had dug and then refilled over the course of the long day. It was nearly sunset, and it had taken that long to lay to rest everyone who had died in the early morning battle. Preacher wouldn't have minded just throwing Cobey's body in a ravine somewhere—that was more than the bastard deserved, as far as Preacher was concerned—but Father Hortensio had insisted that everyone be properly buried, even their enemies.

Somehow, Wick Jimpson didn't fall into that category anymore. Preacher hoped that somebody would put up a marker for the big man. He had a feeling Juanita would see to that.

"What are you going to do now, Padre?"

"My task is to rebuild the mission and bring the word of God to this land once again," Father Hortensio said. "With

Esteban and Juanita to help me, and with the Lord's blessing, I am sure I will succeed."

"They've forgiven you for what happened up in the mountains?" Preacher asked.

Father Hortensio smiled. "Of course. God has filled them with His mercy and understanding."

"Well, I reckon I understand," Preacher said. "I ain't quite so forgivin', though."

"Then it is fortunate for me that I do not require your forgiveness, is it not?"

Preacher just grunted. Him and the padre weren't ever goin' to get along that good, but he reckoned that was all right.

He started to turn away, but he paused and looked again at the grave where Professor Rufus Chambers was buried. He supposed Chambers had redeemed himself, too, there at the end, at least a little. Preacher couldn't bring himself to feel any real regret for the man's death, though. It was Chambers's greed that had started all the trouble in motion. But in the end he had come up empty, just like Cobey and Arnie and the others. Preacher suspected that under different circumstances, Arnie wouldn't have been such a bad fella. They might have even been friends. As it was, though, all Preacher could do was feel a little grudging respect for the man.

The four of them walked back slowly toward the mission as the sun lowered toward the peaks in the west. Audie asked, "What are your plans, Preacher?"

"Mosey on back up to the Rockies and go after a good mess o' peltries, I reckon," the mountain man said with a shrug. "You and Nighthawk headin' that way, too?"

"No, I believe we've decided to stay here for a while and help see to it that Father Hortensio gets his mission rebuilt. Then I'd like to see Santa Fe before we head north again."

"Ummm," Nighthawk said.

Preacher paused and extended his hand. Horse was already saddled and ready to ride. Dog sat waiting beside the big stallion. There was some light left in the day, and Preacher wanted to use it.

"Reckon this is so long, then," he said.

"You're leaving already?" Audie asked in surprise as he clasped Preacher's hand. "Esteban and Juanita will be disappointed."

Preacher thought about what Audie had said that morning about Juanita. If she really had any romantic notions about him, it would be better for her sake if she put them out of her head.

"You can say my good-byes for me," Preacher told him. "I never was much for things like that. Rather ride on without no fuss."

"I suppose we can honor your wishes."

Preacher turned to Nighthawk and shook hands with the Crow warrior. "I got a feelin' we'll be runnin' into each other again, somewheres down the trail," he said.

Nighthawk nodded and said solemnly, "Ummm."

Preacher started toward Horse, but Father Hortensio stopped him by saying, "Wait."

Preacher turned back. "Sorry, Padre. I figured you wouldn't want to shake hands with a heathen."

"Even a priest makes mistakes from time to time," Father Hortensio said as he held out his hand. "Though I still find your name somewhat improper, you are no heathen, my son." With his other hand he brought a small pouch from somewhere inside his robes. "I want you to have this, too."

Preacher clasped the priest's hand and then took the pouch, frowning at the little clinking sounds its contents made. "Some o' the lost treasure?"

"No longer lost, thanks to you. Take it with the Church's gratitude . . . and with mine."

"Well, I wouldn't want to insult the Church's generosity," Preacher said as he slipped the bag of coins inside his buckskins. He added, "Or yours."

A moment later, he was mounted up. He turned Horse and

rode north, with Dog trotting alongside. Looking back, Preacher lifted a hand in farewell, and Father Hortensio called after him, *"Vaya con Dios!"*

Preacher smiled and rode on, heeling Horse into a ground-eating lope. By the time night fell he would be miles to the north, well on his way to somewhere else, content in the knowledge that despite what he had left behind, he had a fortune of his own in this wild, beautiful country that would forever be his home.

AFTERWORD

Notes from the Old West

In the small town where I grew up, there were two movie theaters. The Pavilion was one of those old-timey movie show palaces, built in the heyday of Mary Pickford and Charlie Chaplin—the silent era of the 1920s. By the 1950s, when I was a kid, the Pavilion was a little worn around the edges, but it was still the premier theater in town. They played all those big Technicolor biblical Cecil B. DeMille epics and corny MGM musicals. In Cinemascope, of course.

On the other side of town was the Gem, a somewhat shabby and run-down grind house with sticky floors and torn seats. Admission was a quarter. The Gem booked low-budget "B" pictures (remember the Bowery Boys?), war movies, horror flicks, and Westerns. I liked the Westerns best. I could usually be found every Saturday at the Gem, along with my best friend, Newton Trout, watching Westerns from 10 A.M. until my father came looking for me around supper-time. (Sometimes Newton's dad was dispatched to come fetch us.) One time, my dad came to get me right in the middle of *Abilene Trail*, which featured the now-forgotten Whip

Wilson. My father became so engrossed in the action he sat down and watched the rest of it with us. We didn't get home until after dark, and my mother's meat loaf was a pan of gray ashes by the time we did. Though my father and I were both in the doghouse the next day, this remains one of my fondest childhood memories. There was Wild Bill Elliot, and Gene Autry, and Roy Rogers, and Tim Holt, and, a little later, Rod Cameron and Audie Murphy. Of these newcomers, I never missed an Audie Murphy Western, because Audie was sort of an antihero. Sure, he stood for law and order and was an honest man, but sometimes he had to go around the law to uphold it. If he didn't play fair, it was only because he felt hamstrung by the laws of the land. Whatever it took to get the bad guys, Audie did it. There were no finer points of law, no splitting of legal hairs. It was instant justice, devoid of long-winded lawyers, bored or biased jurors, or black-robed, often corrupt judges.

Steal a man's horse and you were the guest of honor at a necktie party.

Molest a good woman and you got a bullet in the heart or a rope around the gullet. Or at the very least, got the crap beat out of you. Rob a bank and face a hail of bullets or the hangman's noose.

Saved a lot of time and money, did frontier justice.

That's all gone now, I'm sad to say. Now you hear, "Oh, but he had a bad childhood" or "His mother didn't give him enough love" or "The homecoming queen wouldn't give him a second look and he has an inferiority complex." Or "cultural rage," as the politically correct bright boys refer to it. How many times have you heard some self-important defense attorney moan, "The poor kids were only venting their hostilities toward an uncaring society?"

Mule fritters, I say. Nowadays, you can't even call a punk a punk anymore. But don't get me started.

It was, "Howdy, m'am" time too. The good guys, antihero or not, were always respectful to the ladies. They might shoot a bad guy five seconds after tipping their hat to a woman, but the code of the West demanded you be respectful to a lady.

Lots of things have changed since the heyday of the Wild West, haven't they? Some for the good, some for the bad.

I didn't have any idea at the time that I would someday write about the West. I just knew that I was captivated by the Old West.

When I first got the itch to write, back in the early 1970s, I didn't write Westerns. I started by writing horror and action adventure novels. After more than two dozen novels, I began thinking about developing a Western character. From those initial musing came the novel *The Last Mountain Man: Smoke Jensen*. That was followed by *Preacher: The First Mountain Man*. A few years later, I began developing the Last Gunfighter series. Frank Morgan is a legend in his own time, the fastest gun west of the Mississippi . . . a title and a reputation he never wanted, but can't get rid of.

The Gunfighter series is set in the waning days of the Wild West. Frank Morgan is out of time and place, but still, he is pursued by men who want to earn a reputation as the man who killed the legendary gunfighter. All Frank wants to do is live in peace. But he knows in his heart that dream will always be just that: a dream, fog and smoke and mirrors, something elusive that will never really come to fruition. He will be forced to wander the West, alone, until one day his luck runs out.

For me, and for thousands—probably millions—of other people (although many will never publicly admit it), the old Wild West will always be a magic, mysterious place: a place we love to visit through the pages of books; characters we would like to know . . . from a safe distance; events we would love to take part in, again, from a safe distance. For the old Wild West was not a place for the faint of heart. It was a hard, tough, physically demanding time. There were no police to call if one faced adversity. One faced trouble alone, and handled it alone. It was rugged individualism: something that appeals to many of us.

I am certain that is something that appeals to most readers of Westerns.

I still do on-site research (whenever possible) before starting a Western novel. I have wandered over much of the West, prowling what is left of ghost towns. Stand in the midst of the ruins of these old towns, use a little bit of imagination, and one can conjure up life as it used to be in the Wild West. The rowdy Saturday nights, the tinkling of a piano in a saloon, the laughter of cowboys and miners letting off steam after a week of hard work. Use a little more imagination and one can envision two men standing in the street, facing one another, seconds before the hook and draw of a gunfight. A moment later, one is dead and the other rides away.

The old wild untamed West.

There are still some ghost towns to visit, but they are rapidly vanishing as time and the elements take their toll. If you want to see them, make plans to do so as soon as possible, for in a few years, they will all be gone.

And so will we.

Stand in what is left of the Big Thicket country of east Texas and try to imagine how in the world the pioneers managed to get through that wild tangle. I have wondered about that many times and marveled at the courage of the men and women who slowly pushed westward, facing dangers that we can only imagine.

Let me touch briefly on a subject that is very close to me: firearms. There are some so-called historians who are now claiming that firearms played only a very insignificant part in the settlers' lives. They claim that only a few were armed. What utter, stupid nonsense! What do these so-called historians think the pioneers did for food? Do they think the early settlers rode down to the nearest supermarket and bought their meat? Or maybe they think the settlers chased down deer or buffalo on foot and beat the animals to death with a club. I have a news flash for you so-called historians: The settlers used guns to shoot their game. They used guns to defend hearth and home against Indians on the warpath. They used guns to protect themselves from outlaws. Guns are a part of Americana. And always will be.

The mountains of the West and the remains of the ghost towns that dot those areas are some of my favorite subjects to write about. I have done extensive research on the various mountain ranges of the West and go back whenever time permits. I sometimes stand surrounded by the towering mountains and wonder how in the world the pioneers ever made it through. As hard as I try and as often as I try, I simply cannot imagine the hardships those men and women endured over the hard months of their incredible journey. None of us can. It is said that on the Oregon Trail alone, there are at least two bodies in lonely, unmarked graves for every mile of that journey. Some students of the West say the number of dead is at least twice that. And nobody knows the exact number of wagons that impatiently started out alone and simply vanished on the way, along with their occupants, never to be seen or heard from again.

Just vanished.

The one-hundred-fifty-and-fifty-year-old ruts of the wagon wheels can still be seen in various places along the Oregon Trail. But if you plan to visit those places, do so quickly, for they are slowly disappearing. And when they are gone, they will be lost forever, except in the words of Western writers.

As long as I can peck away at a keyboard and find a company to publish my work, I will not let the Old West die. That I promise you.

The West will live on as long as there are writers willing to write about it, and publishers willing to publish it. Writing about the West is wide open, just like the old Wild West. Characters abound, as plentiful as the wide-open spaces, as colorful as a sunset on the Painted Desert, as restless as the ever-sighing winds. All one has to do is use a bit of imagination.

Take a stroll through the cemetery at Tombstone, Arizona; read the inscriptions. Then walk the main street of that once-famous town around midnight and you might catch a glimpse of the ghosts that still wander the town. They really do. Just ask anyone who lives there. But don't be afraid of the apparitions, they won't hurt you. They're just out for a quiet stroll.

The West lives on. And as long as I am alive, it always will.

GREAT BOOKS,
GREAT SAVINGS!

When You Visit Our Website:
www.kensingtonbooks.com
You Can Save 30% Off The Retail Price
Of Any Book You Purchase

- **All Your Favorite Kensington Authors**
- **New Releases & Timeless Classics**
- **Overnight Shipping Available**
- **All Major Credit Cards Accepted**

Visit Us Today To Start Saving!
www.kensingtonbooks.com

All Orders Are Subject To Availability.
Shipping and Handling Charges Apply.

THE FIRST MOUNTAIN MAN SERIES BY
WILLIAM W. JOHNSTONE

__The First Mountain Man
0-8217-5510-2 $4.99US/$6.50CAN

__Blood on the Divide
0-8217-5511-0 $4.99US/$6.50CAN

__Absaroka Ambush
0-8217-5538-2 $4.99US/$6.50CAN

__Forty Guns West
0-7860-1534-9 $5.99US/$7.99CAN

__Cheyenne Challenge
0-8217-5607-9 $4.99US/$6.50CAN

__Preacher and the Mountain Caesar
0-8217-6585-X $5.99US/$7.99CAN

__Blackfoot Messiah
0-8217-6611-2 $5.99US/$7.99CAN

__Preacher
0-7860-1441-5 $5.99US/$7.99CAN

__Preacher's Peace
0-7860-1442-3 $5.99US/$7.99CAN

Available Wherever Books Are Sold!

Visit our website at www.kensingtonbooks.com